FLY WITH THE ARROW

Other Series by Sarah K. L. Wilson

Dragon School

Dragon Chameleon

Dragon Tide

Bridge of Legends

Fae Hunter Series

Empire of War & Wings

FLY WITH THE ARROW

BLUEBEARD'S SECRET
BOOK 1

SARAH K. L. WILSON

PUBLISHED BY SARAH K. L. WILSON, 2021

All rights reserved. This book or any portion thereof may not be reproduced or used in any manner whatsoever without the express written permission of the publisher except for the use of brief quotations in a book review.

This is a work of fiction. Similarities to real people, places, or events are entirely coincidental.

FLY WITH THE ARROW
First Edition. March 1, 2021
Copyright © 2021 Sarah K. L. Wilson
ISBN : 978-1-7772645-5-0
Cover Art byKristen De Palma
Written by Sarah K. L. Wilson
www.sarahklwilson.com

For Melissa who loves Bluebeard
almost as much as I do.

And for my sister Kathryn
who wrote a very serious article ,
inspiring me to write this not-quite-
so-serious book.

PENSMOORE
SALAMOORE
ROURANMOORE
AYYADMOORE
QARAMOORE
PTOLEMOORE
ILKANMOORE
MORAVIDMOORE
MORTAL LANDS

BOOK ONE

Fly with the Arrow

Dance with the Sword

Give your Heart to the Barrow

Die with your Lord

"There was once a man who had fine houses both in town and the country, a deal of silver and gold plate, embroidered furniture and coaches gilded all over with gold. But this man was so unlucky as to have a blue beard, which made him so frightfully ugly that all the women and girls ran away from him."

- Charles Perrault, Bluebeard,

1697 as translated by Andrew Lang in The Blue Fairy Book 1889.

CHAPTER ONE

Some laws are talked about by all – featured in story and song – and as a result, it's easy to know that if you turn traitor to the king, you'll soon see your head mounted on the battlements of Pensmoore, or if you steal another woman's horse, a hempen noose will be the last to embrace you.

It's not those laws that are the problem. It's the other kind of laws. The laws no one talks about at all.

Like the Law of First Greeting.

And it is those laws that bite you in the end, just like that law bit me.

"Izolda must come to court with me this season," my father had declared one day before riding out on the hunt. When he said that, I had never heard of the Law of First Greeting.

"You must be careful to be very polite to the fine ladies of court, Izolda," my mother warned as she packed my fur robes and velvet gowns into a small chest. "Remember what I taught you. They will all be above your station. Try to be meek. Try not to judge others so harshly. And whatever you do, don't decide to go out shooting or riding with your brothers." She was wiping tears from her eyes, as she always did when one of us left. She would miss us sorely – though even she could have had no idea how long I would be gone for. "Be a good girl. Help the women with their weaving and stitching and they will be pleased with you. You are young and very beautiful." She paused to stroke my face lovingly as she said that. "But trust me Izolda, that beauty will fade in time and you will be sorry if you haven't made use of it while you had the chance. Have some fun. Flirt. Enjoy yourself." She paused as if worried she'd said too much. "But do no more than that because your father will be working very hard to secure a wise match for you. It's high time we found someone suitable. You can't live here forever and you're already nineteen."

"Don't worry so much, Mother," I said, kissing her cheek. I was not worried. I was excited. I never got to go anywhere interesting and I doubted my father would procure me a husband in just one visit.

Since we were a very small martial family on the outer edges of the King's territory, my father would have to be very clever indeed to find a match. I'd be lucky if he found a sober man of forty who still had all his teeth, but I didn't bother to mention that to my mother. After all, I was supposed to be dazzled and delighted by pretty faces at this age and they were supposed to be my folly and ruin. No point in proving that was true.

"Don't forget to check on Brueller in the stables," I reminded her as I put some pine scented soap and a comb in the chest. My mother would forget those. Practical things were not her specialty. "If I am gone, he will have to help Sasa foal all by himself."

"You think too much of horses when you should be thinking of being wed," my mother said with a sigh.

All of that advice, and no mention whatsoever of any Law I must be careful of. No mention that the Wittenbrand might come to the castle, too, tearing through it like a winter storm with all the same icy rage. If she'd said any of that, I might not have even believed her.

Which made sense in a perverse sort of way. If I had been a beautiful but brainless girl of fine fortune and the perfect heroine for a story then I would have been warned of the Law and I would have known not to break it, but I would have been courageous and headstrong and done it anyway. But since I was sensible and calm in a crisis and of mediocre appearance – despite my mother's assurances of my beauty – no one had bothered to warn *me* of a pit that only a heroine could possibly fall into. Girls like me didn't have to watch out for Laws and traps.

The next day, my little bay mare stamped with excitement in the swirling wind and I tried not to tug on her reins even though my own heart was just as exuberant. I was bouncing on my toes as my mother kissed my cheeks. Flurries of snow swirled around her as I said my goodbyes. Her lips were faintly blue in the cold and her eyes were filled with sadness to see us go.

"I shall miss you, my Izolda," she said, pushing strands of my long dark hair back behind my ear.

"We should not be gone for more than a turning of Moons, mother," I said because she always kissed us goodbye like she thought we would all die of the plague while we were gone. My cheeks were hot from her attention already.

If I'd known this would be the last time that I saw her, I would have taken more time to treasure it.

"It's always been you and me standing here holding hands as they go and now it will be only me. I will feel an ache in my heart until you return," she said, and my cheeks flared even hotter. I wouldn't be feeling any aches. In fact, I was so excited to see court for the first time that I could hardly keep my breath careful and measured.

"Be safe and healthy, Mother," I said. "Know that you hold our hearts."

"Be careful not to go off on your own," she said, cupping my cheek in her warm hand. "We don't want the Wittenbrand to snatch you away."

"You know those are only fairy stories." I shook my head, laughing the laugh of the young and hale. I'd been hearing tales of the Wittenbrand all my life, but I'd never seen one and I didn't believe the religious fervor of my people. I cared about facts and logic, not superstition and legend.

"Fairy stories are sometimes true," she said, kissing me again.

My bay stomped and huffed as my mother moved on to my father to exchange goodbyes. He'd end up as red-faced as me if she had her way.

While they were distracted, my brother Svetgin edged his gelding in close to mine as he double-checked the straps holding his bow and quiver in place. He was watching the hills around us as he worked. Winter storms could blow down in a moment's notice and no one took fair weather for granted. Or fair fortune.

"You women fuss too much," he said, rubbing his unshaven face as if he thought there might be a beard there by now. "Men know that traveling is normal and natural."

"How nice for you," I said dryly. "Hopefully all your heavy man-knowledge doesn't make your horse too slow."

"In Pensmoore, we will drink honey ale and dance with big-eyed women," he said smugly, ignoring my jab. "And you may even be favored with a dance, sister, if you can rein in that tongue."

"Big *eyes*?" Rolgrin, my other brother asked, waggling his eyebrows suggestively. Like me, he was dark of hair and eye, unlike Svetgin who had our mother's pale hair and complexion. "Is that what you've been noticing, brother?"

I ignored their banter. Perhaps, were I a boy and able to pick my bride someday, I might be weighing the merits of *eyes,* too. But I was not a boy. I would have to allow my father to negotiate a suitable situation for me and the likelihood of me having any say in it was slim. The likelihood of the man being only double my age was also narrow.

I did not resent my father for this. He was a practical man – I had inherited that from him – and he would choose well. Even if the thought of marrying a stranger he chose for me still put me into a cold sweat.

He had already told my mother that he would prefer a man with enough wealth that we could live without fear of hunger, but too little for him to be tempted to keep mistresses. A man with a good reputation in the court, but not enough reputation to keep him often from his hold. A man old enough to see sense, but not so old as to be unfit company for his daughter. That he considered my feelings in regard to faithfulness and company was a relief. Not all daughters could depend on such good grace from a father.

And since I was an expert at self-control, it would be easy to pretend that what I really wanted wasn't deep, dark eyes and broad shoulders. That daydreams of dashing knights on horseback with flashing swords were only for other girls and not for me. I felt my cheeks growing hot again. Of course, I could manage that.

I sat my mare with a straight back and skillful hands and smiled serenely at my brothers – both younger than I, and yet both more familiar with court. Boys always got the best opportunities. Svetgin had already been to court once before and Rolgrin twice.

At nineteen years of age, I was old to have never been, but my mother was very fond of me and had not wanted to see me married too soon. She had the romantic notion that I may even fall in love or have a whirlwind romance. It was a kind thought – but ridiculous. What had she expected would happen? Had she thought some stranger would appear in the night? Someone dashingly handsome who demanded my hand in marriage for the smallest of dowries? That kind of thing didn't happen outside of stories.

And it certainly didn't happen to minor nobles who had to embroider flowers over the holes in their dresses so that no one at court would know how tight the purse strings had to be in Northpeak.

"Ready to ride, daughter?" my father asked as he mounted his dancing gelding. Storm was too energetic to be a good mount, but he suited my hearty father well. It always surprised me that Father – being such a practical man in all other respects – chose my high-spirited, dreamy mother and then this unsuitable horse. It was a weakness of his. And one that made me all the fonder of him.

If I was allowed to do any choosing for myself, I might choose the same.

The ride from the Hold of the Savataz of Northpeak to Pensmoore City takes eight days, and though we stayed in inns and keeps of other Landholders along the way, we were worn and dirty by the time we arrived. I'd made careful mental notes of each inn we had stayed at. The people as we moved closer to Pensmoore City wore finer clothes – even the commoners.

They ate finer foods. Drank finer mead. Their swords and shields showed more polish and their furs less wear from moths and age.

It was foolish to feel smaller just because my father's hold in Northpeak was poorer than these holds of the plains' folk. The sensible thing would be to be glad we were a part of a prosperous nation where many holds were strong and wealthy. After all, if it came to war with the Salamoore or the Ayyadmoore along the borders, or the strange islanders of the east, it would be favorable to have such strong allies. And yet, I felt smaller. I felt shabbier. I began to understand what my mother meant when she said my father would have to be very clever to find me a good match. Any dreams I had of a whirlwind romance – however carefully tamped down – were quickly smothered and buried where I could no longer blush in shame that I'd ever had them at all.

In Northpeak, the people held us in respect. Here, we barely garnered a look and those who did look at us often wrinkled their noses. We were plain and bluff people with simple clothing and weapons. We were nothing now that we had left our land.

I could almost feel the smart of being without it – as if everything I had ever been was wrapped up in those trees and snows, and now I was a living ghost haunting these other lands without body or succor.

By the time we reached Pensmoore City, I was eager for any distraction from this constant reminder of my place in the Kingdom of Pensmoore. I tried not to let a stab of jealousy pierce me when we reached the city gates and were spattered with mud by a passing coach. A girl my age looked out between the curtains, her fine golden hair pulled back into an elaborate dressing and a large emerald hanging from a chain over her forehead. Her eyes didn't even focus on us as she drifted by – as if we were nothing more than trees or goats along the horizon.

"We should hurry before night falls," my father said practically. "The steward will be expecting us, and it will make more work for everyone if we are late."

I felt something cold on the back of my neck as he spoke. I glanced over my shoulder through the city gates. The snow swirled thick and heavy, dampening sound and sight like a warm down blanket in the winter. And yet, something felt wrong. Was that a figure I saw in the whirling snow?

There were a handful of shapes that almost looked like men riding horses, though there was something wrong with the horses' heads. I squinted at them, trying to see clearly enough to make out the shapes. Perhaps they were just fellow travelers journeying to court. But if that was true, then why did they leave little shivers along my spine? Something was not right. I had the oddest feeling that winter had opened its jaws and was trying to swallow me up.

I pulled my fur cloak in tighter as if it could shield me from the malice I felt in the swirling wind and the darkening storm.

"Don't dawdle, Izolda," Rolgrin said, tugging on my rein. When I looked back behind my shoulder, there was nothing in the swirling snow except my imagination and a single black raven.

CHAPTER TWO

Pensmoore City rolled over the plains like a bank of snow pushed by a shovel. It clumped and heaped, with one building seeming to be built almost on top of the next so that it was as much layers as it was rows. I tried not to gape, but just looking at the high towers made my belly flop. Had the carpenters been wise in their choices of timbers and how to place them, or would they fall down on my head as I was riding beside them? It seemed that cities required a lot of trust in strangers and I was not good at trusting.

And to think, in the darkness, I was seeing only a sliver of the city! These signs – so close I'd barely finished reading one before the next appeared – and the ornaments and cobbles and banners were just a small piece of the whole. It was almost too much to take in. Most of the city and the royal stables passed me by in a blur of grandeur.

We saw nothing of the palace except the back corridors leading from the stable to our rooms and a small part of me was disappointed not to have had the chance to properly gawk.

By the time I was tucked away in a very small but warm room, I was too tired to think of much beyond stripping off my travel-soiled dress, brushing it quickly and readying myself for bed. My head was spinning from seeing the city and I was still just a little queasy at the thought of so many layers of palace above and below me.

At least I had the privacy of my own room. My father and brothers were sharing a room next door, their beds so close that they almost touched.

"Quarters are tight, I'm afraid, Lord Savataz of Northpeak," the Head Steward had told us. "Of course, his Highness welcomes all his loyal landholders and bids you rest and warmth, but the whole of the court is gathering for the princess's presentation ball and that leaves little space unclaimed. We've had to put you in the old servants' wing – to our shame, but no other place was available."

"Do not worry yourself, Head Steward," my father had said. "We are practical people. We are pleased to have a bed and the warmth of a fire. There will be no complaints from us."

The Steward had looked relieved, like a man who'd already dealt with many of those complaints today and was just grateful not to have to repeat the experience. Svetgin opened his mouth as if he was going to complain anyway, but my father stepped on his foot, grinding his heel into the arch, and Svetgin's mouth snapped shut as he gritted his teeth against the pain.

"Do no fear," the Steward said hastily. "They have been thoroughly aired and checked by our head housekeeper."

My father nodded gravely.

I found my room to be well enough, but that night before I went to bed, I opened the small window and looked out into the dark sky beyond.

"If I was a man, I would be a soldier or horse farrier and I would work hard for my kin," I said, trying not to sound too wistful as I looked up at the same moon my mother would be looking at. "But as I am a woman, my lot is to marry well for the good of my family and nation. I only wish that the benefit others receive from the marriage would be in equal measure with my sacrifice in giving it. But since the sacrifice is so great, I expect this cannot be."

A raven gave a cry so close to my window that I gasped, and turned until I saw him there, sitting just a little below the window on the peak of an overhang. I frowned, narrowing my eyes. What was he doing there? If I had been very ambitious, or very foolish, I could have reached out and snatched his black wings. It was almost as if he'd been planning to eavesdrop on me.

Instead, he tilted his head, looking right at me as if he was sharing my secret, and then he flew away in a flurry of black feathers.

I didn't know then that the Wittenbrand are said to watch through the eyes of ravens and hear with their ears. Had I known, perhaps I would have been more guarded with my words. Perhaps, I would have thrown a rock.

I was prompt to rise the next day and carefully brush my second-finest wool gown before dressing, braiding my long dark hair, and joining my brothers and father in the hall. The dress was dark charcoal and perfectly serviceable, and I'd embroidered a pine branch over a tear in the skirt.

"We must attend to men's business, Izolda," my father said gravely. "Can you find the place of women on your own?"

"Yes, Father," I said dutifully, and I was rewarded by his smile.

My feet were eager to explore and the castle was bustling with preparations for the princess's Presentation Ball. It was an affair meant to be so lavish that it would be talked of for the next generation. My mouth was already watering at the thought. Delicacies – and sweets especially – were rare in Northpeak, and if the princess gave me the chance to eat something sugary tonight, I'd be more than happy to play the plain wren next to her bluejay.

I dodged out of the way of rushing servants as I made my way through the castle, peering curiously into the empty rooms. The servants were harried and exhausted even though it was early morning, their arms full of tablecloths or chairs, ducks and geese, cheeses and candles and everything else.

I was far too fascinated and delighted by their preparations to ask after breakfast. Instead, I slipped through the halls letting my curiosity guide me, peeking in at the servants hanging garland in the wide man hall, watching in fascination as a group of musicians practiced in the ballroom, even slipping through the stables and peeking at the grooms tending the snorting horses.

If I was never going to have a ball thrown in my honor then I was certainly going to enjoy Princess Chasida's ball in every way I could, from studying the clever way the servant hid tied-up bundles of fragrant pine bows to sneaking a glimpse at the palace library that was being dusted and cleaned with the fervor of a religious practice.

This might be my only time to see court and I meant to see all of it.

I paused in the stables long enough to slip a carrot to my bay mare and check her hooves. She was in good health and as frisky as I was, and I longed to take her out into the yard for exercise, but I had promised my father I would find the ladies, so I made my way up through the castle, dutifully looking for where the women would be doing the weaving and sewing that would make them all pretty for the coming ball.

I found the women in the ladies' work room. They held little bits of handiwork, and most of them were gathered around piecing a large quilt, but no one was sewing.

"I'll be wearing my hair in the Rouanmoore style," one of them announced to impressed gasps. "My father bought me the pearl combs needed."

They hardly even noticed me slipping into their midst.

"But won't it cover the laced back of your dress?" another girl asked the first one. That set off a flurry of chatter.

I watched one of them practicing her posture, carefully checking to be sure that her figure was displayed perfectly. Another girl had her chin resting on her woven fingers and she was stealing little looks at herself in the large mirror that filled one of the walls. She made little adjustments every time so that she slowly appeared more coy and mysterious as the minutes passed.

I narrowed my eyes and looked around me, shocked to see she wasn't the only one. Well now. Who did the sewing around here if everyone was more worried about how they looked than getting anything done?

Shaking my head, I set into the quilt the group was meant to be sewing. I'd have to do the work of five women to make up for those girls and their careful posing. I glanced around and met the eyes of an older woman who smirked at me. I didn't know if she was laughing with me at these preening girls or laughing at me for working so hard.

After a moment she pointed at the flower sewn over a rip in the cuff of my dress and my face went hot. My embroidery had not fooled her experienced eye.

The girl closes to me dropped her needle and eyed me up and down before turning away again.

Was it possible that they weren't here to quilt at all?

Or was this just how they let someone new know her place was at the bottom of the heap?

"Tell us about the last time a princess was presented!" one of the girls said to an old woman in the corner. She was looking dreamily at the piece she was embroidering – a fanciful scene of castles and flowers. But those flowers were blue. I felt a chill wash over me. I wasn't usually superstitious, but one thing everyone knew was that blue flowers – blue anything – called down trouble. The Wittenbrand considered blue their color and legends said that anyone found wearing it would be claimed by them in soul and body. Nobody with sense wore blue or bought blue or even so much as looked at anything blue in a peddler's cart.

But those kinds of thoughts were just superstition. I knew that. It was just a reflex to be worried about it. There were no Wittenbrand and there would be no stolen souls. I knew better than to believe things that had perfectly reasonable alternate explanations I shook my head at myself and stitched the quilt.

The old woman began to speak. Her voice was surprisingly melodic for a woman of her age.

"The last princess to be presented was Princess Margaretta. And she was your great aunt, Princess Chasida," she said to the girl beside her who sat with a placid smile on her pretty face. Her hair was spun gold and her figure perfect in a blue silken dress. A red gem dangled over her forehead hanging from a golden chain and her eyes were faraway and dreamy like a princess from a storybook. I felt smaller than ever at the sight of her. The old woman was still speaking. "And I was her lady in waiting, as you all know. But that was long before your time.

"The snows were heavy that winter, and the wind bit us, and howled in the trees and it was through the trees that the Wittenbrand came."

I startled at her words. I'd just been thinking of the Wittenbrand and now she told a story about them – it was too strange of a coincidence.

"They took what they willed from us – cattle, horses, gold, and finery. People too. And the tricks they played! Cruel tricks. Things that trapped the mind even when the body was healthy and whole, and tricks that made the body waste away even when the mind was sharp and eloquent. A deal with the Wittenbrand was a deal with death.

"All of the Kingdom of Pen were worried, the wheat was gone, and still there was no spring, and now what was left was being stolen from us. But despite all of that, the King decided to make merry and celebrate the coming of age of his daughter – sixteen-year-old Margaretta. She was in the flower of her youth, young and beautiful with hair like spun sunlight and eyes like slices of a summer lake. He presented her to them all in a gown of gold – a gown much like yours, Chasida, except in color."

Princess Chasida's round cheeks blushed prettily and she glanced across the assembly and sighed. Around me, the other girls sighed with her and again my eyebrows wrinkled. Did none of these girls have any common sense? That thing that let you see through the surface to what was beneath. They all saw a pretty girl sighing beautifully, didn't they? And it warmed their hearts. All I saw was a very spoiled and pretty girl who would be traded by her father for power and influence and a bunch of fools who wished the same for themselves.

My cheeks burned hot at the thought, because I would be traded, too and for considerably less and knowing about it wasn't doing me any favors.

"But that night," the old woman said, "disaster struck, for the Wittenbrand came."

Tales of the Wittenbrand were always full of disaster. No one ever mentioned all the work it probably took to clean up after them. Oh, it might make a fine story to come striding in and tear out the city gate with your bare hands with nothing more said about it but a wink and a smile, but no one mentioned the stone masons and woodcarvers, locksmiths and pursers who had to get involved after that. No one spoke of Jamus, the gate guard who was let go because he couldn't guard a thousand-stone gate without it getting stolen out from under him. No one told those stories.

I chuckled in the privacy of my own mind. If I were a storyteller, those were the stories I would tell, and in those stories I would marry the princess off to someone or something truly hilarious. I would have her marry a toad so that her father could stave off a plague of the creatures, or a fire-breathing steed so her father could equip his military with powerful mounts, or better yet, I would have her marry the Lord of the Wittenbrand and then we would see how much good her sighs and pretty poses were.

In retrospect, it was probably those generous thoughts that led to the curse that fell on me that night.

"What were they like?" the girl beside me asked, clutching her hands to her chest in anticipation.

"The Wittenbrand were far too beautiful – beautiful in the way that the coldest days of winter are – perfect, brittle, and deadly. They swept into our court in silence and in silence we received them. But Princess Margaretta's bells on the end of her golden slippers made a jingling sound, and at the sound of her bell, they froze us to ice and stole away the Princess Margaretta in her golden dress and never have we seen her since."

"But why did they take Margaretta?" the girl beside me asked.

It was a silly question. She'd been there in a golden dress, hadn't she? In the middle of a famine. If the stories of the Wittenbrand were true – that they loved sparkling things and beauty, that they were made of arrogance and haughty desires – then who else would they take? But I did not believe in Wittenbrand or in golden princesses stolen away or in any of that nonsense. Much more likely that this Princess Margaretta had simply run away with a lover or been disgraced and hustled out of sight by her worried family.

Likely, Princess Chasida would wear her fine dress tonight and find herself well-matched to a promising warrior or a prince of a nearby nation, and her life would be well and prosperous. And we would not be frozen unless the servants had forgotten to light the fires in all their excitement.

"Princess Margaretta was bold and bright, unafraid of anything," the old woman said fondly. "It was her bright, bold spirit that drew them in and mesmerized them. They could not help themselves. They were enchanted and so they made enchantment and took her for their own. And when she was gone only one of her golden bells remained in the center of the dance floor."

"Will Princess Chasida be taken, too?" the girl asked.

I almost rolled my eyes. Really? The only threat to Princess Chasida was likely jealous ladies like the one beside me. At least

I could be grateful that my meager hopes came with common sense. I had no need to be envious of the princess, since I never had a chance at what she would have. You couldn't be disappointed if you didn't hope for anything.

"She will not be taken," the old woman said, "for one of you will wear the bell that was once Princess Margaretta's and that will prevent bad luck from befalling her."

There was a gasp of horror from around me and really, I would have liked to pretend I thought it was real, but it was obviously staged. They'd all been expecting this.

"But who will wear the bell?" the girl next to me asked, batting her eyelashes and looking right at me.

And that was when my heart sank, because it was immediately obvious to me that the chair I was sitting in hadn't been empty for no reason.

"Luck shall decide," the old woman said. "Look under your chairs, ladies. The woman with the golden bell under her chair shall wear it tonight for the sake of the princess."

Yes. I was clearly the goat who had been staked out for the false mountain lion.

Wryly, I reached under my chair and drew out the golden bell I knew would be there. The room broke into happy smiles.

"Such an honor!" the girl beside me said in a whisper.

"And don't forget to return it when the ball is over," the old woman said placidly. "It's worth quite a lot."

CHAPTER THREE

We broke to eat in late afternoon. The servants had pulled together a hurried lunch for everyone in the dining hall and most were standing to eat or hurrying in and out. The King and Queen had taken lunch in their rooms so no one need stand on ceremony. I looked for my father and brothers through the masses of moving people and as I did, I heard a girl beside me talking with another lady of fine breeding. The girl was the one who had been practicing her poses before the mirror in the ladies' work room. Her voice had the same bell-like quality I expected. Which reminded me, I'd left the bell in the workroom. I was afraid of losing something so valuable. I'd have to remember to go back and get it before the ball.

"I have heard rumors that a special suitor for the princess will be arriving tonight, Lady Allise. Who do you think that could be?" the girl asked, her words clearly concealing the fact that she was quite sure *she* knew who it would be.

"A foreign prince perhaps?" Lady Allise suggested from behind a carefully placed hand. Her bright eyes sparkled and the emerald hanging over her forehead swayed as she whispered. "They say the king has fine hopes for her. Perhaps the foreign prince will bring some of his lords with him and you and I could have our pick for the dancing. Wouldn't a fine exotic lord be exciting? Perhaps they kiss in a different way in foreign lands."

"I've heard that it's not so much a matter of *how* they kiss but that they do it with a passion that would put a Pensman to shame!"

They were giggling together when I caught sight of my family and hurried to join them at the dinner table. My father was glowing with pleasure.

"Two reasons to celebrate, sweet Izolda," he said, ruffling my hair affectionately. "We went to the practice yards with the aim of finding a place for Svetgin in the military and to our delight the commander was there and has offered him a place as squire for one of the King's own knights."

Svetgin grinned at me broadly, barely able to sit still he was so excited. "I will train with Rodham the Brave, Izolda. Is that not wonderful news?"

"It is." I smiled broadly to share his pleasure with him, but I noted the faint tinge of sadness in my father's eyes at the news. He must make this move now before Svetgin grew older if he wanted to secure a strong place for him, but we would all miss my brother. His enthusiasm and boldness were a welcome reprieve from the sternness of our hold.

Rolgrin smiled, too, though I was certain there was envy mixed in his warm congratulations. He must stay and learn the running of the keep and hold for he was to inherit, but there would be no riding out in glorious armor or swinging a sword with fellow combatants. My father already had him working his tallies and studying the rotation of crops for summer.

"But you said there were two reasons, Father," I reminded him, hoping to cheer Rolgrin up. Perhaps the other news was for him. A blacksmith who could make finer swords.

This time the sadness in my father's eyes deepened further.

"It so happened that while we were in the practice ring, the Landholder of the Fallowplains arrived with a delivery of horseflesh and we spoke together. He is in need of a bride before the spring and his offer was a reasonable one. You'll find Fallowplains a well-suited place for you, daughter. The hold is close enough that you may visit your family every year and you have always done well with horses – the breeding of which is their main occupation."

I schooled my expression to calm, hiding the sudden flare of panic in me. I felt so suddenly cold that it made my head light. Spring? That was only two months from now. And a return to Pensmoore before spring would be impractical. Which meant he would have me married here and now without even a goodbye to my mother first.

I swallowed down a sudden stab of sorrow. After all, this was very sensible. Even knowing nothing of the man in question, I knew that his status as landholder and the fine nature of his holding was the upper limit of what my father could hope to secure for me. He had done very cleverly indeed.

One sad little passion-tinged hope sunk deep within the waves of my heart. There would be no torrid romances or soaring love affairs for me.

I forced a small smile. "Thank you, Father. It is a fine match."

My father's face softened slightly, and he spoke quietly so he would not be overheard. "I think you will find the man acceptable, also, daughter. He is young at only one and thirty, and his first wife died leaving him no heir. He seems as though he is lonely, but he spoke long and well of horses and the keeping of them, and I think you will find that in his single-minded passion for his work, he is unlikely to have acquired many vices. You can see him there now at the line beside the food tables. He is the man with the long black coat and the short beard."

I followed his nod and saw a large, wide man with a round weathered face and a short blond beard. He was not good looking, but he did not look wicked, and his gaze was turned inward, not lingering on the ladies of the court. I could not ask for better.

"You've done very well for me, Father," I assured him, taking in a long breath. I must ready myself. There was work ahead and a marriage and family to face. Fortunately, the things my mother sent me could serve as a trousseau. and while my future husband looked a little worn, his clothing was of good quality. We would not live in poverty. I could work with that.

Right? I didn't need someone good looking or passionate or brave like a warrior from a story. That was all just window dressing for men who usually thought women were temporary entertainments or bargaining chips. But a tiny rebel part of me had been holding out hope for just that kind of man and it was wailing deep within me, refusing to die quietly. Just die, you fool hope! And would you be quiet while you do it for pity's sake?

"I have promised to introduce you tonight at the princess's presentation ball," my father said earnestly. "Adorn yourself well and prettily, daughter."

I nodded my head, but though I was a sensible girl who knew a good thing when she saw it, I still couldn't help the little pang of sadness in my heart that sprang from a wish to be whisked away by a handsome lover and who would speak golden words into my ear and sigh my name with longing.

I think that perhaps, it was that very wish that doomed me. Along with all the other things, obviously.

CHAPTER FOUR

By evening, even *I* was excited for the princess's presentation ball. I had cleaned my traveling clothing and had them packed away again, ready for the inevitable wedding and travel to my new home. I put on my finest wool gown – a deep green, beautifully woven creation of my mother's that hugged my figure nicely all the way to the floor. Over that, my embroidered, sleeveless overdress was laced into place and I carefully braided my own hair in the most elaborate style I knew. It wasn't much. I still looked like the daughter of one of the poorer landholders, but it was my best, and hopefully both my father and my newly betrothed husband would be pleased with my appearance.

I tried very hard not to think of that round face smiling at me. A girl should probably want her future husband to smile for her, but the thought made me just a little ill. It occurred to me that tonight he would be sizing me up like he sized up his brood mares. Would he wonder if I would carry well? If my feed needed to be adjusted?

I took a deep breath. It wasn't sensible to be ungrateful for this opportunity. I would watch for his smile with the same curiosity that I'd employed when I watched the servants set up the ball – and hopefully the same sense of distance.

It didn't do to get too invested in your own life. That only led to disappointment.

I realized as I was leaving my room, that I didn't even know his name. I was going to marry a man whose name I did not know. My heart leapt into my throat again, but I carefully breathed it back down. Vapors and excitements were for girls with money and position, not for those who had to think judiciously of their futures. And not for those who were going to be measured in hands.

My father opened his door, and my brothers exited their room with him. They wore clean, brushed clothing and my father had taken the time to comb his beard. A little shiver of sadness rolled through me. This may be the last time we were all together. After this, I would be married and living in a hold far away and my brother Svetgin would be serving in the King's army.

I hugged him on an impulse.

"What has flown into your head, Izolda?" he said, batting me off. "I'm dancing with beautiful ladies of the court tonight, not sisters!"

Rolgrin was slightly more tolerant. Perhaps he understood what was happening. He let me hug him briefly before hurrying down the hall after Svetgin.

My father was misty-eyed as he embraced me, and he even placed a small kiss on my brow. "Were this your ball and were you princess here you could look no finer, daughter."

I was surprised by his compliment but secretly pleased. It took the edge off the worry I felt as we sallied through the long winding corridors and staircases toward the Great Hall, where the ball would take place. Our rooms in the old servants' quarters were the farthest possible from the hall and I was almost ready to sit down for a while by the time we finally made it into the massive room.

"Lord Savataz of Northpeak and his daughter Izolda," the herald said as we entered.

No one turned to look except for the Lord of Fallowplains who bowed to his companion and strode toward us. I kept my face calm and quiet as his eyes studied me and I saw them linger on my hips.

Yes, get a good eyeful. They're very narrow indeed if you're comparing them to a horse.

It was hard not to feel resentment as he clearly was checking for the pink of health in my cheeks and any sign I could breed well, but I was being unfair to him. He must be clever in his choices just as my father must. Perhaps he had married for love the first time and had come to regret it when his wife died without providing an heir. It was a sad thought and I tried to tell myself it was true if only because it made me feel compassion toward him rather than anxiety.

"Lord Savataz," he said, bowing slightly to my father.

"Lord Danske, may I present my daughter Izolda."

Lord Danske bowed nicely to me and I forced my lips into a smile.

"Greetings to you, my Lord. It is a fair night." My voice sounded too fragile. It should be strong and powerful. It should tell the world I held the reins of my future strongly in my hands. Instead, it told them I was terrified.

"May I be bold, beautiful Izolda," the Lord of Fallowplains said awkwardly, clearing his throat partway through his speech. "May I, ahem, be bold and request a dance from you this evening? The akul, if you would favor me, as it is the only one I know."

No one may now say that I do not have the restraint of a saint. No one. Because the akul involves a great deal of prancing and those who dance it look like they think they are horses. And still, I did not snort a laugh or so much as twitch a lip.

"It will be as you please, my Lord."

"You may call me Leonid," he said, and for a moment he looked like only a nervous man and not a Lord arranging a marriage for himself. I softened.

"If you prefer not to dance, Leonid," I said gently, "I do not require it of you."

He sagged with relief.

"We should suit admirably, if you don't think me too bold in saying so, Izolda." He looked around nervously. "If you don't mind, I'll beg my leave for the moment. I was called away to the stable – my horse had a hot leg and none of the fool stable boys noticed – and so I missed eating at midday. It has left me ravenous."

He was gone as soon as I was done making my bow. I was trying very hard not to imagine life with the ravenous Lord Fallowplains – or Leonid, as I supposed I would have to get used to calling him.

"Daughter?" my father asked, watching me carefully. "You are pleased with the match?"

"Of course," I said with a smile. I was about to take his hand when the herald spoke again and this time, the whole room went still.

"The King, the Queen, and Princess Chasida!"

We fell into bows and curtsies but not before I caught a glimpse of Princess Chasida. She was indeed the sparkling gem of the nation. And she had not brought bad luck on herself by wearing gold like her great aunt Margaretta. Instead, she was dressed in a gown like a sparkling cloud that flowed around her such that it made her look half magic. It was made entirely of blue cloth. Blue.

I was not superstitious, I reminded myself as I sank into my curtsy. But I was also very glad not to be wearing blue. It was so much worse than gold.

I had barely managed to rise when a finger and thumb grabbed my ear, pulling me to my feet, and I looked right into the eyes of the old woman from the work room.

“The bell, girl,” she hissed. “Where is the bell?”

CHAPTER FIVE

I rushed from the ballroom, not even stopping to give my father an explanation for my strange behaviour. I'd forgotten the bell! And while I didn't believe in any of these superstitions, there was just something about tonight with the Princess so bright and beautiful, and the whispers and the wind howling around the castle and that blue, blue dress that was making shivers run up and down my spine like a squirrel on a tree branch.

I lifted up the skirts of my woolen dress and sprinted down the empty corridors and up the lonely staircases. Every noble and servant in the castle was in the ballroom or the kitchens or the coach house right now. There wasn't a soul to slow me.

My breath heaved in my lungs when I finally reached the work room. I snatched the bell from under my chair where I'd left it and paused for one gasping breath to look out the wide window.

I could hardly make out the rooflines of the surrounding buildings. The wind roared cold and harsh, sending gusts of glittering snow puffing with its every movement. It was cold enough that the snow sparkled like shredded diamonds and frost filled the air. I couldn't even see the moon above.

I thought I heard hooves on cobbles and a shout from below, but I didn't recognize the harsh consonants of the words. Perhaps the princess was going to receive a foreign prince after all.

I drew in a second rasping breath and then spun on my heel and paused.

Somehow, impossibly, I could hear the swell of the orchestra, through the open workroom window, and for a bare moment I thought I had turned to confront a dark-haired girl with high color in her cheeks and a sharp, intelligent look in her grey eyes. But it was only my own reflection in the large mirror.

I shook my head and sprinted back down the halls and through the stairways and corridors, my feet echoing loudly through the empty castle wings.

I slowed as I drew nearer the Great Hall. I needed to catch my breath. I must be a sight after that run. The bell jangled merrily as I carefully patted down my braided hair and tucked a loose strand behind one ear, the sound of the bell the only thing I heard.

Jingle. Jingle. Jingle.

My heart was slowing down. My breathing returning to normal.

I plastered a cheerful smile on my face.

And then hesitated.

Why could I hear the bell so clearly when I was just outside the hall? Shouldn't I hear the orchestra? The party?

I stepped past two men standing on either side of the doorframe, their eyes fixed on something within.

And then I froze.

Everyone in the room was standing perfectly still and silent, though they swayed slightly, their chests rising and falling just enough to tell me this was not a trick of my imagination or a spell.

I had a perfect view of the ballroom from the door, almost as if someone had parted the crowd just for me.

I saw my father first, a look of panic on his face as his eyes met mine. I had to tear my gaze away so I could see the rest. I could not find my brothers in the crowds, but I was surprised to notice that my betrothed was watching me with an identical look on his face to that my father wore, as if he, too, was worried for me. It was surprisingly endearing, and it warmed me in a pleasant way. Perhaps being married to Leonid would not be so bad after all.

But I snatched my gaze from his, too, looking to see what was going on.

My bell still jingled slightly as I took a step forward and finally saw King Feolin Pensmoore and Queen Illandre Pensmoore standing just in front of their thrones on the other end of the room. It was as if they had risen in surprise only to find themselves stuck on their feet. They were mirror images of shock – each with a hand reaching toward their blue-shrouded daughter who stood before them facing the ballroom. Her face was so pale that I was afraid she might be dead, and her lips were as blue as her dress.

Her mouth quivered slightly as if she longed to speak but was fighting against an equal longing to keep silent. A single tear streaked down her cheek.

But it was not the princess who had my full attention.

It was the five men standing in the middle of the room. Foreigners, for certain. The crowd had parted so that there was a ring of empty space all around them, and at their very center there stood a man, no taller than all the rest, and yet somehow he seemed to take up more space.

If I were being quite honest – which I probably wouldn't be no matter what the circumstances entailed – he was almost exactly like the fantasy man I'd envisioned falling passionately in love with. The one I was currently trying to mentally murder in my psyche. That one.

He had the same strong shoulders and neatly narrowed hips. He had the same corded arms and sharp jawline. The same black hair and dashing good looks. The same sharp expression that seemed to stab to the heart of your secrets. The exact same smirking irreverence that so often painted my imaginary lover's face.

He was tailor made for my dream-world, except for one small detail that I would certainly never have added.

He had a blue beard.

Not blue like a jay, but blue like a hound or a horse. It was trimmed so close to his face that it was more stubble than beard, and yet I felt frozen by it.

Only the Whittenbrand wore blue.

And it was with that thought that I realized they were all wearing blue in varying shades. Some of their clothing was dusky dove grey-blue and some a powerful peacock. Some a thick blue-black that was so dark it was nearly midnight, and some a light, airy blue that sang of faraway oceans.

The man with the blue beard wore a coat of that deep midnight with a high collar and a small white neckerchief at the throat. He wore a waistcoat under it that clung to his frame in a way that made me swallow. It was a brilliant cerulean. His breeches were just as revealing as the vest and were a smoky Prussian. I did not let my gaze linger on those.

If there had been any doubt about who these men were, all doubt was removed.

Legends had come alive. The Wittenbrand were here.

The bearded one – who I was beginning to think of as "Bluebeard" – made a sudden move toward the princess and wrapped his hand around her throat.

He was inhumanly quick and inhumanly graceful. It was as if a pillar of smoke had come alive and leapt at her. Or perhaps, as if a falcon had morphed into a man. Or whatever a Wittenbrand was.

"So beautiful," he said silkily. "Will you not greet me, Princess? Have you not prayed for a powerful husband, and one rich as sin besides? I have gold of such quantity that your father could fit his soldiers in golden breastplates and greaves. Your mother could sew it into the gown of every maid in the castle. You could gild your very walls with the stuff. Will you not speak and greet me as one of your own?"

His eyes seemed to dance and laugh at her.

The princess's throat bobbed as she swallowed. Her eyes met mine across the room, filled with terror and, when she noticed the tiny golden bell in my hand, filled with hate.

And she was right. I hadn't been here with the bell and now the Wittenbrand were here to snatch her away. But why was no one speaking? Were they under some kind of a spell?

I took a step forward, not sure what I could do and yet feeling responsible to do *something*. After all, it was my error that had allowed all of this. My oversight. My tardiness.

I couldn't let her suffer for me.

I took a second step, and the bell sang out. Bluebeard spun, releasing the princess, and stalked toward me.

In Northpeak, we lost a man almost every year to cougar attacks. I couldn't help but think – as he took that predatory step toward me – that perhaps the men who died were so fascinated by the cougar that they couldn't run or even scream. I knew I was.

He tilted his head, his eyes lighting with delight.

"What a singular golden bell you bear, maiden. But your manners are very poor. Will you not greet a visitor to your King's court?"

My eyes met his. His were blue – of course – and so light they were almost white. My stomach flipped as I realized they were the eyes of a cat, not a human, with black slashes for pupils. They pierced into my own and I could hardly look away.

"Will you not speak and bid us welcome?" He bit his full lower lip after he said that, his cat's eyes dancing as if he were laughing at a joke I hadn't heard.

It seemed suddenly as if he were balancing along a high branch. A bare movement on either side and he would fall to his death, and only my greeting might prevent that. People in such a dire state had a tendency to do wild things. He took a step backward and grabbed the princess by the hair, jerking her head back and exposing her throat.

"Or perhaps we'll wait and see what you say when we're done with this pretty trinket."

My heart leapt into my chest, racing so hard that my breath was coming in ragged gasps. All my fault. If he killed her, it would be on my head, and all because I disregarded a silly princess and her silly friends.

The only sensible thing to do was to try to calm him down.

"I greet you, foreign Lord, and wish you well on this winter night." My voice as clear as a crystal bell. Where had that voice been when I met my betrothed?

As if my words had broken a spell, Bluebeard dropped Princess Chasida. She fell to the ground in a heap, sobbing loudly. Around me, there was a sigh that sounded almost like regret or guilt. My eyes narrowed. Something was going on that I knew nothing about.

Bluebeard smiled – a wolfish, wicked smile.

I felt something tighten in my chest that I couldn't identify. My hand reached up to clutch it, but I'd barely managed a gasp of my own before I caught the eye of my father. His mouth was hanging open in an agonized expression. He took one stumbling step forward and suddenly Rolgrin was there beside him, supporting his arm and whispering urgently in his ear.

"The Law of Greeting," Bluebeard said, his grin widening so now he reminded me of a fox. His eyes seemed to be fixed on me still, which made no sense. What was the Law of Greeting?

Though they had started breathing and murmuring again, the court was still. But this time it was not the frozen stillness of fear, it was the waiting stillness of anticipation. Fear crept up my spine like a slow spider.

To my shock, the Lord of the Fallowplains moved forward, a determined, purposeful look on his face.

"You may not take her, Wittenbrand," he declared. His awkwardness had been shed, and in this one moment he looked like a hero of legend rather than a backwoods breeder of horses who needed an heir.

I bit my lip and tasted blood.

Bluebeard's grin turned to fury. "By the Law of Greeting you know I may take whatever greets me upon my arrival. It is the long-standing agreement between the Court of Pensmoore and the Wittenbrand."

My heart stuttered painfully.

"But you haven't been here in generations," the King said, finally speaking. He had positioned himself before Princess Chasida, shielding her with his own rather substantial body. As if she were still in some kind of danger. Maybe she was. No one had bothered to teach me about the Law of Greeting. Maybe there were more laws I did not know. I was finding it just a little hard to breathe.

"Be glad I have not," Bluebeard said softly, his low voice rumbling like the thunder of a coming storm. "I could have visited you many times over the years and yet I have reserved this moment for a special need. I have come for a bride."

A *bride*?

"The girl is promised to me," Lord Fallowplains – Leonid – said, striding through the crowd toward Bluebeard. My eyes widened and my hand reached up to clutch my chest over my heart. I had not expected so much loyalty from a man who had only just met me. My father had chosen very well indeed.

So why was I still finding it so hard to take a breath?

Bluebeard smirked. "Well, now the promise is broken by the Law of Greeting. Be on your way, hale mortal."

"I will not," Leonid said, swallowing nervously. "It is my life for hers. You will not take her."

He was within reach of Bluebeard now, arms crossed over his chest, squaring his stance, his round chin thrust forward. I had thought he was a large man when I met him, but he seemed small in front of Bluebeard, even though he had four inches at least on the Wittenbrand.

Bluebeard sighed and made an expression of distaste. "What is this? A duel? Over a woman not yet your wife? How horribly last century. I thought we'd moved past that. Haven't we moved past that, Sparrow?"

One of the figures with him snickered unkindly.

Leonid cleared his throat. "I am offering a duel, yes."

"No," I said quickly. "You don't need to do this for me, Leonid."

He made a gesture to quiet me, and Bluebeard snarled.

"Do not silence my betrothed, mortal." His hand shot out, grabbing Leonid by the neck and shook him so quickly that I hardly realized what was happening. Leonid's large head snapped back and then forward like a doll in the mouth of a very large dog.

Princess Chasida screamed so loudly that I heard nothing else and her guards finally came to their senses, rushing forward to surround the royal family.

Bluebeard flung Leonid's limp body aside and I struggled to see him. Was Leonid dead or merely unconscious? How had Bluebeard done that with just one hand? To a man larger than he was?

My hands flew up over my mouth and the little golden

bell dropped to the floor, rolling across the shining marble to Bluebeard's feet.

Bluebeard snatched the bell up, bouncing it on his palm like a toy. It rang every time it struck his palm again. Like a death bell signalling to the town that someone was gone.

Around me, people were shuffling backward, making the gap around me wider and wider. I looked to my own father and he looked back at me, sadness and resignation in his face. Resignation. That was what hit me so hard. What was he going to do? Was he going to try to step up and fight, too?

I shook my head at him, but he took a determined step forward.

I glanced at Leonid. He was very still on the ground. I wasn't certain if he was dead – but he might be. I glanced back at my father pushing through the crowd, his face drained of blood. If I didn't do something fast, that would be him, too.

"I will be your bride," I said. The words had tumbled out of me so quickly that everyone seemed to freeze, listening. "I will be your bride and go from here with you. Only let me say goodbye to my family, and gather my things, and let there be a proper wedding before I leave these lands with you."

Because if I was going to lose everything, I should at least be sure we were properly married and I was not to be a slave or a concubine.

"Done." Was that sorrow I saw in Bluebeard's eyes as they met mine? It must have been a shadow because his eyes immediately shifted to trickery as he turned to the King. "Go find whatever holy man you use and bring him here. There will be a wedding before the hour is gone." He turned to his own men. "Sparrow, Grosbeak, gather her things and take them to our mounts. When the ceremony is completed, we ride."

"This man was so unlucky as to have a blue beard ... Adding to their disgust and aversion was the fact that he had already been married to several wives, and nobody knew what had become of them."

- Charles Perrault, Bluebeard,

1697 as translated by Andrew Lang in The Blue Fairy Book 1889.

CHAPTER SIX

The King cleared his throat. I couldn't even see him anymore behind all his guards. "By the Law of Marriage, you must spend at least one night with your new bride under the roof of her guardian. Since she is of my land, this castle may stand in stead of her home."

Bluebeard waved a mocking hand. "Is it not night? Have we not spent it here beneath your roof? Why ask me to meet conditions that are already met?"

The King's voice sounded strained. "We have laws, and you have laws. The Law of Greeting is where they meet. If you ask us to respect that law, we must respect all the laws."

"This was not required of me the last time I came to claim what is mine."

"A different man was King then. Perhaps he had less fortitude than I do. We will honor the laws. But we will not be dogs before you rolling in the mud. We have laws of our own and we will uphold them. Be ye noble or craven, of sound purpose or twisted, she will be your bride but only if you marry her properly."

My legs felt weak beneath me. The realization that I was actually going to marry this man – that the King was negotiating that the marriage be legal and binding – was suddenly becoming far too real. I met my father's eyes across the room, and I let one moment of my fear show, let him offer his strength in the shared misery in his own eyes, and then I dropped my hands from my mouth and stiffened my spine. I lifted my chin and forced my face into a calm expression. I could be sensible about this.

Bluebeard was here right now in the Court of Pensmoore. He had already killed my betrothed. My family would be next, and then the simpering girls from the workroom, and the King, and Queen, and Princess Chasida, who was having hysterics on the royal dais, and the soldiers and grooms and servants and everyone else. I had no doubt that he and the four others with him could accomplish that. No doubt at all. They wouldn't swagger in here demanding brides – and talking to kings as if they were grooms – if they couldn't enforce their will. Which meant that if I cared for my family and had compassion on these other people, if I cared for the stability of our nation, then there was only one sensible thing to do and that was to marry this foreign blue-bearded murderer and keep them all safe.

It was even a clever match. After all, I was the daughter of a very minor house, and quite dispensable, and he was a threatening foreign lord. A foreign lord of the Wittenbrand. He was one of the strange long-lived beings of legend who scared us in tales told on long winter nights. He was one of the ones rumored to steal children from their cribs and carry off grown women to be their wives. I paused at that thought.

Well now. It was hardly a rumor, was it? It was happening to me. Perhaps I'd been too quick to label things superstitions when they were not.

I'd barely finished the thought when my father and Rolgrin finally made their way to me.

My mouth was very dry.

"You don't have to do this," Rolgrin said as soon as they'd joined me. He shot a furious look at the Wittenbrand, his sword hand grasping at the empty spot on his belt. No one had worn weapons to the ball.

Bluebeard heard him and leaned toward us in a very feline way. One of his eyebrows quirked upward like he was going to share a delicious secret. "If she does not, then the Law of Greeting says that your kingdom is mine from the stones to the rooftops. Every speck of dust of this place will belong to me, and then I could still marry her – and every other woman in this land – for she would be mine, too."

I shuddered.

"But then why have you never done this before?" Rolgrin demanded. He was young and furious, determined to protect me. I shot my father a worried look and he put a hand on my brother's shoulder.

"Who says I have not?" Bluebeard asked. "I'll take that man's lying tongue."

My eyes were so wide now that they stung.

"Princess Margaretta," I gasped. "You were the one who took her."

"Was that her name?" Bluebeard asked indifferently. "Golden-haired round little thing, like that girl who wears our colors so boldly?"

He spared a glance for Princess Chasida and her bright blue dress. I almost thought I saw a glimmer of disgust on his face. He must not like to see mortals wearing his color without warrant.

"I hardly remember her," he said indifferently, and Chasida shrieked in terror.

My father's face grew whiter and I grabbed his other hand, hoping he would see sense.

"Girls are married all the time for the safety of their nations," I whispered to him. "Usually they are princesses and not lower nobles, but it does happen. Even with people like us."

I was surprised by a clinking sound behind me. To my shock, a pair of the King's guards were there with Svetgin between them, locking him in manacles.

"What –" I gasped, and then the King's guards moved fast, ripping my brother and father from me and chaining them with Svetgin. "What are you doing?"

I felt suddenly bereft.

It was the King himself who spoke. As his voice echoed out to me, I realized that the hall was emptying. The pretty girls in their dresses were gone. The band was nowhere to be seen. The Queen was helping the hysterical princess out of the room and most of the guards were going with them.

Chasida gave me a look of pity before she was escorted out the door. She had stayed silent. She had known the law. I didn't know if she pitied me for being ignorant or being a fool but at least I hadn't had hysterics in front of everyone. And that was something I could comfort myself with in the wee hours of the night.

"We don't want anyone else to die, Izolda of Savataz. I'm sure you can understand that." The King's tone was not unkind. "It's for the safety of your brothers and father. They cannot decide to do something heroic under lock and key. They cannot be killed by the Wittenbrand if we keep them from being fools. I promise you, fair lily, I will release them all the moment you and your bridegroom are out of sight of the city walls. Until then, they will be kept comfortable, but they will remain under guard."

One glance back at the red in my father's cheeks told me the King was wiser than I had guessed. My father *had* been planning to fight for me. Perhaps he had been waiting for the right moment or for Svetgin to join them so they would be three to five. Either way, in that moment I was grateful to the King. My mother would get to keep two of her three children and my father as well. This was better. Rolgrin was but seventeen and Svetgin only fifteen. They did not need to die for an older sister when they hadn't even tasted life properly.

One death in exchange for their lives – and also the lives of thousands of others – was a small price to pay.

"As you say, my King," I said respectfully, and he gave me a rueful smile. His craggy face and reddish nose looked almost comforting. Which was saying something. Truly, this was an odd day.

The King hadn't left the dais. Now he gestured, and my family was carefully brought to one side below the dais.

"If we are to have a wedding, let us do it properly," he said stiffly. "The bride's family are on this side. And the bridegroom's on this side."

Bluebeard chuckled, still bouncing my golden bell on his palm like a cat playing with a toy.

"I do not think you wish to see my family, little King. They would give you nightmares that may kill you in your sleep."

He rubbed his blue beard and considered me in a way that made me think again of a cat. This time, of one eyeing a mouse. I stood even straighter to show him I was no mouse. He smirked.

He could smirk all he wanted. I was not the one with a horrendous blue beard or the need to trick people into marrying me. I'd had someone who actually wanted to marry me.

I shot a guilty glance to where Leonid lay – lifeless – on the ground. I wanted to believe he had merely swooned. I was almost certain I was wrong.

He'd been a good man, though I'd barely known him at all. He hadn't deserved to die honorably defending a woman he'd only just met. He deserved far better. What would his hold do now with no heir and no Lord? I felt a stab of worry for them, but I must not let that distract me. There was nothing I could do to help, and I knew the King would take care of them. He would install one of his best knights there to manage the hold and people, and in time the wound would heal. Though likely Leonid's horses would miss him for the rest of their lives. I had a feeling that they were very attached to him.

"Gathering wool?" someone whispered in a rough voice at my ear.

I startled and turned with narrowed eyes to see the wicked glint in Bluebeard's.

"I was mourning the death of my betrothed before marrying another. It seemed fitting. Especially since my new husband was his slayer." I made my words icy cold.

"Is that who that was?" He said the words like they were maple candy he was turning over on his tongue. "Your betrothed. What a shame. You could have borne his gigantic babies."

"You know he was," I said acidly. "He told you so."

"I wasn't listening. I rarely bother listening to mortals. They speak and speak, but in the end, they just die before they're even done talking," he said, waving a hand languidly. "Speak to my riddle, fair mortal. What keeps you waiting until it dies?"

"Hope?" I asked.

He chucked in delight. "A better answer than mine. I was going to say 'kings.' Can we get on with this ceremony?"

"Yes," the King said, and I saw the bitterness souring in his eyes – but there was relief there, too, and guilt whenever he glanced at my father. He knew how close he had come to seeing his own daughter wed this way. And he knew that he'd have no trouble from my father over it. My father was a loyal King's man. He'd be loyal to the point of death. Even now. Even when his daughter stood substitute for the princess in a wedding meant to protect the kingdom.

Someone shoved an old man in a robe forward and I startled. I was too deep in my own thoughts. Had my heart ever sped this fast before?

He looked priest-like, but I wouldn't know. We only had monasteries up in Northpeak and the monks only came out in the summer to sell honey mead and, three other times a year, to sing to us of holy things and perform marriage and death rites all in one big batch. They preferred to divide life into slices like a goodwife with a pie.

The old man tottered slightly, blinking as he looked around him.

"It's a wedding, brother," the King murmured.

"Ah yes," the old priest said, "And we'll do the traditional vows, of course."

"No." Bluebeard snapped the word. Behind him, his men shuffled like nervous horses.

Of course, he wouldn't want to do traditional vows. There was no way this ravager of kingdoms and thief of maidens was going to promise fidelity to me.

"You promised the marriage would be legal," the King prompted. "There must be vows."

And for just a moment, I saw a glimmer of pain in my enemy's eyes. Now, what was that? I had a mind to draw it out further and examine it. It could be useful in keeping me alive.

"I have never said vows before," he said in a way that made me think of snakes hissing.

"But you will say them to me," I said firmly. I didn't need the king to stand up for me. I could stand up for myself. "Or we will not be wed."

He looked at me for a very long time and behind him, one of the men spoke in a language I did not know. It sounded like a curse.

Bluebeard bit his lip and then said, "And what will you give me in return, mortal woman?"

"The same vows," I said, my cheeks flushing. "You give me yours and I give you mine. Is that not what marriage is?"

There was a glitter in his strange cat's eye, as if he'd never considered such a thing, and for a moment his hand strayed to the hilt of his sword. My breath caught in my throat. I didn't dare let it out. I had the feeling I was a heartbeat away from him drawing the sword and slicing my throat, but after a moment he tilted his head slightly to the side and then he laughed.

He smirked. "I will offer the vows of my people."

Behind him, one of his men shut his mouth with a loud click and the other gasped.

I darted a glance to him. There were three remaining, as one had gone to gather my things. All three wore stony expressions on their beautiful faces. They were all of swarthy of skin and hair with brilliant blue cat's eyes – but while their coloring matched and their beauty was similar, each had his own appeal. One was a woman. One had a huge scar that twisted up from either side of his mouth. My future husband seemed taller than the rest of them – though he was not – and with his blue beard and a scar that cut down across one brow, he looked the roughest and cruelest of all.

"Then let us say our vows together," the priest burbled happily. "The groom may begin."

Bluebeard was staring at me like I should realize how significant this was. He leaned forward slightly, looking as if he might leap at any moment. Seeing as it was my wedding, I was very cognizant of its importance.

"As long as rivers run and moon shines, as long as the earth has bones and death has claws, as long as the ages pass and fail – that long shall I be husband to you. Flesh of my flesh and bone of my bone you will be. Spirit of my spirit, heart of my own heart, fall what may, we shall be one. Your days shall be mine and your happiness my own. My body I dedicate to none other. The bounty of my wealth is yours. If ever it be otherwise, may I waste away with sickness and may famine eat my strength, and may my enemies overtake me, and siphon from me the blood of my life."

Well, that was somewhat extreme.

Perhaps I should have been horrified. A smart girl would have been. But mostly, I was just fascinated. This vow was deeper than any I'd heard before. It seemed to match the tightness that had surrounded my heart since I spoke my greeting. It was just as immobilizing. Just as binding. Just as deadly terrifying.

“And now the wife,” the priest said. “Say your vows, kind lady.”

I looked at Bluebeard and paled.

“It was you who wanted a real marriage and I have complied with your wishes, you ambitious climber.” He said the words like he was spitting them. “You ask for things above you and I have granted them and now you reject my gift?”

“I reject nothing,” I said carefully. I didn’t know why he thought this was some kind of maneuver on my part, but I wasn’t ready to see blood spilled over it, and there was violence in his eyes. “But I will need your help. The words are unfamiliar to me.”

With his prompting, I repeated his vow.

“As long as rivers run and moon shines, as long as the earth has bones and death has claws, as long as the ages pass and fail – that long shall I be wife to you. Flesh of my flesh and bone of my bone you will be. Spirit of my spirit, heart of my own heart, fall what may, we shall be one. Your days shall be mine and your happiness my own. My body I dedicate to none other. The bounty of my wealth is yours. If ever it be otherwise, may I waste away with sickness and may famine eat my strength, and may my enemies overtake me, and siphon from me the blood of my life.”

I felt a chill wash over me at my words. When I glanced behind me, my father’s face was wet with tears and my brothers’ expressions were sickened.

“And so, I declare, man and wife,” the priest said, still seeming to be oblivious to our situation. “And you may kiss your bride.”

“There will be no kisses,” Bluebeard said.

And for that one thing, I was thankful to him.

CHAPTER SEVEN

"You should say your goodbyes now," Bluebeard said, his shining cat's eyes never leaving my face. He had an odd look on his face like he was trying to read my mind right through my skull. "We leave at first light. I think that counts as spending the night under your roof, little King."

The King's mouth tightened but wisely, he said nothing. What could he say? We all had heard of the power of the Wittenbrand – even if I'd been a skeptic until today.

A thousand years ago, they waged a war against humans and nearly destroyed us completely. We still didn't know why they'd called a truce and relented. We only knew that we were bound by some old treaty to allow them into our mortal courts if they asked it and to provide a tithe to them if requested. And apparently, there was this Law of First Greeting no one had told me about and now a Law of Marriage no one had seen fit to mention. Because obviously, you wouldn't mention it to the one person who likely should have been told. Where would the fun be in that?

Whoever had designed this world of Kings and Wittenbrand had been like the ladies in the workroom – not very interested in the consistency of their work.

I kissed my father's cheeks gently, ignoring – for the sake of his pride – that they were so wet and his eyes so glassy that he likely saw only a blur instead of a daughter.

"Your honor is not besmirched," I whispered to him. "Tell my mother that you did all you could do and paid a high price for the sake of the kingdom. And do not forget that the King owes you now. It could have been his daughter who was taken. Be sensible. Demand a knighthood for Svetgin and a good bride for Rolgrin. Tell my mother that I love her and will miss her and that she must not blame any of you."

"My Izolda," my father began, but I kissed his cheeks again, embraced him, and his voice broke. He need not say anything, for I knew his heart and that he loved me and that he wished beyond anything that he could save me from this.

"I absolve you of any guilt," I said. "Live in peace."

I kissed each of my brothers and murmured to them, "Live well and be prosperous. Your sister is proud of you."

They seemed stunned as they spoke the words of goodbye back to me, their voices hollow with shame and their faces pale as death.

In time, they would forgive themselves. There had been no way they could protect me from this. I had sealed my own fate. It would have been silly to think otherwise or to expect the impossible from any of them. A part of me found it interesting that they had been willing to risk me to a marriage that only had a dice roll's chance of success as long as it was within a world they were comfortable with, but they were terrified to offer me to this foreigner and found it shameful, though the risk was similar to me. The difference was only in degrees and not in kind. For all I knew, this inhumanely beautiful monster also loved horses and spent his time breeding them. For all I knew, he could also be so obsessed with them that he thought of little else.

It was unlikely, but still possible.

But even though I could see all that, I loved them too much to want to leave them with sadness or shame.

"Cheer up, my father and brothers," I said bravely, "for though I may never see you again, you have given me in marriage to a foreign lord for the sake of our nation and should feel no shame in it. Indeed, I'm sure your King and country thank you."

I looked at the King. He swallowed and his face turned red almost instantly. There. I'd planted a sliver into his mind. He would always remember how he owed my family a debt.

Oddly, he leaned in for a fatherly kiss on the cheek. "Go with our blessing, daughter of Pensmoore."

And then I turned and faced my fate.

My new husband wore a strange expression on his face and a darkness in his eyes that made my heart speed, and my knees turn to jelly. I took one wavering step before I forced the iron of my will into my legs and managed a straight back and steady steps again. It took an effort of will that consumed most of my energy.

We were all silent as the King himself led us down a short corridor to a suite of rooms as fine as his own – perhaps they were his very own.

"Your men will be given appropriate accommodations," he said tightly. "And you are free to leave at dawn, having consummated your marriage and made a legal binding out of what has been offered nation to nation."

And now it was my face that was hot as fire as I realized why he'd insisted on a night beneath his roof and a wedding chamber for us both. And if I'd been irritated at my people for trading me off as tradition demanded, I was even more horrified at a King who offered my innocence up as the price of security for his kingdom.

And yet the practical side of me was impressed. It was a very tiny price for a kingdom to pay for security. And it cost the King almost nothing at all. He was getting a very clever bargain. Even if my cheeks flamed at how it would be paid. I doubted I could be so cold.

I did not meet his eye as my new husband growled in answer and opened the door.

"How hospitable," he spat. "Your laws, mortal man, are as delightful as your city."

The King seemed mollified by that – which was ridiculous. Could he not see that the Wittenbrand mocked both his laws and holdings?

At Bluebeard's curt nod into the room, I entered the suite before him and managed to hold myself together long enough for him to follow and lock the door behind us.

After that, it was all I could do to make it to the nearest flower pot before losing the lunch I'd hurriedly eaten at midday when my life seemed settled, and the supper of dried meat and hardtack I'd eaten on the road the night before, when I'd been excited to see the city for the very first time. With the contents of my stomach, I brought up every hope I'd ever had of living a happy – or even a quiet and relatively peaceful – life.

"How very mortal of you," Bluebeard said with a grimace when I was done. He shoved a pitcher of wash water toward me and strode away as I dutifully washed out my mouth.

I was grateful he'd given me the whole jug. One more glance into the room and at the massive four-poster bed with its thousands of pillows and silken bedcoverings and I was heaving up the last of the acid in my belly. It turned out I needed most of the pitcher to rinse my mouth before I made it any farther into the room. Just the sight of that bed was enough to make me queasy again. I wasn't ready for this. Not with a man who had just killed another with his bare hands. Would he snap my neck, too?

"I will promise you very little beyond what promises have already been made," Bluebeard said from a chair by the fire, where he was reading a book entitled *Marvels of Modern Accountancy,* "but I can promise you this. I will feed you food that sits better in your stomach and has not soured. The ladies of my court do not spend most of their time bringing up what has been fed to them."

At least he thought I'd eaten something bad. That was a good thing. I swallowed down another wave of nausea. I doubted he'd be pleased if he learned the real reason for my sudden attack of illness. I didn't have much experience with men, but likely the idea that I was sick at the thought of him consummating our wedding would irritate him.

At the very least.

Possibly even enrage him.

The sensible thing would be to hide my feelings on the matter.

It was hard to do when he was already half disrobed, his jacket and shirt unbuttoned and open to his breeches and one of his legs slung up over the arm of the chair.

I looked around the room warily – trying to put my eyes on anything other than him. He was not entirely human with his too-quick movements, his flickering facial expressions, and those strange eyes mesmerized me.

He twitched his nose just a little when he spoke like a cat might. But none of that took away from the very masculine lines of his body or the way his muscles – laced with silvery scars – were taut and well disciplined. No, it would be unwise to let surface things influence my opinions of the violent murderer who had married me. If I did that, then I'd be like those girls preening in the mirror and I'd fall into a worse trap than I'd fallen in already.

It was worrisome enough to be married to an unpredictable man of violence. It would be much worse if I allowed myself to let my emotions swirl when he was around. A clear head was my last weapon.

Better to focus on the room. It was massive – which gave me a lot to look at. Bigger than my parents' apartments and all of their children's put together. It was also grand – filled with objects of curiosity and fine craftsmanship. I could spend all night going from one to the next and not have time to give each its proper due. They were stored on shelves and in cases, on little tables and in opened chests. The chest nearest me held a helm and mail shirt made entirely of gold and adorned with gems made to look like peacock feathers. It was utterly impractical – and beautiful as a summer's day.

There was a wide door to one side, and I could see through it a brass tub and stack of cloths for drying. The enormous bed sat on a raised dais, a window with a small balcony on one side of it, and a huge fireplace with a roaring fire on the other. Beside the fireplace were a pair of high-backed chairs and a stack of books.

Bluebeard was skimming the books and then throwing them into the fire one by one. I tried very hard not to be appalled. It didn't work. Instead, I bit my lip.

He was not just a murderer, but also a book murderer, which felt similar in an odd way.

"Not a single worthy page in the lot of them. As if economics is not a black art of magic controlled by a few demon summoners. And this one! A treatise on morality. From a group of people who sell me delicious young women as brides for nothing more than the promise not to kill them."

He looked up at that and smirked. I tried to keep the fear from my expression as I opened my mouth to ask him how old he was, but he raised a hand to forestall me and leapt up from his chair, flinging the book he'd been holding into the flames. They burst into sparks that shot out into the room like a thousand orange stars.

He was in front of me – inches from me – in a heartbeat. His finger covered my lips and his beautiful eyes looked into mine. All of a sudden that tightness in my chest drew me to him as if I had been fitted to a yoke pulled inexorably to his breast by a dozen oxen. I fought the feeling and kept my feet firmly planted in place.

"As of the moment we were married, the spell of magic and its curse has fallen upon us," his voice oddly breathy. "I must warn you not to break the spell under any circumstances, or the curse will come to pass and with it, the goodwill I have for your people will end. I will turn on this place and ravage the cities and lay waste to the towns. I will burn every home and any place where two sticks have been set on one another. I will sow the fields with salt so that no crops will grow. I will slaughter the inhabitants and lay them out head to foot across the kingdom and write in their blood that these souls were lost because of Izolda of Savataz. Is that clear? Don't speak."

I swallowed, nodding carefully. He was a madman.

"Good. I see you understand perfectly." He smiled one of his foxy smiles.

I understood *perfectly* that he was utterly insane.

"There are terms to our marriage that go beyond the vows," he said.

Even I knew that. Why did he think I was vomiting into the flowerpot?

"I have not the patience to tell you all of them."

What a surprise. No one had bothered to tell me *any* of them, which was how I ended up here.

"Would you like to hear one term, though? The one that matters most tonight?"

I had to look away from his eyes. They were too intense, as if he could peel back my layers and expose my core.

I looked nervously at the bed, but he caught my chin between his finger and thumb and brought my gaze back to his deadly and beautiful face.

"The curse is this – I may not speak a word to you in the day and you may not speak a word to me at night or the spell will be broken and, with it, our marriage. You must heed me on this."

I blinked at that. Stunned by such a very strange request.

"And if the curse is triggered, I will have to enact the horrors I just enumerated. Do you understand?"

I nodded. But seriously, the threats were going to have to slow down or I was going to pass out from how ill I felt.

“I think that will do for tonight,” he said, releasing me. His eyes seemed to be weighing me like he was going to purchase me by the pound. “I didn’t ask my men to bring your things here and I don’t think I will. Take something from the King’s wardrobe to sleep in.”

He nodded to a tall armoire, and wordlessly, I stumbled to it and opened it. Robes of silk and fur in every color known to man, embroidered with scenes of hunting and fishing filled the wardrobe. All of them could have fit three of me. I stretched an arm out to take one and he reached past me, snatching up a royal blue robe in shining silk that was trimmed with white fur.

“I’ve changed my mind. You should wear this,” he said with a wink.

Icy cold shot through me.

I paused for a moment, not taking the robe. I’d agreed to the silence and agreed to the marriage. But if I didn’t put my foot down somewhere, I’d be nothing more than a doormat. I looked him squarely in the eyes and reached past the blue robe to pull out a gaudy bright red one trimmed with orange fox fur, and covered all over with scenes of a particularly bloody hunt.

I turned on my heels and went to the dressing screen without looking back, though I heard his growl behind me. As I stripped out of my dress and wrapped the robe around me, the growl turned to a laugh.

I hung my dress up carefully and stepped out from behind the screen, the hood of the robe pulled up over my head.

He smirked and gestured toward the bed. “I’ll take the chair. Go to sleep. It will be a long ride tomorrow.”

Wait. What? He wasn’t going to … My cheeks heated again.

He raised a single eyebrow.

"Fifteen wives I have had of mortal blood and fifteen wives have worn what I told them to wear that first night. But I sullied myself with none of them and I will not sully myself with you either, even though you are clearly no mortal woman but rather a demon sent to torture me."

And with that insulting declaration, he stalked over to his chair and sat down much more energetically than necessary, picking up yet another book, cursing, and throwing it into the flames.

I seized the opportunity, ran across the cold flagstones, and flung myself into the massive bed, gathering the blankets around me like the walls of a keep and burrowing into them so that nothing of me showed but my eyes.

I do not know how long I waited like that, afraid and close to being ill again, as he cursed at book after book, but eventually, sleep stole me away more thoroughly than the Wittenbrand could.

CHAPTER EIGHT

The next morning, I woke still shrouded in blankets. My legs ached from being curled up under me all night and my eyes were surprisingly puffy. I wiped them awkwardly. I might have been crying in my sleep and I did not like that at all. If he'd seen that, it was a sign of weakness.

The sun was not yet up, and Bluebeard was asleep beside the dying fire, his head hanging over the high back and his mouth wide open as if he were a particularly expensive fly trap.

By the candle clock on the wall, it was five bells of the morning.

I crept from the bed, slipped into the bathroom, and poured water quietly to clean myself. It was cold – of course – and brisk in the winter room, but I scrubbed myself carefully and wiped away all signs of tears, combing out my long hair and braiding it in an elaborate double-woven braid – the fanciest I knew how to make.

I was not vain. I knew well enough that I was not the fairest girl of the court.

My face was long rather than round, my eyes tilted slightly instead of wide and large, and my mouth had an unusual bend to it, so it often looked like I was smirking when I was not. And my figure – such as there was of it – was more bony than properly curvy. I had a serviceable body and a face that expressed my thoughts, and a woman could hardly ask for more when she had her health and family.

My thoughts stuttered at that part because I no longer had a family, though I did have a very strange husband.

I would simply have to make do with him.

And, I would have to look the best I could, and hold my head high, so that I at least kept my dignity, even if all else had been plundered.

I turned, meaning to collect my dress, and gasped when I saw Bluebeard leaning in the door.

"You move very quietly for a noble woman," he said, narrowing his eyes. "I don't know if I trust that."

I bit back the response that rose in my throat. I was hardly the untrustworthy one since I was not the one who was going to be stealing *him* away today.

He raised an eyebrow. "Don't speak."

I was trying not to speak, but it was very hard to keep all my questions inside.

How long had he been standing there? Only long enough to watch me braid my hair or long enough to watch me washing myself, too? I tried to think back to how much skin might have been shown and I couldn't remember. I'd thought I was alone. I dared not make that mistake again.

"Be that as it may," he said with a strange, almost hungry look in his eye. "I will need to stop speaking to you when the sun rises, so I must remind you that if anyone asks, you should tell them that we consummated our marriage, or they will think this wedding was a sham."

I felt my face heat at the thought of confirming that to anyone.

He paused, rubbing his short blue stubble with one hand. "I see you are of two minds about it. Well, there is still time." His expression turned wolfish. "If you prefer not to lie about it, we can consummate it now, and then you can blush prettily about the truth instead of a lie. Does that suit you, wife?"

It did not suit me. At all.

Though I did find myself swallowing a lump in my throat that hadn't been there a moment ago. This was the first time that a very beautiful man with his hair tousled from sleep and had lounged against a doorframe and suggested an intimate act to me. And it was the first time I'd been called 'wife.' It was a powerful word – a word that left little chills running up my legs.

I needed to remind myself that he was not human, that he had stolen – or perhaps bought – me as one might acquire livestock, that he had ridiculous rules about our lives together, that he had threatened the death of thousands if I disobeyed, and that he had likely killed the honorable man who had tried to defend me. That last part cleared my head admirably.

I shook my head and he smiled as if he'd just solved a problem and expected to be congratulated.

"Well then, that's cleared up. Tell them I was a delight. Tell them I was a better lover than any you could have imagined."

He seemed absolutely sincere about that. I felt my jaw dropping in shock. As if I would ever say any of that!

He turned and padded back into the room, and I realized his

feet were also bare and that there was something strange about them. It almost looked as if the floor was mossy where he had stepped. Ridiculous.

He looked over his shoulder and called a parting shot. "Speak to my riddle, wife of mine. Or rather, don't, but do contemplate it. What does the ship feel when the tide turns? What does the bird wish when the wind shifts? What does a man think when his fortunes reverse?"

He didn't stay to wait for the reply, which was good, because I might have been tempted to answer with the only answer I could agree with right now – *fear*.

I shook my head and dressed quickly before any other dangerous offers were made to me.

But I couldn't help but think that I was biting off more than I could possibly chew with this husband I'd acquired. Even if he didn't kill me before the week was over – which he very well might – he may just break me and leave me in pieces.

I needed to wear my good sense like armor and keep a close watch.

True to his word, at the first ray of dawn, Bluebeard rose and bathed himself. He had none of my concern for modesty, and one glance at the bathroom told me to keep my back firmly to the door. I fed the fire in silence, trying very hard not to remember what I'd seen in the split second I'd noticed him in there. He was my husband, and I supposed there was no harm in looking, but he had also been very clear that he was my enemy and his sheer beauty was a weapon he could use against my maiden mind. I would not so easily fall into its trap.

I didn't turn when he was done until he tapped me on the shoulder and smirked, waggling his eyebrows at me.

"I suppose we're leaving now," I said carefully, testing to be sure it was allowed and wouldn't end in sudden bloodshed and rampage.

But he didn't even acknowledge that, merely slipping on his boots and jacket as if I were a fly buzzing around his head. "I have a lot of questions. About things you said last night."

Still nothing.

"Perhaps tonight you can tell me why you've had fifteen wives. It seems an inordinate number for one man to have, don't you think? Are they still living? Am I to meet them?"

What had gotten a hold of me? It was a *very bad* idea to poke at the man who held my fate in his hands. And yet the longer he was silent, the bolder I felt.

"And if they are dead, did they all die of being around you? That doesn't recommend your company."

At that he looked up, fixing me with a devilish glare made all the more devilish by how the sunlight caught his nearly white cat's eyes. I gasped and he leapt up, seized me by the throat, licked his lips, and hovered so close to me that for a moment I wasn't sure if he was about to break my neck or kiss me. He released me suddenly and strode to the door, opening it so hard and fast that it hit the wall, bounced, and nearly smacked him on his smart behind.

Well, then. No more teasing about the wives, perhaps.

Unless he really bothered me.

I followed him out into the hall, where his men were already waiting. Two of them held my chest and the female one had a saddlebag in her hand. She was armored the same as the others, and for a moment I was envious of her thick armor and sharp sword. I could use a sword like that.

"Let's see her things," Bluebeard said briskly.

They opened my chest.

"What are you doing?" I asked. But, of course, he couldn't respond to me. He just started throwing my plain dresses to one side and the pretty to the other. I had very few of either, but it made sense. If we were traveling by horseback, then we would need a light load.

"At least let me take the necessities," I said, pushing past him to take a small woven bag of soaps and combs and other needed things from the chest and put it in the bottom of the bag. I added my handkerchiefs and reached for a plain shift.

He ripped it from my hand, snorting, and took a lace one from the chest instead. Something my mother had added to my chest, for reasons unknown to me.

"That's impractical," I objected. "There's hardly enough there to keep me warm!"

He batted me backward and to my horror, shoved the lightest, fanciest dresses into the saddlebags, and threw the practical gowns aside.

"Wait! You've left all the useful ones."

I scrambled for the warm woolen shifts, but he kicked them aside, tossing my fur-lined cloak to me. I caught it and put it on. At least it was warm as well as pretty. To my surprise, he added a book to my bag. A book of tales. One from our room last night that he had not chosen to burn. He did not choose a single practical item except a small mirror.

"Leave the rest," he ordered his men. "My wife will ride on my mount with me."

"I have a very good bay mare of my own," I objected. "She is well suited to traveling and will be no bother."

It was like he didn't even notice my words. He strode past and his men fell in behind him as if they practiced walking down corridors together. His female warrior was no different. She didn't even look twice at me as she snatched up my saddlebags.

I stood frozen in place until they stopped, waiting for me.

One of the Wittenbrand turned – a little too quickly for a human. "Will you come, or must you be carried, girl?"

"My name is Izolda," I said, clenching my fists at my sides.

He grinned a creepy grin, with those scars that cut up from his mouth, like the grin of a toad. "Must you be carried, Izolda? I have stolen many a mortal from this world. I can sling you over my shoulder and have you dreaming pink dreams and sighing purple sighs before we reach Wittenhame."

In answer, I hurried to catch up to them. There would be nothing more undignified than being carried by them out the doors and through the city like an ill-tempered child. And I didn't want to know anything about pink dreams or purple sighs.

If there were servants in the halls, they ducked out of the way before we reached them. I saw a streak of black dart into one door and a white apron edge into another, and both doors were quickly shut.

"There was only one welcome for us in this Hall," Bluebeard said the third time it happened as one of his men put a hand to a sword hilt. "And it was the only welcome I required."

And the only welcome that could doom me to losing my life,

but we wouldn't mention that.

He paused and his men paused with him in the empty, vaulted corridor. I looked up at the groin-vaulted ceiling. I still wasn't used to the grandeur of this place. And perhaps I never would be, since I was unlikely to see it again.

Bluebeard looked to the man right beside him. "We are not all armed as we should be for the journey."

His man looked curiously from one of them to the next, his brow wrinkling and with good reason. They were all very, very armed.

Swords hung strapped across backs or down the sides of their legs. One man had a small axe at the waist and another a quiver of silver arrows and a bow. Bluebeard had his own quiver and bow and a sleek sword at his waist. Their weapons – oddly enough – were made almost exclusively of a metal that shone like bronze. Little knives were strapped at the tops of boots or their hilts peeked teasingly out jacket cuffs. Not a mote of iron was on the lot of them.

And there was only one of us who was not armed.

"He means me," I said after the silence stretched out. "I am not armed."

"We don't arm mortals. We never have," the man closest to him said.

"We will arm this one," Bluebeard said. "As soon as possible."

His men frowned in a way that looked close to rebellion, but they touched the opposite shoulder with a hand, and it looked like a salute.

Interesting. So, he wouldn't talk to me, but he was … sort of caring for my needs. In the most ridiculous way possible. I could have used my chest of warm dresses – or even just one of those double-thick wool woven gowns. Instead, he'd tossed those, kept the lace, and now he was acquiring a weapon for me. He was a puzzle.

That paused my thinking.

He was a puzzle I was going to have to figure out if I had any hope of making my life last longer than the ride to his lands. That was my goal. I must pick this Wittenbrand apart and know him up and down.

It was the only way to survive this madness.

The king was waiting for us in the Gatehouse with most of his court arranged behind him and a line of palace guards in front of him.

I craned my neck, looking for my brothers and father, but I could not see them. Bluebeard whispered to one of his men and the man grabbed me roughly by the arm and pointed to a balcony above. My father and brothers were there – their chains removed but naked blades pointed at them from four guards.

I waved up at them and schooled my face to calm. They would prosper and be at peace – as long as I was wise and did not tempt them to action.

"The marriage has been completed?" the King asked, looking at me.

My cheeks flamed and my eyes widened. I was not sure what to say.

"It must be completed, by the Law of Marriage," he insisted and behind him one of the girls tittered nervously.

A sinking feeling stabbed through me at that. But when Bluebeard's eyes shot to the offender, his hand gripping the hilt of a sword, I raised a staying hand.

"All the Laws have been fulfilled, my King," I said.

There was a growl behind me from my husband and one of Bluebeard's men leaned in close. "No wife of my master calls a mortal their King."

I swallowed, waiting for a tremor of fear to pass, and I was surprised to see that the king was doing the same thing.

"I do not know his given name," I said cautiously, "nor have I the right to use it. What would be a proper mode of address?"

No one answered my question.

Without looking at me, Bluebeard met the King's eyes and made a declaration.

"The agreement of the ages has been met. Peace will remain with you until we meet again. Do not forget the Laws."

"We thank you," the king said, and maybe his voice was a little breathy when he said it.

"Where is the sword?" Bluebeard asked with a frown.

"Sword?" the King asked, perplexed.

"The marriage sword, as is tradition the morning after a wedding. Where is hers?" Bluebeard looked around at everyone nearby with his brows drawn down and fury on his face.

The King snapped his fingers and one of his guards rushed forward. There was some whispering and then after a few minutes, a fine sword was produced in a silver-worked scabbard. The king tried to hand it to Bluebeard, but he scoffed.

"No, *she* gives it to me so that no knife may cut our bond. Do you not exchange swords in this barbarous mortal world?"

My husband was nearly shaking with some sort of pent-up emotion that I read as rage.

The King offered me the sword with an air of great care, and I offered it to Bluebeard just as gingerly.

He grunted in satisfaction, accepting the sword and scabbard and slipping off one of three belts he was wearing, adding the sword and scabbard to it.

He knelt before me so suddenly that I gasped, and in a moment, he was unbuckling a second sword from his waist – one the length of my forearm and made of that odd coppery metal. It was very finely made indeed. He wrapped his arms around me and as my face went hot – again! – he placed the belt around my hips and tightened it before buckling the sword on.

"It is done," he declared to those around.

That was it and then he was striding through the gates and one of his band – the woman – was guiding me out behind him, and I couldn't tell if she had my arm to guard me or to keep me from lingering. I shot one last look at my brothers and father on the balcony and then I was torn forward again, being hurried through the gatehouse and out to the mist beyond.

Oddly, it seemed as though Bluebeard's men had formed a ring around me rather than him – as if it was my life they were guarding. I shook my head but then stopped. As ridiculous as that might seem, I was certain that it was fact. For some reason, I was valuable to them. And that they thought I was in some kind of danger.

"It shouldn't be misty," I said aloud. "Not after all that snow."

No one listened to me. That was starting to be the new normal. Instead, Bluebeard gave a piercing whistle with his fingers in his mouth while one of his men spoke low and fervently to the gate guards. He came back with a pair of daggers on a man's belt and handed them to Bluebeard, who – without any ceremony at all – turned and slipped his arms around me a second time.

I gasped and one of his eyebrows rose like he found me amusing. The belt slid around me, and he buckled it for me in the front. Even buckled on the tightest hole, it hung loosely over my hips. He made an irritated sound in the back of his throat, produced a knife from his sleeve, and cut a new hole for me before cinching the belt.

"Thank you," I said, because what else did you say? I was very well armed indeed and almost half again as heavy as I'd been an hour ago.

Around me, there were looks of approval – as if I'd been undressed until this moment and someone had taken the time to clothe me decently.

And then I caught sight of our mounts.

They appeared through the mist blazing a bright white and shaking snow from their beards, their red eyes flashing. They were antlered elk. Massive ones – but they didn't seem anything like the elk that we hunted in Northpeak. They were half again as tall, for starters. Their coats were the blue of my new husband's beard and their antlers were inlaid with gold and silver. They were saddled and haltered, and I gasped as Bluebeard put his hands around my hips and threw me up onto the back of the nearest beast.

"The answer to your riddle," I said, looking down at him, "is fear."

He sucked in a breath, bit his lip for a moment as if something was bothering him and then leapt into the saddle behind me. Before I could catch my breath, we were off.

CHAPTER NINE

"Are we going to your home?" I asked, though I knew he would not answer me. In the deep fog, I had lost track of his followers and I could see nothing but fog and elk and the hands of my husband on the reins on either side of me. He rode with me pressed against him and if I tried to wiggle to create a space between us, he pressed me firmly back to him again.

"In the mortal world, we have stories of people stolen by the magic of the Wittenbrand. Stories of how they come back and they are never the same."

I glanced over my shoulder and saw there was a small yellow bird on his head. My eyes widened as four more landed on his shoulders and head.

"You seem to be very attractive to birds," I said dryly. It was a worrisome characteristic for a man who reminded me so much of a cat.

He lifted a single brow in response and I could almost imagine him saying, "Just birds?" because that seemed to fit with the kind of person who had suggested I tell everyone at court what a delight a night with him had been for me.

I turned back around, trying to think. I was married to a man who either currently had or once had fifteen wives. I did not know his name or the names of his friends, the name of his court, or why he had such a penchant for human brides. I needed to know these things before I could decide what to do next.

There was no sound of the elk's feet on the ground and it worried me that we seemed to have been riding in a straight line since we mounted. That should have taken us straight into the side of a building or the castle wall. But we'd been riding for hours with no breaks and no lifting of the fog. I had a very eerie feeling that magic was involved, and I didn't like the idea of that at all.

"What is the name of your kingdom?" I asked him. I glanced over his shoulder and he gave me an acidic look. "Oh, I don't expect you to answer now, but it might be gracious of you to inform me of the most basic information when eventually you find your tongue has loosened … what are you doing?"

I slapped his hands away. He had taken my braid and had begun to unweave it. I snatched it away and quickly rewove the braid.

Were the Wittenbrand obsessed with hair? And birds? I tried to remember what I knew of them.

Most of the tales were meant to terrify. That, at least, seemed accurate enough. There were the tales of travelers who were lost in a winter storm. They may find that they had stumbled into the lands of the Wittenbrand and when they returned to us, they were not the same. They dreamed strange dreams and saw visions with startling accuracy. Some would be gone for twenty years and not age a day. Others would be gone a day and return to us elderly and withered.

There were the tales meant to convince us they were at the heart of every problem – every stolen pie, every woman with child while her husband was on a long journey, every illness sweeping through the town. All those things were laid at the feet of the Wittenbrand.

Though I couldn't imagine Bluebeard stealing pies, I *could* imagine him poisoning them. My face flamed when I moved down my mental list. I shot him a dirty look over my shoulder and his smoldering gaze matched mine. No, I would not think of unexpected pregnancies. My cheeks were already hot enough.

He certainly didn't look like he spread illness. He'd been fastidious about his cleanliness and he smelled so sharply of cedar that I thought he might keep sprigs in his pockets.

Every strange occurrence in our world was blamed on the Wittenbrand and every bit of magic came originally from them.

And yet.

My father had never seen one until now. And neither had his parents or their parents.

I knew nothing about him or his people.

The Wittenbrand had just been a story to me. Something to explain when things went bump in the night. Something to blame misfortune on. Something to curse when the crops failed, and the lambs were stillborn, and a man died without an heir.

I paused there and thought sadly for a moment about the man who had died without an heir just last night. The man who had died trying to protect me.

I sniffed back a tear, and a finger reached out and turned my chin until I was looking into a pair of very light blue eyes. They narrowed with a frown at my tear. I knew what he wanted to ask.

"You can hardly murder someone who sprang to my defense

last night and then expect me not to mourn him. And you can hardly expect me to leave my family forever without shedding a tear."

He glowered.

"Perhaps, when we stop tonight, you'll deign to tell me where we are going and what you plan to do with me. I find it very hard to know how to feel about all of this when I do not know how I will be spending my days."

He ignored me, releasing my chin and wrapping one of his arms around me to snug me close against his chest. I was about to object when he kicked the elk and it lurched forward, leaping like a deer over a fence, its antlers bobbing. And yet, the ride was perfectly smooth. I looked down to try to see the ground, but it was swallowed up in mist.

There would be no answers from my new husband. So. I would need to concentrate and investigate if I was going to find out the nature of what the Wittenbrand were or why they had ventured into the human world to get me.

Why did people go a long way to acquire an item? They did that for precious things. But if he'd done this fifteen times already, it hardly seemed that mortal brides were rare. I remembered a knight who had visited us telling of the cargo that came off a ship in Porthaven. He'd claimed to see pearls the size of my fist and eaten a creature with a hard red shell.

Eaten. I shivered. I hoped very much that I was not meant to be a delicacy.

He had my hair out of its braid again and he was running his fingers through it as if he was charmed by the length. This time, I let him be. If he was a cat obsessed with a strand of yarn, then at least he wasn't a cat ripping the heads off sparrows.

The rest of the morning was spent in silence. I had nothing to say to my captor and he could not speak to me. It was hard to make conversation with someone who could not speak back, and I couldn't discuss my hopes and dreams about a future that was more opaque to me than the mist.

I judged it to be close to noon when we landed somewhere. It worried me that it felt like landing. One moment, the elk was carrying me without a jostle or lurch and the next moment, the sound of thudding hooves met the earth, and I was jarred in the saddle. This entire journey seemed incredibly impractical and I wasn't sure how to operate in a world that was so odd.

A large spreading tree was just ahead of us, ringed in grass. Two of my husband's followers were already there and one was kindling a fire. I could only see a few strides in any direction, so wreathed were we in mist.

We slowed to a stop and Bluebeard dismounted, helping me down graciously. As the elk's back was nearly half again as tall as me, it was still a rough landing.

"We need to move faster," the man by the fire said. He was the one with scars around his mouth that made it look like he was grinning twice. "I'm getting an itch between my shoulders. The game will begin soon and on it rides the fate of this mortal world."

"You should be nervous, Vireo. We did not plan to spend a full night in the mortal world," Bluebeard said

"Then why do it at all?" Vireo grumbled. He was filling a kettle with water. "You shouldn't have taken Wittenbrand vows with her or agreed to their Marriage Laws. Not only are you wasting time, but you're also tying yourself like never before."

His mouth shut with a snap as another one of the

Wittenbrand arrived, pulling food from his pack as if it had been arranged ahead of time. His hair was longer than the others and pulled back into a knot at the back of his head. He grinned in a wicked way, almost leering when he came to me.

"Do you want to eat?" he asked, leaning against the tree as he offered me a small loaf of bread.

I did want to eat, but I didn't trust this Wittenbrand.

"They call me Grosbeak," he said, letting the name tumble over his lips like he was kissing it.

I looked away sharply. Had he no respect for Bluebeard? Or was my new husband not powerful enough to keep his men in check?

"You could call me that, too," he pressed.

There was a growl from the fire and when I looked back, Grosbeak had his head bent low.

Bluebeard handed me a small mug of hot tea with a dark look on his face as if I had been the one to start that conversation.

"Speak to my riddle, Grosbeak," he growled, his eyes never leaving mine. "What has one hand and one eye?"

Grosbeak laughed, as if the riddle didn't bother him at all. "Me, if I push you too far. Is that what you want to hear, Arrow? I can be a good Wittenbrand. I just don't have to *like* it."

Arrow. So that was what his men called him, but that didn't mean it was his name. I liked Bluebeard better.

I sipped the tea carefully, watching Bluebeard from the corner of my eye. His moods changed faster than the weather – faster than my brothers' moods when they'd first begun to grow beards.

And last night he'd killed poor Leonid. He could shake me to death just as easily. I needed to be very, very careful about what I did next.

"We must move more quickly after we eat," Bluebeard said, his voice more growl than the sound of a leader commanding troops. What manner of man was he? "The Sword will make every attempt to catch us while we are vulnerable."

At that comment, Grosbeak side-eyed Bluebeard so briefly that I almost didn't notice it. Did my husband see that? It put me on edge. Like the look you get from a town cur right before it bites.

"Is my husband a prince in your land?" I asked Vireo.

The woman at the fire snickered. She'd been quiet until then.

"In a manner of speaking," Vireo said. "Though he may wish otherwise. He is the Arrow of Wittenhame, Lord Riverbarrow, and a prince of Wittenhame, though not blood to the Bramble King. He flies to the heart at the order of his Sovereign – as we all must for the great game."

He was a prince? And an arrow? And a lord? But he didn't wish he was a prince, so I would avoid that part. It still made me feel a little dizzy. It was strange enough to be married to a foreign lord, but princes were dangerous. People wanted them dead.

"The Arrow?" I asked carefully. "That's an odd designation. Is it like a knight?"

I didn't want to infuriate my new husband. I wouldn't mention the prince part.

"Not quite," Vireo said, considering. "Close, but a little more significant than that. He is lightning rod and blade, both." At my confused look, he rolled his eyes at Bluebeard and then sighed and turned back to me, addressing me as you might address a particularly annoying child. “There are several named roles in the Wittenhame. Your husband is the Arrow. Your task should be to meet them all and figure out what they do without troubling me to explain it.”

“Do you think it’s unlikely that I will?” I asked. His tone had suggested it was an impossible task.

“The Arrow has had fifteen wives. You are only the most recent. None of them has lived long enough to complete that task.”

A chill came over me. I knew I was in danger with this husband and his strange, barbaric followers, but I had expected I would at least survive – however miserably. I had assumed too much.

“Did he kill them? The other wives?” I tried to keep my tone bold instead of terrified.

“All but the one just before you. She died by her own hand.”

“Did she have a name?” I asked.

He shrugged as if he didn’t care. Around us, the sound of the others eating was all I could hear. They were watching us intently as if our conversation was entertaining.

“How long ago?”

“Six months ago.”

I gasped. “So soon?”

“There is a toll you pay for being married to the Arrow. A price for marrying him. It is possible that the price will be too steep for you to complete even that small task. It’s possible it will be too steep for you to see tomorrow."

He didn't sound particularly concerned about that.

I shivered in horror. Six months since his last wife died and he was already married to me. And his friends – if that was who these were – thought nothing of the fact that I might not survive through the night.

I glanced over at Bluebeard, but he did not seem to be paying attention. He was jingling the little golden bell for a yellow bird, drawing it ever closer as it fell slowly under his enchantment until it crept right up and sat in his hand. He closed his fingers around it so suddenly that I flinched. And then opened his hand and the bird flew away.

"He certainly seems keen on marriage," I said lightly. "And what is my role as his wife? Am I to be some kind of Arrow?"

That earned me a harsh laugh from the whole party. I noticed that Bluebeard did not laugh. Instead, he looked longingly after the bird as if he wished he could fly away with it.

"You, an Arrow? I think not," the woman Wittenbrand said. "The Arrow is our Backwards Man. While everyone is moving forward, he is walking backward and that is how he can see the future – because he's facing it."

"That doesn't make any sense."

"What does?" she asked with a wink.

"And what of the rest of you? Are you his court?"

They all laughed at that and she answered me. "We're bound to him by blood and oath – like your sworn arms men but deeper than that – and he'll spill our blood if we falter. We do his bidding and kill by his word. Does that make us his court? I suppose it does. His Court of Fools."

I swallowed, wondering at that. He was like a prince. And these were like his knights. But none of them acted like that at all.

"Leave off, Sparrow. We need to get moving," Bluebeard said, throwing the water from the kettle over the fire. It hissed as if it were a living thing being smothered.

He was tending to his mount when the first arrow flew through the air, landing in the moss beside the fire.

"To horse!" he cried, and I was thrown to the back of the elk before I could gasp. It stamped its blue foot and sprang into the mist at almost the same moment that Bluebeard hugged me to his chest. It was almost as if he was huddled around me to protect me from the arrows – but that was madness. What was one more wife when you'd had fifteen?

CHAPTER TEN

The arrows did not relent even though I couldn't see our pursuers. They flew and flew until I wondered if they were magical in some way. Twice, our elk shrieked, stumbling to the side. Each time, we pierced the mist to where another of the Wittenbrand were riding and nearly collided with them.

I tried not to scream as I clenched my jaw tight and held on to the saddle with all my might.

Bluebeard cursed in his own tongue as an arrow sliced so close that it nicked the elk's neck, leaving a thin streak of red blood.

My heart was in my throat and it made my chest ache every time I heard the sound of the arrows hitting trees or grass nearby.

Slowly, the arrows grew more sparse and then eventually stopped.

"I would like very much to know who is shooting at us," I said as calmly as I could, but there was a tremor in my voice that betrayed me.

There was no response, of course. Perhaps, I would learn to be quiet, too. I shook my head wryly to myself at the thought. My father had hoped to find me someone who would be good company. I could almost guarantee that his choice would have been far, far better, even given the fact that all our conversation would have been of horses. I could have learned to enjoy that. I rather liked horses. Perhaps, in time, Leonid would have come to value my thoughts on the matter. But none of that mattered now.

I had a mute for a husband during the day and a villain by night. Perhaps we'd find our own things to discuss – but any discussion we had would be like mailing letters to play a game of merels.

We slowed after what felt like hours. My muscles were stiff from tensing at every turn and I was grateful when Bluebeard practically shoved me off the elk. The poor thing had two arrows in its flank, and he turned, ripping one out.

"I'm going to walk that way to – to relieve myself," I said, pointing to a nearby patch of bushes, barely discernible in the fog.

He spun, frantic-eyed at the same moment that Grosbeak's elk plunged from the mist to join us.

"A good ride, Arrow. It's been long days since the Hunt chased me in the mists of memory, and here I am running beside the famed Arrow." He paused, glancing from one of us to the other, realizing that neither of us was listening.

"I'll only be a moment. It's just that it's getting urgent." I felt my face heating. Still, Bluebeard stared at me with intense eyes, his hands holding that one bloody arrow.

"I'll take her," Grosbeak said, seeming to understand what I meant. "No Wittenbrand arrow will fell her while in my care."

Bluebeard didn't seem convinced, but I shook my head and stalked to the bushes. Some things just couldn't be ignored forever. Even for very practical girls – maybe especially for very practical girls.

I found a well-sheltered spot between the bushes. When I'd finished, and I was tucking my cloak back around me I felt something in the pocket.

Odd. I hadn't put anything in there. I fished it out and found a small fabric packet tied up in string. With care, I unfurled the packet and found a little round, dull mirror smaller than my palm with eyes stamped all around it and a thin letter. I jammed the mirror back in my pocket and opened the seal on the letter. It was written in a magnificent hand.

To Izolda Savataz of Northpeak,

Though your marriage to this foreign lord comes as a surprise to all of us, it is our royal hope that you will choose to act as our eyes and ears in the Wittenhame. Were this a usual wedding of convenience, we would have had time to provide you with adequate tutelage as to what to observe and how to report it, but as this is all done in a great deal of haste, we can only send you this mirror and hope you can use your good sense to note what might interest us in the courts of our ancient neighbors.

The king wanted me to spy. I felt a chill at the thought. But the letter was not finished.

As you are your father's daughter and therefore must be loyal as he is, we trust you will accept that this is your role without question, just as we will honor your father without questioning why you were the one chosen.

The threat there was fairly explicit – the implication that I had greeted Bluebeard on purpose, knowing what that would mean. I didn't even think he believed that. It was just a courtly bargaining chip. And then the offer: spy, or we'll blame your parents for your failure. I would have accepted that, but the King could have offered his own daughter – or even himself. After all, Bluebeard had not specified a young woman must be the one to offer the greeting. Perhaps the fat king could have been the one riding an elk nestled in the lap of my dear husband. I had to suppress a snicker at that image in my mind.

This mirror is the only way we have of contacting you, but its magic is weak. Be ready with it on midsummer night.

Midsummer? That was six moons from now! Was he mad?

And then it was signed with the King's royal signature.

I was not fool enough to keep the letter. I buried it with the waste. But I kept the mirror. I had a decision to make about whether I would use it. Under normal circumstances, I would be insulted at the suggestion that I would spy on any husband of mine. But this husband had murdered a good man in cold blood last night. It was hard to weigh whether it was he or the King who best deserved my loyalty now. And, of course, there was the threat to my family.

A hand reached through the bushes and drew me out so quickly that I was still gasping when I came face to face with Grosbeak. His eyes glittered as he pulled just a little harder than he needed to and I stumbled.

"We're stopping for a moment while the mounts are tended. And I doubt the Arrow will notice you gone for a few more moments. So. Let's see how well you play games, mortal."

I tried to find my voice, but it came out a little too high. His pupils – narrow slashes rather than the round of human eyes – were expanding and I felt like I was caught in the gaze of a snake.

"What kind of games?"

"My favorite kind of all," he said with a nasty grin. "The kind that leaves scars."

"I'm not interested," I said curtly. I tried to rip myself from his grip, but he held me fast.

I opened my mouth to scream and his hand slammed around it, cutting off all sound. He had my back to a tree before I knew it and I squeezed my eyes shut knowing that whatever happened next, I would be powerless to stop him. I was defenseless in his grasp, tiny as that bird in Bluebeard's hand and just as easily crushed.

I knew my eyes were welling up with tears, but to my shame, I couldn't stop them any more than I could stop my panicked breathing. He was tugging my skirts up and I tried to shift to the side, but he had me pressed too hard against the tree. All my struggles were not enough to move even a bare finger-width.

I opened my eyes, frantic to find a way out – any way at all. And then his blade was out, copper bright in the light and my heart was hammering in my ears. Pain blossomed in my upper thigh as the blade cut into the tender flesh. Stars shot across my vision and I gasped in agony.

He was knocked away. One moment his face was hardly a breath away from mine, the next he was gone. My hand felt for my thigh, clamping tightly over the welling wound. Tears flowed and my breath came out as a shudder. My blood was thick and hot, pouring through my fingers. I fell to the ground as if my very life was seeping out of me.

And there he was – my new husband – kneeling with one knee on Grosbeak's chest as he removed his head from his body with a single slice of the slightly curved, silver-inlaid sword the king had given him. Horror flashed across his face. He sprinted to me, and for the barest moment, I thought he was coming for my head, too. Instead, he dropped his blade on the mossy ground and ripped my hand from my leg, cursing violently.

I heard voices as the others arrived, but my eyes were caught on Bluebeard's. He gritted his teeth like he was dying to say something and then with a hiss of frustration he put a hand on my head, and everything went black.

CHAPTER ELEVEN

I blinked awake to find myself lying on a soft cloak with another one wrapped around me. With my face pressed to the ground, the scene in front of me looked odd until I realized the Wittenbrand were digging a grave for the headless corpse of Grosbeak who had tried – perhaps – to kill me. That's what it meant to try to cut the femoral artery in the leg, right? I'd heard of men on the plains who were gored by wild boars and bled out in minutes when that artery was sliced by a tusk. That could have been me. So, why wasn't it? I felt for my leg and hissed when I found the flesh completely smooth.

My hiss drew Bluebeard's attention. He threw down his shovel and strode across the cold ground to sink into a crouch beside me. He examined my face with what looked like concern and then offered a hand up. I realized, belatedly, that it was his cloak I was wrapped in on top of my own.

"Let's speak these rites and get out of here," Sparrow said as she threw the body into the pit they'd dug. They seemed horrifyingly unaffected by the death of their comrade and a new chill tore through me. Was life of so little value in the Wittenhame?

Bluebeard took my hand gently and placed it on his arm, guiding me to stand beside the grave. The gentleness tore something loose in my mind and made me want to laugh hysterically. That one, ridiculous contrast made everything else seem that much more insane in comparison.

"You were taller than me by almost a hand," Sparrow said and then drew a finger down forehead, nose, and chin in some kind of sign.

"You were the lord over the Mudhills and you owned a herd of Clay Horses," Vireo said soberly, making the same sign.

What sort of memorial was this? I felt my eyes widening.

"You were husband to Derlia, now deceased, son of Gorath, also deceased," said the only one whose name I still didn't know. His eyes were dark, and he shot a poison glance at Bluebeard. Maybe not everyone was as calm about this brutal murder as the rest. He made his sign grimly.

"You were a traitor and likely a spy, but you played cards as well as any I've known. And you died with me owing you two silver," Bluebeard said grudgingly, making his sign. He threw two silver coins into the grave.

All eyes turned to me. I supposed I was supposed to say something. But there was very little I knew. Seeing as Sparrow had only mentioned his height, I could say anything, really. Height. I again felt the hysterical urge to laugh. He was shorter now, wasn't he? What was wrong with me? I was losing my mind. And they were all still staring at me.

"You were very quick with a knife," I said acidly, and there were nods of agreement around the circle as I made the sign the others had made.

"Cover him up while I settle my wife on our mount," Bluebeard ordered in a low, furious tone. "When I find out who has betrayed me, it will be more than their head that I take from them."

The man whose name I still didn't know looked up at that. "Maybe no one has betrayed you. Maybe he just acted on what we were all thinking. You shouldn't have married her in our way. You never have before. How are you supposed to spend her if she is your Wittenbrand wife?"

"In the same way that I spend them all," Bluebeard said, and his hand on mine was suddenly cold as death. "I was married to them all or none of this would work."

"You weren't married to them our way. You didn't give a vow. You didn't put them in your room for a night. We took them from this world, you kept them sleeping the pink sleep until we crossed, then we brought them to your home, and you put them in their rooms and that was it. They lived out their brief days like birds in a cage. But this one you keep awake. And you ride her in front of you. You act as if she is your wife in fact as well as name!" The look of pure hate on the other man's face made me shy away. "Put her in the hole with him. Go back and get another. One like the others. The Bramble King will approve. We all will."

"I'm collecting heads today, Ibis," Bluebeard said, looking away into the distance as if none of this meant anything to him. He drew my bell from his pocket and bounced it on his palm, rolling it over his knuckles like a man at the fair might do with a coin. "Would you like one of them to be yours?"

The other Wittenbrand looked away and spat and Bluebeard moved with inhuman speed. The bell fell into a sleeve and disappeared, and he scooped me up into his arms and strode through the mist to where the elks huffed in the cold under a sprawling clump of cedars. His elk bore two wounds from arrows in his haunch but seemed unconcerned as it tore up frosty grass.

Bluebeard set me delicately on the elk's back, arranging me in the saddle in a way that seemed fussier than I thought my situation warranted. I was very light-headed. So light-headed that little sparks danced across my vision, but I was not in immediate danger. He turned to retrieve something, and I gasped. There was an arrow stuck in his shoulder.

This would be shocking in any circumstance, but this man had killed and buried another, healed my wound by some sorcery, and carried me through the woods – all with an arrow shaft stuck in his flesh.

"Your shoulder," I gasped out. "Let me help you."

He grunted impatiently, reached up to where it stuck out of his shoulder and broke the shaft close to the skin with no more than a single grunt of pain.

My hands flew up to cover my mouth. If he had been my father or my brothers, he would be sweaty and white-faced, laid out on a table while someone cut the barbed head from his skin.

Bluebeard winked at me, looking for all the world like the beautiful devil the monks spoke of – the one who thought so highly of himself that he fell from heaven into the underworld. And then he was gone, striding through the woods.

He returned with a grisly trophy, the head of Grosbeak, hanging from his hand by its long, blood-drenched hair. I gagged into my hands but fortunately for me, I had nothing in my stomach to vomit up. I had the most terrible precognition that I might need to stay light on the meals for the days and weeks to come.

He leapt into the saddle behind me, still clutching the head, shifted until we were pressed against each other again, and then made a satisfied sound and flicked the reins. Our elk leapt back into the mist as if it carried riders holding heads in their fists every day of its life. Maybe it did.

A wave of nausea rolled over me at the same time that my hysterical laugh bubbled up. I couldn't hold it back this time. And why should I? If I was going mad, then what was the point of hiding it?

"Is it always like this with you?" I asked as my teeth chattered together.

He tilted my face around to see his – oh so gently, as if he were a lover and not a monster. I felt his palm reach up and cup my face and then everything went dark again.

"This little one here is the key to the closet at the end of the great hall on the ground floor. Open them all; go into each and every one of them, except that little closet, which I forbid you and forbid you in such a manner that, if you happen to open it, you may expect my just anger and resentment."

- Charles Perrault, Bluebeard,

1697 as translated by Andrew Lang in The Blue Fairy Book 1889.

CHAPTER TWELVE

When I awoke, it was dark. I opened my mouth, but a hand clamped around it.

"Remember, you must not speak to me."

I thought about biting his hand, but then what? Would he chop off my head, too? I certainly was no match for him with the sword he'd given me.

"We are about to land at the Evergreen Inn. I will take a room there for us. I stole a few of your hours to heal you, but that is not real rest, and you will still need sleep to refuel yourself. Do not speak to the denizens of the inn. Do not speak to the Wittenbrand who ride with me. I will tell you what you need to know when we are in private again."

I would have been more resentful of those orders if I hadn't still been in shock over watching a man beheaded after he tried to kill me. My head swam at the memory of his bronze knife cold on my thigh and then the hot pain that followed. Little stars still danced across my vision. I'd lost a lot of blood.

I was very, very careful not to glance to my left. I caught occasional glimpses of Grosbeak's severed head out of the corner of my eye. I didn't want a better look. Every glimpse made me feel ill all over again with a kind of gripping queasiness that made all the illness I'd felt so far pale in comparison.

The elk touched down in a flurry of snow, landing in front of a well-lit inn with a jolly green sign and snow frosting the roof and the edges of the diamond-paned windows. Music poured out from the common room – a tin whistle and a snare, a woman's lilting voice, and the sound of clapping and foot-stomping. I realized, with a start, that it was a human inn.

Had we not been traveling to the Wittenhame?

And yet, here we were in what was obviously a human town. Rooftops with curling smoke spiraling white against the black sky made a sloping curve down the hill from the inn. In the distance, the wide moon shone on the glare ice of a lake. Through the diamond-paned glass of the inn, regular people were dancing and laughing, red-cheeked, smiling, and whole. They wore bright reds and yellows – both men and women – and the women wore bonnets embroidered heavily around the brims in bright colors. Their pale braids hung down from these bonnets, like spun gold against the scarlet and marigold of their clothing.

Rouranmoore. I'd heard of this nation. But it was many days' ride from my home and then one must take a boat across the wide channel. My breath froze in my lungs. That misty world we'd traveled through – had it somehow been outside our world? And now we were dipping back in to rest at a common inn?

I made a strangled sound in my throat.

"Don't fret, pretty wife," Bluebeard whispered in my ear. "No harm will come to you while you are with me and I will be with you until the end of your days. You are far too precious to leave without protection."

I gave him a long, dry look. I wanted to say that the only protection I needed was from him. But that wasn't entirely true, as evidenced by the head he still carried in one hand.

I looked at him and then glanced at the head and then back to him again.

"Oh no, bell of my heart, the head I keep. It is my due." He winked one of his terrible cat's eyes and I shuddered.

He was going to bring the head into the inn.

My cheeks flamed with the horror of it, but he snatched up my spare hand, kissed the back of it, hopped down from the elk, and drew me into the inn as if nothing was wrong at all.

And what could I do? Could I steal the elk and run? I looked over my shoulder at the exact instant that it winked out of sight. One moment it stood, stamping in the snow, the next minute it was gone. No, I could not steal our mount. Could I run out into the snow? In these clothes, I would freeze to death before morning, but even if I did not, he was inhumanly fast, and the snow was deep. I would leave tracks and he would find me so quickly that all I'd get for my trouble was my new husband's distrust. I would simply have to bear all this.

Bluebeard strode straight to the bar where a man a head taller than him and twice as wide was polishing glasses and watching the dancing with an indulgent smile.

"A room I'll have and a dram of your wine," Bluebeard said.

"There are none to be had," the man said without looking at us.

Bluebeard set the severed head on the counter and looked the man full in the face while around us the dancers slowed to a stop and the tin whistle squealed a wrong note.

"Three decades and four years ago there was a man who

operated this inn by the name of Rubken. And that man asked me for a barrel of wine that never runs dry. And in exchange, I asked him for a room always kept free for me. Now … I ask *you* … is there a room? Or is there an empty barrel?"

The man went pale as a ghost. "There's a room, of course, noble Wittenbrand. And food to go with it. My daughter Sarcha will take you there immediately."

He must not have cared much for the poor girl to offer her up like that. It seemed a lot of men were willing to offer up their girls rather than bear the risk of the Wittenbrand themselves. I raised an eyebrow.

The innkeeper snapped his fingers and a girl with eyes round as those of a fresh-caught fish hurried over, wiping her hands on her tidy white apron. She bobbed a curtsy and practically ran up the stairs with Bluebeard striding behind her. I had to speed up to almost a trot to keep up with them.

Bluebeard had kept the head. The thought of sleeping in the same room as it made something inside me start to whimper.

The room the girl showed us was on the highest floor and took up the entirety of it. It was long and low, with an exposed beam ceiling and the thatch right there sitting on the rafters. It had its own separate bathing chamber with a door that locked. Someone had white-washed the walls nicely and even put a braided rug on the floor beside the bed. A fire burned hot at one end of the room and a wide hearth surrounded it.

Sarcha bobbed another curtsey and then she was gone, running down the stairs as if her life depended on it. My legs itched to follow.

Bluebeard set the head down by the door and stalked to where I stood by the fire.

"I can understand being upset over the misunderstanding with your betrothed." He paused as if thinking. Oh yes, it was night now. He could say his piece. I straightened, lifting my chin to show I was not afraid. It was a lie but I would need to get very good at lying to be around this man. "Well, I really can't, but I can *try* to understand. What I cannot at all fathom is why you would be upset about Grosbeak over there."

He flicked a finger at the head. It rolled slightly to the side, looked up, and scowled at him.

"You'll have to wait on vocal cords, Grosbeak. I've about used up my reservoir of magic."

I gasped, my hands flying over my mouth. The head was still alive? And now it turned its furious gaze on me. I backed up until my shoulders hit the wall. Bluebeard scowled.

"Don't be such a fainting violet. He has no limbs. He cannot harm you or betray you now."

I was in hell. I was being punished for sins uncommitted and crimes unrealized. That must be what this was. My breath sawed through my lungs, leaving them ragged.

Bluebeard pulled the bell out of his pocket as if it was significant, and bounced it on his palm a few times, biting his lip before looking over at me with what could almost be a soft expression.

They'd been right about the bell. It really did attract the Wittenbrand. A laugh swelled in my throat, threatening to escape. It took all my presence of mind to force it back down.

He strode over until the tip of his nose nearly touched mine. He placed his hands either side of my face, palms flat against the wall, eyes looking deeply into mine.

It was impossibly unfair that he smelled of lavender and his breath – which ought to be rank from travel – smelled of mint. It was also impossibly unfair that his blue stubble had not grown at all and was just the right length to make him look more rakish than anything else.

My breath hitched in my throat.

His eyes twinkled as if we were about to share a delicious secret. It was all I could do not to tremble slightly at his decided beauty and the uncommon way his ears came to a very faint, barely-there point. He reached into his shirt with a sudden motion and pulled out a small golden key on a chain around his neck. Drawing it off, he placed the chain over my head instead.

His fingers trailed lightly over my throat and I shivered. My good sense was screaming to me that now I was mixing fear and attraction and if I wasn't careful, I'd be drunk on them, and once drunk on that deadly brew, I may never be able to feel one without the other – which would be very dangerous indeed.

I agreed, but there wasn't much I could do to prevent it. It was carrying me along like a swollen river after the spring melt.

His hands pulled away and settled back to the wall on either side of me. I swallowed and reached for the key so I could focus on something – anything – other than the powerful man caging me between his arms.

The key felt heavy, and when I lifted it, I saw it was the length of my pinkie finger, crafted of woven gold as if someone had magicked a thousand fine wires into a key instead of stamping one in a mold. It was impossibly fine workmanship, incredibly valuable, and it weighed far more than it should have.

"You will wear my key as some women wear rings," he whispered as his cat's eyes locked on mine. There was a sudden desperation in his eyes when he said, "but whatever you do, you must not enter the room the key unlocks. You must not open it. You must not use the key at all. Do you understand me?"

I nodded nervously and he exhaled a long, desperate breath.

"I have tried. Let it be known and remembered that I have tried." He looked like he was in turmoil as he spoke, his eyes thick with something very like pain. Unconsciously, I reached toward him, stopping myself just before my hand touched his arm.

No, no, Izolda. You must not be sucked into his story. That will only complicate things. Remember who this man is – a murderer, a trickster, and a thief. And do not be drawn by pity or anything else.

"Well then, that's the day," he said briskly, startling me, and leapt from where he stood to the bed in a single massive jump, as if he were a large cat jumping on prey. He kicked off his boots and threw himself under the covers with so much violence that I could hardly catch my breath.

My mouth was still hanging open when there was a knock at the door. I had the foresight to draw my sword before opening it, but it was only Vireo.

"Your bag, Lady Arrow," he said with a smirk, handing me my saddlebag.

"Thank you," I said a little breathlessly.

"It's not a gift," he said harshly. "It is payment for the entertainment earlier. I haven't watched the Arrow claim a head in so long that I almost forgot that he collects them. The opportunity you afforded will keep me entertained for many nights to come."

I took the bag wordlessly – because what could you possibly say to that?

He *collected* them? Like interesting rocks or trinkets?

I was very careful to bar the door before I slipped my sword back into the scabbard, snuck into the bathing room and barred that door. That done, I sat on the floor, and sobbed until I could sob no more.

"Then she took the little key and opened it, trembling."

- Charles Perrault, Bluebeard,

1697 as translated by Andrew Lang in The Blue Fairy Book 1889.

CHAPTER THIRTEEN

There is only so much crying a girl can do, and eventually, I sobbed myself to sleep. I woke with a muzzy head and looked out the window of the bathing chamber to see it was still dark. I changed into the nightdress in the bag – the ridiculous filmy lace one that Bluebeard had chosen – and worked to wash my dress of dirt and blood. It was the only practical one I had, and it would have to do for tomorrow. If Bluebeard left the inn in the same hurry that he'd entered it, I'd have to be ready to leave in the space of a heartbeat.

When the dress was clean, I did the only sensible thing a woman in my situation could do. I drew the key out and wondered to myself how one could use a key to open a door that was not there. I examined it from every angle, searching for clues and finding nothing. There seemed to be a very small bow and arrow placed somehow under the golden wires but that gave me no clues. There was no writing on it, no symbols, nothing to give away what manner of door it might open.

I put it between my thumb and forefinger, miming turning a key as I considered it.

To my shock, the air in front of me shimmered and then a rectangle of space opened up in front of me. I dropped the key in shock, and it fell to the end of the chain, thumping hollowly against my chest.

In my mind, words seemed to whisper as if the room before me was welcoming me.

I am sudden death to calm.

My roar breaks the hush.

My song, the mind's somnolence.

I was no longer looking at the bathing chamber. Rather, I was looking into a large room with no windows. It was lined with fifteen glowing pillars set in alcoves, and before each pillar was an open book chained to a pedestal reader. The center of the room was carpeted with the layered skins of many animals I recognized and many I did not. I would not like to meet the one with the orange and black stripes on a dark night, that was for sure. Neither would I like to meet the scaled one with the very long jaw.

Each book glowed a faintly different color than the next so that some were pinkish and some golden, some spring green, and some the purest white. One was even faintly purple. And each book matched the glow of the pillar behind it.

At the very end of the room was a very large hourglass with the top bulb completely empty and the bottom bulb full of what looked like uncut garnets. As I watched, the hourglass slowly spun until the top bulb was now the full one. The first garnet hit the floor with a clatter, and then someone began to pound on the bathing room door. In a panic, I leapt into the mysterious room.

The pillars, it turned out, were not pillars at all. They were women, frozen in place, eyes shut as if they were sleeping, but utterly still. They stood on pedestals that brought their feet to the height of my waist.

I stared in horror at the one nearest to me, whose face was bathed in a very soft pink light. She was wearing a golden dress and had a face so much like Princess Chasida's that they could be sisters. And one of her shoes was missing a golden bell.

I raced to her alcove and reached for her, but my hand met something that felt smooth and slick as glass surrounding her. There were no seams, no top or bottom, as if the once-living Princess Margaretta had somehow been blown into invisible glass. She still looked nineteen years old. The same as me.

My belly rolled uncomfortably at the thought.

I hurried from her to the next girl – a girl with a very impressive figure and flowing dark curls. Her red dress dipped low in the front in a way that made my cheeks hot.

I rushed on to the next in line – a girl with sharp, authoritative features and a very bulky dress with an elaborate belt as thick as my forearm ringing her waist. Her hair was white – but her features as young as my own. The book on her stand was signed on the exposed page and a tiny brass plaque on the alcove she stood in bore the same inscription. Ki'e'iren. Was that her name?

The next woman was curved perfection with full lips and cheeks and such an abundance of curls as I'd never seen before. She wore a two-piece costume too indecent to wear in society and her skin was flawless wherever it was exposed.

I fled down the line of beautiful women – one after another, stuck in perpetual beauty forever – as the pounding on the bathing door finally turned to the sound of wood cracking and splintering.

They were his wives, I realized. The wives of Bluebeard, encased in … magic?

Dead. All dead. And there was one empty pillar with an empty pedestal and no glow in either located right next to the door.

Was it getting hot in here? I felt almost faint with the heat.

By the time I reached the hourglass, my breath was caught in my throat and little white stars were dancing across my vision. I collapsed in front of it as Bluebeard strode through the room, his face a thundercloud.

"Where trouble is, look for the woman," he growled, his lip twisting up in a way that made his beautiful face look like a devil's. "Speak to my riddle? What creature must plumb every depth, turn every stone, tempt death and defy him to his face and all that only to reap what she never sowed and gain what she never earned? Whose curiosity devours like an army of locusts and mind seeks out danger as a man seeks out a lover? I will answer for you – it is a wife."

He reached the place where I was crouched on all fours, reached down, and pulled me up by the roots of my hair so that I was looking into his eyes.

"I had hoped to spare you this, Izolda." Fury and pain filled his face. "Do you long to dance with death? Does your heart yearn for the barrow before its time? Fifteen times before, I have watched this story unfold. Fifteen times before, I have given a key, and fifteen times before, it has been turned in the lock. I had hoped that perhaps you were too clever to fall into this trap, but oh how you have disappointed me, wife."

He turned my head with my hair and pressed my face to the glass, his chest heaving with his infuriated breath.

"The proverb says, "*Teach us to number our days.*" See these garnets? They are the days of your life, Izolda. And because you opened this door, they are mine now irrevocably. Mine to spend as I want. Mine to rule over. Mine to direct. And when they are gone, you will be on that last pedestal and your days will be no more."

I knew my eyes were wide and pleading. I wanted to speak more than anything. No, I wanted to stop crying even more. It was humiliating to let him see me cry.

"Your tears cannot save you," he whispered, his gaze catching mine, and for a moment his fury faded away, replaced by a dull misery that ached out of him and seeped into me. "Even *my* tears will not save you now. You are well and truly trapped by magic too great for you. All that now remains for us is to see how we will spend the time you have."

He swept me up into his arms as if I were his lover rather than his enemy and carried me from the haunting room. As he went by the last pedestal, I saw that it now bore my name. *Izolda Savataz.*

When we left the hidden chamber, the door vanished as if the room had never existed at all.

Bluebeard carried me through the ruin of the door, through the horrible room of the inn where Grosbeak's eyes followed us, to the large bed where he laid me on the mattress and stepped back for a moment, catching his lower lip between his teeth before he tugged up the eiderdown and tucked it under my chin.

"Sleep, treacherous one. You cannot break our hearts more tonight."

For the second time, I cried myself to sleep.

CHAPTER FOURTEEN

I woke to a hand clamped over my mouth. I barely bit back a scream when I saw Bluebeard's pale cat's eyes staring into mine.

Something slammed against the door and wood crunched behind us.

"No time to dress, wife," he said, shoving my fur-lined cloak into my hands and the pair of belts with my sword and knives. "Hurry. They've found us."

His blue coat and shirt were completely unbuttoned and untucked, revealing skin so crisscrossed with scars that I gasped at the sight of them. They were worse the more skin I saw. What had happened to him? Another key – silver – dangled on a chain around his neck. I shuddered, wondering if it led to the same kind of place as the golden key hanging inside my lace nightdress did.

I finished clasping the cloak and buckling on the belts over my filmy nightgown at the same moment that Bluebeard slung my saddlebag over my shoulder. He had his own hanging over his.

"Hold this for a moment," he said, trying to pass me Grosbeak's severed head.

I shook my head violently. I was *not* going to carry the head!

The door shattered and fell into the room with a boom. I jumped, squeaking in an embarrassing way in my surprise.

Little bits of wood and straw rained into the room like a sandstorm. I backed up until my head hit the thatch roof above and Bluebeard threw the head back at me as if he expected me to catch it. I dodged out of the way, letting it hit the ground with a dull thump. I had my limits. I was not going to cart around a dead head for him – especially not one that was scowling up at me from the floor. Just the thought of it made me ill.

But there was no time for being ill.

Two men leapt into the room, and Bluebeard's curved swords appeared in his hands as if by magic. He was so fast! One of them was his own bronze sword and the other was the one the King had offered for me to give him, inlaid in silver and sharp as winter. He spun the swords on either side of his body, as if he were a performer for the King's court and not a man in the room of an inn.

The men brandished their own swords, not bothering to be dramatic. They were human just like me. Dressed like minor nobility – just like me. They were both breathing heavily, as if they wanted to be there as little as I did. The younger of the two – barely older than my own brothers – caught sight of me and cursed vehemently.

"He has already taken another."

"This has never been what you thought it was," Bluebeard said silkily. "You still have time to leave. I don't want to kill anyone."

The other man – this one older and bearded – spat. "We don't believe your lies, kidnapper."

"I keep trying to tell you all that I'm not a kidnapper,"

Bluebeard said through gritted teeth, but there was no time to say more. Both men attacked as one and his swords whirled in his defense. He fought like he was dancing, a quick step back and then another to the side. The blade in his left hand came up and twisted just so, flinging the man on the left backward. Then a step forward, a pivot, and he knelt with precision, sword up just in time to block the double handed swing from the other opponent. He stepped forward twice, still on his knees – knee to foot, knee to foot, sword up like the thrust of a horn. He tossed the inlaid silver sword up in the air in a way that made it spin and then caught it by the grip so that it curved back along his forearm. He lunged to his feet, his first sword blocking a fresh blow, followed quickly by a back-handed slash from the sword now facing the wrong way. Blood sprayed across the room, coating our bed.

My hands found my face, my breath coming out in a rush. I didn't even think of the sword or knives on my belts. I wasn't thinking at all.

Hands seized my shoulders, covering my mouth. I barely bit back a scream and then I was yanked up through a hole torn in the thatch and pulled onto the roof by Vireo. He threw me in one motion onto the blue elk stamping and huffing on the thatch. In front of him, Sparrow sat her elk, and there was one other elk with a long, dark bundle slung over its back.

Vireo ducked through the thatch again, came back with the severed head of Grosbeak, and strapped it behind my saddle. I didn't move to stop him. I could hardly keep myself from shaking head to foot already. I didn't know if it was the searing cold or the shock of another attack – of more bloodshed. Vireo took my saddlebag from me with care, as if he thought I might bite at any moment, and attached it to the side of the saddle where it belonged.

"There was one more of you," I said through chattering teeth.

He nodded his head to the bundle tied to the saddle of the riderless elk. "The Brotherhood of Stolen Sisters killed Ibis on our way here. They took us a bit by surprise tonight."

"I thought you were immortal. I thought you didn't die."

"We die neither by age nor by disease, but violence and poisons may end our lives like a string of pearls severed. Who would have thought they could guess we'd be here on this of all nights?" Vireo said with a savage grin. "Never a dull moment when you ride with the Arrow. Always an adventure."

"You consider death an adventure?" I asked. My tongue was thick between my frozen lips. The lace nightie was not warm enough for a winter's night.

Vireo cocked his head to the side, brow furrowing. "What else would you call it, then? Is it not the great adventure? The sea each must one day sail?"

He'd just finished with me when Bluebeard vaulted up onto the roof, flicking the blood from the tips of his swords and then wiping them on the thatch.

"Thatch shouldn't hold something as heavy as an elk," I said, my teeth still chattering. Hysterics didn't make sense. I needed to stop them at once.

"It's magic, wife of the Arrow," Vireo said, winking this time. "Get used to it."

Bluebeard sheathed his swords and threw something at Vireo, who caught it and examined it. He was close enough that I could see it, too. It was an iron medallion with the words "Forever the Faithful" etched on the back and a pair of crossed swords on the front.

"Brotherhood," Vireo said with a nod, as if he'd been expecting it. He glanced at Bluebeard as my husband mounted behind me, his hot breath gusting across my neck. "Dead?"

Bluebeard didn't answer directly. He made a whooping sound, both Sparrow and Vireo replied with the same as Vireo hurried to mount his elk, and then we were leaping into the sky. I bit back a scream, but we did not plummet to the ground outside the inn. Instead, we disappeared once more into the thick mist, the elk seeming to run through it as if they were running on a well-packed road.

The frosty air bit through my lace nightgown until my skin smarted all over like little needles were being jabbed into every inch of my skin. The night sky above us was crystal clear, the stars spilling across it like a spray of water on a hot summer day – glittering, bright and sharp in beauty. Our elk's breath gusted into the air, almost tinkling from the cold. My breath gusted with his, like a silver chain hanging from my mouth and nose. My eyelashes froze together a little and I had to wiggle my nostrils to keep them from freezing.

Bluebeard reached around my throat, and I froze, terrified that he might strangle me right here, drain me of days, and put me in that room with all his other wives.

He tossed my long braid over my shoulder and I felt the lightest brush of something warm on the back of my neck before my cloak fell, pooling between us. I grabbed for it frantically, but already he was slipping a dress over my head – I reached my arms through the woolen sleeves, greedily grasping for warmth, and as I tugged it around my hips and under my bottom, he already had the cloak back up and was clasping it around my shoulders. It was a narrow warmth, but more than nothing.

"You are likely wondering what those men wanted," he

whispered in my ear. "I shall salve your curiosity. They want you."

A chill shivered through me. But how could that be? Who in the world would want me?

"When you opened that door – against my warning, I might add – you unlocked my access to your days and now I may spend them as I please. Each one opens for me new powers and skills I cannot access otherwise. I had but a bare brush of them before, but now they are my possessions, every one. Your kind have stories about the Wittenbrand and the great feats we may accomplish – but magic, my glorious wife, has a price, and the price is paid by the wielder. He pays with his life. He pays in the length and breadth of the days allotted to him. But a married man is one with his wife. And as one, I can pay with your days. With the allotment of your life's breath and the span of your soul's time on this garlanded globe."

And that explained why he had sixteen wives. Sixteen seemed awfully excessive, even for him.

I glanced back at his sharp, pale eyes. They had a fey look to them but even with his blue beard, he didn't look much older than thirty years. And if he was only thirty years old – or perhaps even thirty-one – and assuming he'd begun wedding wives as early as fifteen or sixteen and that there were no overlaps between his marriages, then he had spent the life of a woman for every year he was an adult. My heart seized inside me. Did I only have a year left to live? Did I have less? Perhaps he drained a wife entirely and then bided his time for a year before he was finally driven to take another. He did not seem like a man much given to self-control.

My brow wrinkled. But hadn't he spoken to the man last night of having been there a generation ago? And had he not stolen Margaretta, who would be aged by now had she lived? Perhaps he was far older than he appeared and more frugal than I guessed.

"The Brotherhood of Stolen Sisters wishes to spare you this."

My heart leapt, startled from fear by this sudden burst of hope. If they came for me again, perhaps I ought to lend them aid. Perhaps if I did, I could go home and leave this strange husband and his terrifying plans for my future. Surely, my king could not fault me for wanting to live the year out. He would not punish my family if Bluebeard was dead and unable to come for me.

And all Bluebeard's threats about razing my lands and slaying my people would die with him.

Something soft was flung around my neck. Bluebeard buttoned it in place, the very tips of his fingers brushing my throat in a way that made me shiver – and not from the cold. It was a fur collar, I realized, thick enough to be a scarf. It must have come from his own bags.

He whispered again in my ear, his words tickling my heart in a way I didn't find at all comfortable.

"You tantalizing creature. You mad folly. You unravel my careful plans and bring care into my unraveling. And yet, I must use you as I have used the rest of my wives – even having given my vow and all that such portends."

I pulled forward, away from his words, but he only leaned with me so there was no gap at all between the warmth of his body and my back. No gap at all between his gusting breath and my frozen ear. No gap at all between the squeeze of his thighs and my seat on the elk. Something tightened in my belly.

"I have decided to offer you something I offered none of my other brides – just as I offered you a marriage vow when I did not offer them the same."

I screamed "*no*" in my head, but he could not hear my fierce denial. And he could not see the tears that might have been fear or might have been rage that froze on my cheeks as quickly as they fell.

"I offer you an alliance. Work with me, wife. Do not be merely something I use up and put away in that closet you found. Be some*one* who weaves this dangerous gilded web with me. A true partner in the spending of your days and the rending of your years." He paused and I felt a light tug on my braid. I frowned, turning, and realized he was fiddling with the end of it again. "You're a wise woman, wife. I can see that about you. Likely, you're thinking about whether it is shrewd to betray me to my enemies. I assure you that it is not. Your best hope of deliverance is in the arms of the very man you loathe. Think on it. I do not need the answer immediately, but I will need it before we next enter the lands of mortals."

Though he was my enemy, his dearest desires in conflict with my own, his offer gave me pause. Had I not wished that someone would see me as an equal, that I could be more than a bride married to a disinterested husband? That in marriage, I could do more than simply sacrifice myself for nothing? And here he was making me an offer of just that. How perverse that it would be him to offer me such a gem when it was also him who wanted to ruin everything else that I loved.

Something made a growling sound in the heavy mist surrounding us and I looked toward it, startled out of my own brooding. A dark shape was moving precisely beside us, neither ahead nor behind – so close that I felt I could reach out and touch it. It rumbled again with the promise of dismembering us in due time.

"Mist Lions," Bluebeard whispered. "They rise again, and all such monsters will rise the longer we linger. We must join the Wittenbrand at the Turning of Ages, the Game of Crowns, and we must join them soon or time itself will begin to unravel."

Well, that sounded like a bad thing. He was just full of pleasant news today.

"I must play the game. For if I do not, this world will be ravaged by those who do. And who knows what evil they may unleash or what chaos may come to rule the mortal realm? And I must take a day from you, wife," he said, flicking my ear sharply.

My hand sprang to my ear, clasping it against the sting. I almost cried out an objection, barely catching myself in time. Instead, I turned, letting all my fury fill my face so he could see how I felt about being randomly mistreated.

His eyes were dancing when I turned, his smile mischievous, like a boy caught stealing sticky buns. My lips were parted in a snarl, but to my shock, the moment I was fully turned around, he leaned in and caught my lips with his own for a sudden, shocking kiss.

I had never been kissed on the lips before. My mother kissed me often on the cheek or forehead, her kisses maternal and safe. My brothers or father had, upon occasion, given me the rare minimal kiss on the cheek, as if to get it over with as quickly as possible so that no one might think they actually felt affection of any kind toward me.

But this was my first ever kiss on my lips and it was far, far sweeter than it had any right to be. Especially since it was coming from a man who had not only murdered fifteen wives but was dead set on murdering me.

Delicious warmth mocked the frigid night and tantalizing

softness dazed me. It was as if he was shaping my lips into a clay pot with all the firm delicacy of a potter caressing the clay. I melted against him despite all my good judgment, my common sense lost in the momentousness of the act.

He drew back, and for the barest second his nose nuzzled against mine, and his forehead gently touched against mine, as if in apology for what he'd stolen this time.

And then he was leaning back from me again. I faced forward as fast as I could.

That was a very, very bad idea. Kissing did not stop with kissing. My mother had been clear about that. Kissing, she claimed, nearly always started an avalanche like the wrong note sung in the mountains and it ended – if it ever ended at all – with fat babies and lines of inheritance.

My face was hot at that thought.

"I always try to give as much as I take," Bluebeard said lightly and I wondered if those other girls had blushed as hot as I was blushing at his kiss. I wondered what they'd given him after that. And if he really had given back just as much in return.

But I could hardly be jealous of a string of dead women, right? After all, I had known that Leonid had been happily married before me and the fact had not left me envious but had made me feel secure in the fact that he was capable of some measure of care for a wife. So why should I feel cheated that Bluebeard had been married before? That he had likely kissed all those women – and more – before, while I had only ever had this one stolen kiss? Perhaps it was merely the imbalance. Perhaps if I kissed the rest of the Wittenbrand he'd brought with him, it might even the balance. But the thought did not help at all and I felt certain that the action wouldn't either.

I bit my lip in irritation. I was being impractical. But so was he. Sixteen wives was far too excessive! And taking kisses from any of them just seemed like an excess too far.

I would be judicious about this. I would not be jealous and I would not remember the feeling of his lips on mine. I would, instead, set my excellent mind to the puzzle of how I should betray him to the Brotherhood of Stolen Sisters, thus making both my King and my family safe while securing some length of future for myself. I let out a long breath and let out all my jealousy and foolishness with it.

I was nearly at ease again when I heard Grosbeak's gravelly voice, and all semblance of composure fled as I covered my mouth to hold back a shriek.

CHAPTER FIFTEEN

"If you think giving me a voice will make me your ally, Arrow, you can think again."

I gasped and craned my neck backward. The voice really was coming from Grosbeak's head. Little gold sparks were popping one by one out of the top of his head like corn popping in a kettle over a fire. They fell to either side of the elk's blue flank, falling into the mist and disappearing.

"I think it will, enemy of mine," Bluebeard said contentedly. "You will soon find that being a head with no body is a boring existence – unless someone finds a way to make it interesting for you."

"I'll chew up your boots and spit them out in a thousand pieces," the head said in an ominous voice. "I'll bite your toes off and laugh as you stumble in your own blood. I'll scream your location to the heavens until vengeance rains on you like the fires of heaven!"

To punctuate his claim, he began to shriek – terrible, soul-shivering screams that struck to my very core. I tried to plug my ears, turning my head away to look ahead again, but it made no difference. Bluebeard ended his screams with a dull *thunk* – but not soon enough. The shadowy lion closed in, leaping for us.

It did not look like the fawn-colored lions I was used to in the rocky mountain clefts. This creature was a silvery-white with jagged black stripes across its fur and a double pair of white feathered wings. It leapt for us, its wings giving it extra lift.

This time, Grosbeak's scream was pure terror.

Bluebeard hunched forward, whipping the reins and the elk leapt ahead. He leaned around me, low so he was hanging almost off the saddle to the right. His sword slid from the scabbard with ease – the sword I'd given him for our wedding – and then he was whirling it in his right hand like a pinwheel.

A lion from that side leapt, wings extended, and he sliced it onto ribbons without slowing at all. Its keening scream faded behind us.

A second lion leapt, teeth and claws gleaming for the brief instant it became solid instead of ephemeral. Bluebeard's sword severed its head cleanly from its lion body, and a tiny, giddy part of me wondered if we would keep that, too. Perhaps we'd tie them all behind the saddle to add growls and purrs to Grosbeak's screams.

And then pain filled my world and I screamed, too.

I tried to look behind me, but I was caught in place, agony ripping down my back.

Bluebeard cursed loudly and then shifted behind me. His blade whipped around my body like my hair on a windy day. Something screamed – a high-pitched animal squeal – and then all was silent except my agonized breath huffing into the night.

I clutched the saddle, eyes gritted shut. I needed to breathe. I needed just a breath. Each attempt was agony.

Slivers of ice and fire shot up and down my back turning my

bowels to jelly and my head to a fizzling mass of chaos.

"Blood of gods and mortals," Bluebeard breathed, and I thought that maybe he was pulling the edges of my cloak aside, but I couldn't tell. All my senses were directed at the searing, endless pain in my back.

"You're clever with the blade, I'll give you that," Grosbeak said grumpily. "But you always let things come to a head. Why didn't you kill the lions *before* they attacked? You could, with all that power just waiting to be used."

"Everything deserves to act before it is judged," Bluebeard said distractedly. There was a note of concern in his voice. "Can you hold on, you stern creature?"

"Of course, I can't. I have no arms." Grosbeak's voice was still bitter.

"I'm speaking to my wife, adversary," Bluebeard said but I barely had the wherewithal to nod my head. It was taking all my strength just to hold myself up in the saddle.

"We'll have to go straight to the Wittenhame, I suppose," Bluebeard said reluctantly.

"And then everyone will know you've made me your creature for no reason but your own pleasure!" Grosbeak crowed. "And they'll know you had to cave and take a short cut!"

"And they'll not lift a finger for you, fool," Bluebeard growled before whistling sharply twice. On either side of us, his men closed in, riding their own elk. Sparrow's elk had claw marks on its hind flanks. Vireo was still flicking blood from his blade.

"Mist Lions," he declared. "If they are waking then there are worse things yet."

But he seemed resigned to it and so did Sparrow, their eyes hard and focused into the mist.

"No," Bluebeard said, sounding a little guilty. "We'll use the key."

Vireo's mouth dropped open and he shut it hard, his eyes widening so suddenly that I thought he might have bit his tongue.

"You've shown us the fruits of rebellion," Sparrow said with a nod to Grosbeak's head, "but even with that trophy I am gravely tempted not to follow."

Bluebeard shrugged. "Suit yourself. My wife needs aid. The lion tore her back."

Sparrow leaned in a little, and I felt cold on my back as if Bluebeard were exposing the flesh to the cold. Sparrow looked green when she pulled back.

"Scars and sires," she cursed. "And with the horns of the Hunt still in my ears."

"We must ride the dangerous paths to reap the gift of speed," Bluebeard said grimly. "Do not die before your time, my practical wife. It would be far too dramatic an end for you."

I gritted my teeth. I'd never want him to know that I absolutely agreed with him.

"What's he planning to do?" the gravelly voice of Grosbeak asked from behind me. "Please, fellow Wittenbrand, assure me that our great Arrow does not plan to dole out madness."

The others were silent. Which should make me worried, but all I could think of was the pain.

"Just watch the rear," Bluebeard muttered. "Call out if you see more lions."

"And if I see horrors beyond the pits of hell? What shall I call out then?" Grosbeak spat back at him.

"Don't worry," my husband told him, "I don't plan to ride past any mirrors, so you won't need to report your ugly visage to me."

Sparrow snickered but then she turned sober. "Maybe you should brace the girl."

The elk shuddered as his feet hit the ground and Bluebeard leapt from his back to a fallen tree just peeking out of the mist where we had temporarily landed. I clutched the pommel of the saddle, feeling sweat break out all over me despite the way my breath still left a spectral plume in the moonlight.

He reached around his neck to pull out the little silver key and looked right at me.

"Every Lord of the Wittenhame has a key like this one. We usually prefer the long ride through the lands of dreams that connect the mortal world with the Wittenhame. It is faster than any human road and contains only limited nightmares."

That must be this fog we kept riding through. Even injured, I could work that much out.

"Just turn the key already," Grosbeak moaned. "No one wants the lecture."

"I do," I said between gritted teeth. "And I have all my limbs, so I win."

A startled laugh escaped my husband's lips and he smirked as he finished his explanation. "I told you there's a price to all magic. This magic can take us directly and immediately to the courts of the Wittenhame. But we each pay a price for its use."

"And the price is insanity, yada yada," Grosbeak said from behind me. "I swear, you cut my patience off with my head."

"The price is a *piece* of your sanity," Bluebeard said gravely. "Fortunately, you seem to be the most sane person I've ever met. You have plenty of sanity to spare."

"Have the rest of you used the key a lot?" I asked Vireo.

He snickered. "Are you asking if your dear husband is insane? Because the answer should be obvious – a thousand times, yes. Now, quit stalling like a girl about to make her first kill and let the Arrow use the key to the kingdom, yeah?"

I swallowed and tried to nod. Instead, it was just a flinch. Little white stars danced over my vision. Again. I was nearly killed a lot when I was with Bluebeard. And he hadn't even tried to kill me himself yet.

Bluebeard gave me one last, grave look and laid his hand briefly on the back of my neck. "Courage now, you solemn creature."

Then he lifted the key – and just like when I had opened the door to his wives' chambers, he turned the key in the air and a door opened before us.

It was like someone had cut a neat door with a curved top out of the air itself, only on one side it was entirely different from the other. On our side, it was the foggy land – the dream world? – and on the other, I saw the glimmer of lights and heard the sound of tinkling laughter. But the door rippled like a troubled lake, as if there was a thick window set into it.

Bluebeard seemed to grit his teeth and then he dropped the key back into his shirt and took a step forward, pulling the elk to follow him through the door. I opened my mouth to protest but then shut it with a click as he disappeared into the rippling view of – whatever it was he'd stepped into. It wasn't sensible to fear something just because it was foreign and hard to see, and yet I felt shivers of dread as the elk stepped forward.

"Whatever pain you're feeling, Lady Arrow, will be nothing compared to the madness of stepping through that door," Grosbeak said, cackling to himself as if he wasn't stepping through with me.

I clutched the saddle horn as my face hit the bubbling surface and I gasped.

Someone was screaming so loudly that I couldn't process any other sense. Screaming, and screaming and screaming.

I looked to the side and saw Bluebeard smiling at me. He was speaking, but I couldn't hear him through all the screaming. And then his head fell off, rolling to the ground.

What happened next wasn't precisely a series of events or visions. When they passed, I couldn't have described any of them later, but I had the sensation that I had experienced a hundred tiny horrors. My hands shook as if they could remember something my mind did not, and my heart was heavy and laced with a sadness deeper than I'd felt before.

I jumped at the sound of the elk's feet on the gravel below and my wide eyes came up to see Bluebeard – with his head on again – trying to speak to me.

After a moment, I realized that the person screaming so hoarsely was me.

I stopped abruptly, but I couldn't entirely calm myself. Instead, I was making tiny little keening sounds one after another. Bluebeard seized my face between his hands.

“Izolda,” he said sharply. And then, again. “Izolda!”

I managed to stop the hysterical sobs so that they were only very heavy breathing.

“There, see? I told you it wasn’t so bad. You’re still mostly sane.”

He laughed in a way that made me wonder if he was.

Then, he let go of my face and I realized I had tears running down my cheeks. They stung in the cold. On either side of me, Sparrow and Vireo were hunched in the shadows, eyes staring into nowhere, their expressions dull and aching.

“It’s almost dawn,” Bluebeard said, not even waiting for them to snap out of their mirrored shock. “We need to move.”

CHAPTER SIXTEEN

Our elk were standing on a wide, flat blue stone, snow drifting over it like a bridal veil. The moment that Bluebeard's elk stepped beyond it, the stone disappeared and a crash like cymbals made me startle despite the pain of my back.

Angelic and harsh all at once, a choir began to sing, their voices first soft and then growing louder and louder, containing within them the anticipation of spring which slowly rose into the blast of dawn light scouring the earth and from there into a roar as though a tempest were rolling across the horizon. While I saw no owners of these voices at all, their song overwhelmed me. I caught very few of the actual words, except for the occasional "glory," "power," or "prince." But I didn't need to hear the words. The very tone spoke of magnificence, of fealty, of worship.

The chorus combined with my pain to leave me in a trance like state of feverish dizziness.

As the elk stepped farther, nearly dancing in his precise steps, red and white petals fell out of the star-bright sky, filling the crisp air as if to celebrate the entry of a conquering prince into a great city. They fell around, in front and before us, creating a carpet of petals for the elk to walk on.

I blinked hard, sure I was hallucinating through the searing agony I fought in my daze. But when one of the petals landed in my lap, I picked it up and stared at it through glassy eyes. It was velvet soft and fragrant between my fingers.

We emerged into a thickly wooded area wreathed in white snow. The world became bright in a strange, too-white way that was nothing like sunrise or noon.

Before us, something like a white marble altar stood and at its center, a single all-white flame burned. Within the flame, a brilliant white arrow was stuck into a jagged stone.

To my shock, my husband leapt from the back of his elk and ascended the steps of the altar in a way that seemed both reluctant and reverent all at once. He bowed low, making obeisance with a gesture and the flame seemed to flicker in greeting. All at once, the singing stopped.

"And so Wittenhame greets her princes," Vireo said wryly.

My shock must have shown on my face. "What is that?"

He snickered. "The Wittenbrand. The white flame? Did you not know of it before? Teeth of the gods, but mortals are a stupid breed."

There was an irritated tick like someone had *tsked* out of the side of their mouth and then Bluebeard was there beside me.

"Watch your tongue, Vireo, or I'll feed it to Grosbeak."

"I shall eat it with relish!" Grossbeak said from behind us and I shuddered and then froze. Even that tiny movement brought tears of suffering to my eyes.

Bluebeard mounted behind me and Vireo's voice was a little more respectful when he said, "Welcome home, Prince of the Wittenbrand."

Bluebeard grunted. We were moving again before he began to whisper to me.

"Let me tell you a story, wife of mine."

And I found that the words of his story seemed to ease the pain of my wounds, so I listened intently.

"The Wittenbrand are called so for the great White Flame of the Wittenhame. No one can tell how the Flame came to be or why it shows favor to some and not others, but all here respect the flame or see ill luck follow. And it is whispered from nurses to their charges and from the lips of mothers to daughters, and the words of fathers to sons, that one day, blood will be spilled on the Wittenbrand. The brand will turn gold and on that day a great hero will arise and he will pluck that arrow from the stone and he will be marked with white and chosen by the Wittenbrand to lead the people to an age of glory."

I wanted to know if that meant people went around slicing their fingers and touching the flame to see what happened. It sounded like the kind of fool thing people would do.

Bluebeard sounded chagrined when he said, "Of course, I've been with the lads to test if anyone's blood could change the flame or pluck out the arrow. They make a bit of a game of it from time to time – particularly now at Eventide."

Of course.

"And it is said that when the Wittenmarked one comes, he will bring us milk and honey to eat, and all will dance for ten years in joy at his coming."

"Tell her another one," Grosbeak said from the back of the elk. "One that's not old and dry from the telling. Played-out stories are no way to win a lass."

"Perhaps if you'd stuck to stories, you'd still have your head," I growled.

Bluebeard laughed, a lovely, tinkling laugh, and then he whispered to me, "And the Wittenmarked will marry the finest woman of the Wittenhame, for she will have been revealed to be true of heart and pure of spirit. And all the land will see peace once more."

As he finished his tale, we left the thick woods, the elk still walking on fallen petals and through heaps of soft snow. We took a turn in the path and I gasped at what was laid out before us.

The forest had not melted away from around us, rather, it had gotten larger so that we were as mushrooms on the forest floor. Around me, between the massive boles of the trees, were the oddest houses. They were small and crooked as if made and then left to dilapidate. They grew moss and fungus all over them, and each was moving. One was strapped with a great band to the back of a toad. Another seemed to walk on four legs of a pair of storks. Yet another, rumbled happily on the back of a painted turtle larger than a palace.

Bluebeard whistled and a house fluttered over to us, half flying and half hopping across the ground. It had grey, tufted bird's feet and a pair of wings on either side that looked like ruffed grouse wings. It was a tall, twisting affair, thatched on the roof and covered all over with thick chartreuse moss and clinging lichen.

"Here we are," he said, and leapt from the elk, snatching Grosbeak's head from the back of the saddle and tying it to his belt by the hair. Then, he gently lifted me from the saddle.

I moaned at the movement. My back was pure agony. My vision swam with the pain as he eased me from the saddle. For a bare moment, I could hear nothing, and I missed the orders

Bluebeard was giving his men. I had the sensation of movement as my eyes squeezed tightly shut and my jaw clenched even tighter, and then he was carrying me up steps. I opened my eyes in time to see him opening a round blue door painted with constellations and then he carried me inside.

"None can cross the threshold of a Wittenbrand house without invitation or magic," he whispered in my ear and despite the agony I was feeling, there was also a little thrill at his words. "In my home, you are always welcome, wife."

He was surprisingly tender in how he welcomed me – or perhaps my senses were merely dulled by pain.

He set me on my feet, and I stumbled to one side, catching myself on a tree – an actual real tree – from which coats and hats were hanging. The inside of the house was much larger than the outside. At any other time, that would have bothered my sense of order. Right now, it was just one more thing I observed and then ignored. Pain has a powerful way of concentrating the mind so that all else seems but a needless detail.

This room was so full of things – shelves stacked so full of books that they were jammed in every which way and crammed into every gap. A series of stuffed birds lined up on the top shelf and arranged in order from largest to smallest. A stuffed wolf beside the bookshelf that I was certain was looking straight at me. Beside him, a window as tall as me was thrown open, but the view from outside it was not at all the view from where we had just left. It showed mountains drifted with snow and bright stars above, swirling with color. The curtains to either side were deepest blue, dappled with silver. And after a moment I realized the silver in them was actually little lights winking and twinkling at me. I'd only examined half of one wall when Bluebeard set Grosbeak's head down on the bookshelf and began to throw off his bloody clothing.

"And now you choose," he said, tossing his sword into an urn as tall as my waist and carved with mostly-naked men grappling with dragons. I would have found them shocking any other time. Right now, they were merely another useless detail. "I can stitch your back with silver thread, and it will heal quickly and soundly, but it will pain you. Or, we can spend a day of yours and I can heal you instantly."

The jacket was next. He tossed it to the floor as if it were nothing. And then his white shirt – stained with blood. Should I be worried that he was undressing before me? I couldn't remember. There was only the pain and the time before the pain.

He whipped off his white shirt, gathered it with the jacket, and walked past me to where an open hearth contained a merrily dancing orange fire.

He threw the clothing in the fire, tugged off his boots, and threw them in, too. They went up in bright red bursts and coiling black smoke and then a puff of smoke filled the room. The fire made a sound like a belch and said, "Thank you."

I must be losing a lot of blood. I was imagining things. Like how utterly beautiful my new husband was without his shirt. He wasn't a large man, but he was all corded muscles and white silvery scars from the waistline of his leather pants to his closely trimmed black hair.

"I bet you'll choose a day,'" he said, stripping off his stockings and sending them into the greedy flames. I could have sworn a flame that looked very much like a tongue licked them up. "But before you do, think hard, my wife."

I was starting to like it when he called me that. No, that couldn't be right.

He turned his silvery eyes to me, and they glinted brightly, reflecting the dancing flames. "A day is a precious thing. Who can say how many you have been allotted? It is easy to spend them like water for trinkets, only to realize too late that you've used up all your precious days on nothing at all."

He plucked a twisted red bottle from the tangle of a human skull and a shed snakeskin wrapped in a string of pearls above the fireplace. Unstoppering it, he poured a single drop onto his fingers and then promptly began to smack his day-old blue beard with his hand. The scent of cloves and cedar filled the room in the most appetizing way. Having done that, he ran his hand through his very short hair like a bird preening its feathers, and then replaced the bottle.

I was still staring at him with wide eyes when a raven flapped down and landed on his shoulder. I gasped and looked up. And up. And up. I could not see the ceiling of this house. What I could see was a chandelier made of deer antlers and strung with black pearls and dripping yellow candles. And … was that an orange cat sitting in the chandelier, hissing at me?

Bluebeard smacked the raven away, irritably.

"Not now," he chided. "Report later."

"I'd take the day," said Grosbeak from his spot on the shelf. He sounded oddly content, as if he was resting now that he had been set on a shelf. "Pain is never worth the price. What is one day for the loss of it?"

"You tell us," Bluebeard said easily. "You are out of days, so you would know best."

"I'm not out of days, I am simply short one body," Grosbeak sniffed. "Don't you want to ask me 'Who sent you?' or 'Why did you try to kill my new wife?'"

"I never ask questions I already know the answer to," Bluebeard said, smacking the lintel over the fire with the palm of his hand. A hidden compartment sprang out. I didn't think my eyes could grow bigger, but apparently, they could. He drew out a spool of thread, that was indeed silver, and a needle that looked to be made of the same material. "Make your choice, wife."

I bit my lip. Even if this thread really did heal me quickly, I would still be in pain the whole time. And what would that be? Weeks? Days? Or I could give a single day and it would all be over.

My head throbbed with the agony of my shredded back and sweat slicked my forehead. But Bluebeard was right. I did not know how many days I had left. What if I offered just one and then I missed something important?

I pointed to the thread and the half-smile he offered me was triumphant.

"Up on the desk," he said, gesturing to a desk the size of two beds stuck together. It was heaped with parchment and quills, ink bottles and books. Books open. Books shut. Books on top of parchment, and under parchment, and in stacks, and in what might have been stacks before they fell into whatever they were now.

I stared at the mayhem. There was no way *to* get up on that mess even if I wanted to. The raven fluttered down and landed on the edge, tilting its head at me.

Bluebeard looked from my wide eyes to the desk and back, and then he stepped forward, and very gently removed his cloak from my shoulders and threw it into the fire.

"Thank you," said the fire.

"This will hurt," Bluebeard said, and he almost sounded sorry for that. But then he lifted me up so suddenly that I couldn't even catch a breath, flipped me in his arms so I was face-down, and leapt.

The leap was impossible. A man his size could not leap into the air from a standing start with a full-grown woman in his arms and land on a desk higher than my waist.

But here we were.

He laid me down on the heaps of papers, and then with a rip that made my cheeks suddenly hot as a sizzling day in summer, he smoothly separated the back of my lacy nightdress all the way down to my waist – and I could only hope no farther.

From the shelves, Grosbeak whistled, and my face grew even hotter.

"Only three claws tore your back," Bluebeard said, ignoring Grosbeak and sitting beside me on the desk cross-legged as his gentle hands worked their way down the slashes on my back. "One is barely two inches long, but the others are longer and deeper."

He breathed across my torn skin and his breath felt cold like the first snows of winter. I shivered.

"Easy now, wife. Easy." He ran a hand over my head and hair as if calming a snorting stallion and then he reached for the needle and thread. "They're horrible wounds, but we'll soon have you stitched. I have marks like this myself."

I remembered those scars, decorating his whole body like netting.

I felt the bite of his needle when it entered my skin, and I clenched my jaw against it, feeling a fresh wave of nausea kick through me and sweat slicking my fists and face in a wave. Had he stitched many people before? I wished I could ask him and hoped he would say yes – because it would mean he knew what he was doing – but also no – because then this would be a rare thing around him instead of a regular occurrence.

The room swam. I tried to look at the papers right under me to keep my mind from dwelling on what he was doing to my back. They were poetry, I thought. One was some ode to snow on tree branches and another one described the wonder of frost on window panes. I had expected something more along the lines of bribe letters or threats. The poetry surprised me.

I lifted my head just a little and saw a door behind the desk that seemed to lead into a dark corridor.

"I wonder how many rooms are in this house," I said a little faintly.

"Best not to ask," said Grosbeak from the shelf. "In a Wittenbrand house, that might change with his mood. It could be large as a palace today and then just this room tomorrow."

I was starting to think I was in a world where I didn't know the rules. And that worried me.

"This is not a very sensible place." I felt like I was pushing through a heavy quilt just to speak the words. "Where does the food come from?"

"Dreams and dreamers," Grosbeak replied glibly.

"Not farms and farmers?"

"Now, what would we want with farms?" Grosbeak asked. "The people on farms are dull. They do not dream of flying like a bird or being gutted by a unicorn. Their thoughts are entirely of crop rotation and putting up carrots for winter."

"Maybe that's because they like staying alive," I said wryly.

"You can't live at all with such a lack of imagination," Grosbeak said. "That's just surviving."

"I don't think you're in a position to scorn those who want to survive," I said coldly.

"Well, I might be dead," Grosbeak said, "but I still am more alive than they'll ever be."

And as horrifying as he sounded, I thought he might be right.

"Let me tell you a tale," Bluebeard whispered in my ear as he set a stitch. I was grateful for the whisper for it distracted me from the pull and tug of his needle. "It's a tale of star-crossed loves. Two warring clans lived side by side."

As he spoke, I could almost see a vision of the tale he was telling me in my mind. Focusing on it eased the pain once again and I found myself sinking into the story.

"They hated each other with the hate you must feel for those who keep accusing you of things you never did and then killing your relatives for it."

That was understandable. I hated the Wittenbrand and they'd only killed one man, who I had met that same day. He wasn't even family.

"Then one day, a Cavr'l was working on a stone wall between their lands when a Hy'lil set on him, and their fight was harsh and swift until the hood of the Hy'lil fell free and her bright red hair shook out long and brilliant. And the Cavr'l's eyes widened and he let go of her cloak and she scampered away."

I felt his needle drawing through my skin and I tried not to whimper at the added pain.

"But the next time their two clans tangled, when she rose from ambush with them to smash the heads of the Cavr'l, the head she was meant to smash had raven black hair and the eyes of the stranger who had let her go, so she did not slay him but pretended to miss her mark."

His gentle hands were drawing my skin together as he worked but despite his gentleness, I could not help the tears that swelled in my eyes and brimmed over onto his poetry.

"The winter grew cold and harsh, and she went out hunting and found nothing. Her belly was empty, and her hands froze to the bone, and she dared not go home to look at her family and their empty eyes and empty bellies unless her hands were full. So, she collapsed against the wall and lay down in the snow to die there, and who should happen to be on the other side but the Cavr'l with the dark eyes? He had with him a brace of hares. One, he gave to her, and their eyes met, and an understanding was made."

I leaned into his words and the rich cedar and clove scent that surrounded him and I tried to think of nothing else.

"And from that time on, when the two were out hunting, they would meet at the wall and share what they had, and also share warmth that turned to kisses, and kisses that turned to true love."

True love was something I would never have. So why did the mere thought of it melt my heart the way the Cavr'l's had melted his enemy's?

"But in the spring, when the snow melted and the clans turned to warring again, their families discovered them one night, wrapped in his cloak, and perched on the wall and though the lovers tried to explain, they were ripped from each other's arms and cursed."

I felt him tie a knot, tugging at my skin in a way that made me bite my own lip.

"And from that day on, the Hy'lil was woman all day long and a red fox at night, and the Cavr'l was man all day long and a dark raven in the day, and never may they speak to one another or find solace in feverish kisses. Except for that one moment at the edge of dusk and dawn when they are both human for the blink of an eye, and sometimes when they meet there, the clouds turn pink for blushing at the passion of their kisses."

He tugged another knot and I bit back a cry.

"Stay still now," he said, stroking my head again, and then a smell of camphor filled the room – pungent and intense.

I winced as he spread cold ointment over my wounds and then again as he pressed something soft against them.

"You'll need to sit up so I can wind the bandages around you." He was so close as he whispered to me that his lips almost grazed my ear.

I sat up with great care, my stitches smarting and the pain a dull constant like the ache in my heart from where my family and home used to be. Like the betrayal in my memory when I saw all those dead women encased in magic. Just like that.

I managed to get myself upright, clutching the front of my nightdress to me. It was tattered and ruined. His hands reached around me and under the dress, grazing the bare skin at the bottom of my rib cage as he ran the bandage around me and wrapped it around my back and then again, and again. It was such an intimate gesture for two strangers. Two strangers who were married to each other. I found it hard to reconcile this Bluebeard with the gentle touch, who never once tried to put his hands in intimate places while he worked, with the one who had so easily lopped Grosbeak's head off and stolen my first kiss from me.

"I think something backless," he said when he was finished with the bandage.

I found him at the side of the desk, rummaging in the bottom drawer. He pulled out a dress made of some soft, rippling material that caught the light and somehow softened it to cling to every curve beneath. It was a soft grey-blue, and trimmed in fox fur at the cuffs and the edge of the high collar. Thick black embroidered scrollwork covered the bodice and fell to spider legs across the full skirt. The back of the bodice was open in a wide keyhole that would have shown most of my back had it not been wound with bandages.

From beside it, Bluebeard pulled out a pair of soft leather boots with very sturdy soles and strong laces. They were so different from the dress that my eyes widened. These were practical boots for living and working in, and while they were finer than those I usually wore, they were just as sensible. I could run or gather firewood in these without worrying about turning an ankle.

"There are underthings in the drawer," Bluebeard said, looking over his shoulder casually at me. "One of my other wives had a whole batch ordered right before her last day."

Those words tore away all the softness and intimacy, shredding it like wet paper. I should never forget I was his sixteenth wife. I should never forget that none of this was real.

He reached over to me and popped something into my open mouth. In surprise, I bit down and tasted mint.

"I'll leave you to dress," he said, snatching a knit hat from the coat tree and jamming it over Grosbeak's head right down to his nose. “No peeking.”

He paused in the doorway and then turned back to me. “When dawn comes, I will need your answer, wife. Will you work with me or no? Think hard on what you will say.”

Then he strode through the door and I watched him prowl down the long, dark hall like a cat going out for the night. I half expected to hear him yowl when he reached the other end, but when all that met my ear was silence, I chewed my soft, gooey mint candy with my eyes as wide as saucers.

CHAPTER SEVENTEEN

After a moment, I came to my senses. Who knew when he would return? I should dress before then. I scrambled painfully down from the table and put on the odd clothing that had been left for me. It was a long, agonizing affair. Every movement tugged and pulled at my stitched skin and my tears flowed freely as I carefully shrugged on the ridiculous dress.

Twice, I had to hold onto the desk to catch my breath and clear my head. Would I work with Bluebeard? Did I dare say no? Did I even want to? Here, so far from the mortal world, spying for my king seemed ridiculous. What would I say? That the houses had wings and the fires spoke and if he found a man to pull an arrow from a stone it would fulfill their prophecy?

I laughed hoarsely at myself for even thinking of it.

The dress was far too fancy for everyday wear and I missed my practical woolen shifts and embroidered overdresses. This one would be cold – especially in the back, despite the fur trimming the keyhole. If I hadn't been in a torn nightdress, I would never have worn it at all. But while I did indeed find a blue silk slip – fortunately, it had a very low back and was trimmed in lace so that if a little peeked into the keyhole of my dress it would not look out of place – there were no other dresses.

I frowned as I put on the slip purchased by another woman.

It worried me that it fit me perfectly. But it was impractical to be fussy when it was my only option and utterly superstitious to think that its dead owner would resent me for wearing it. Or for marrying her husband, for that matter. When I was done, I marched over to Grosbeak, and delicately pulled the hat from his eyes.

"Bluebeard may know why you were trying to kill me, but I do not," I said to him. I needed an ally here. One I could be sure wouldn't run out on me. "And if you don't tell me right this instant, I will throw you into the hungry fire."

There. That should get me some answers for once. I needed to be smart about this. I wasn't used to fires that belched or bodiless heads, but I could still find ways to be sensible in a nonsensical world.

"Bluebeard? Is that what you call the Arrow?" His snicker was nasty. "Oh, he'll like that. I guarantee he will."

"Fire or confession," I insisted.

"You won't do it, a big-eyed wisp of a thing like you with tumbling dark waves of hair – oh, you're a pretty one, and you can hold your tongue, but you're mortal, and all mortals are but a blossom that lasts a day and then is gone. You've no value at all. You're just a stone in a game of merels. Something to sacrifice. Something to use. The Arrow will use you for your days. I planned to use you to delay him."

"Delay him?" I asked in a deadly voice.

"I'll say no more."

I lifted his head by the hair and held it as far from my body as I could. It was heavier than I'd expected and lifting it pulled at the stitches in my back so that tears brimmed in my eyes again.

I took three wavering steps toward the fire before he hissed.

"I'll talk." The words came out in a rush. "I'll tell you why."

I finished walking to the fire and set his head on the hearth. His eyes were wild. "Not here. It's too hot here. Don't you know that corpses burn?"

"You're not a corpse yet," I said in a cool tone. "But you could be."

"Yes, yes, I understand." He looked resentful. "It's about the Great Game of Crowns, the Turning of Ages. They play it every five hundred years and it's due to be played again. Tomorrow. If the Arrow does not arrive in time, he does not get a seat at the table. If he does not come with magic, he will surely lose the game. So, I tried to kill you because it would force his hand. He would either have to play without magic – for he draws that from you – or he would have to go and find a seventeenth bride and marrying takes time. The mortals like it done right. Either way, he's out and he can't win and ruin things for the rest of us."

He was right, I realized, suppressing the cold fear that washed over me. I was only a tool. A thing. Or at least, that's what I was to them. But imagine if you were trying to use a tool and it came to life? What if the axe started to chop at you or the blade twisted in your hand? I might be a tool to them, but I was a living tool. I would find my way to chop.

Besides, Bluebeard had asked me if I was on his side, and would he do that if he only saw me as a thing? Unless maybe it was a way to keep his things orderly and malleable. I frowned as I thought.

"And was this plan your own?" I asked, keeping all that out of my cold voice.

"Of course not. I worked for the Sword. Your husband will know that by now. It's no secret that they are rivals."

So, Bluebeard had powerful enemies. Which meant I did now, too.

"And now you work for me," I said.

"I *certainly* do not."

I lifted his head by the hair again and moved it closer to the flames. The fire murmured something that sounded a bit like begging.

"Not the fire, not the fire!" Grosbeak pled.

I pulled him back.

"I know perfectly well that terror only gains you obedience while the fearful thing is there," I said calmly, marching him back to the bookcase and setting him down there. He was still steaming.

I walked over to a small alcove where someone had thoughtfully placed a bowl and pitcher. They were both encrusted with round, red gems. Uncut rubies, I thought. I ignored the king's ransom I was using as a tool and washed my hands thoroughly. Dead things were disgusting.

"What is it that you may still want, dead as you are?"

His face took on a thoughtful expression. "Revenge on your husband."

"Besides that." Hurting my husband would not help me at all.

"There is nothing besides that," he declared boldly.

"Very well, then I will find some other ally."

I moved back to the desk, examining the papers there. Anything to keep me distracted from the grip of the pain in my back.

"Perhaps …" Grosbeak let the word hang in the air, but I didn't take the bait.

I kept shuffling papers and reading them as I went. My husband was very fond of stories. Not a single paper here was nonfiction. They were all tales or poems, songs, or stories. How interesting. What sort of a man did that make him inside his mind? He was both murderer and poet, brigand and storyteller.

"It's possible that I also want revenge on the Sword for putting me in this position," Grosbeak admitted eventually.

I turned to him and smiled.

"Your smile is crooked," he said. "And your face too narrow. And your nose is too thin."

"And you're a bit on the short side these days," I shot back.

He snorted.

"I will give you revenge on the Sword if you work for me. Be my ally. Be my helper."

"Why do you want that?" he asked suspiciously.

"I am new to this world and I can't ask my husband questions in the night or receive his answers in the day. You can help with that."

He pursed his lips, seeming to consider my words.

"You will never get revenge for me on the Sword," he said eventually. "It is impossible."

"Nothing is impossible if you approach it with systematic logic and careful observation," I said as I flipped through my husband's papers.

"You must get it for me before the Game of Crowns is finished," he said. "Or our bargain is void and I will spill your secrets to all who listen."

"Done," I agreed.

"What is done?"

I turned to look at Bluebeard. He was leaning against the doorway, one shoulder propping him up as he examined his nails. He wore a midnight blue jacket thick with bronze frogging across the breast and narrow, tailored blue trousers with bronze scrollwork running up the outsides of the legs. The jacket was hanging open and under it, he wore a white shirt trimmed in red fox fur that he'd left open and a tailored vest embroidered with arrows of many styles. Again, he'd only buttoned it partway, as if to show he didn't care. Most of his chest was left exposed so that his many crisscrossing scars were bare to the world on the surface of his pale skin.

I looked him up and down and raised an eyebrow at his smirk.

"Yes," he said, "I'm a fine specimen of a Wittenbrand. Now, what deal has she struck with you, Grosbeak?"

Oddly, he had the tiniest cut on his cheekbone under his left eye and a thread of blood ran down his cheek. His leaning had turned into something that looked more menacing.

"Only that I am to be her creature," Grossbeak said bitterly.

"In exchange for?" Bluebeard asked, stalking forward and rubbing his beard with one hand. It was so short now that it was nothing more than stubble, and yet he had not shaved it completely. I wondered why. Maybe there was something wrong with his skin underneath.

"She said something about revenge," Grosbeak muttered. "And she needs some way to carry me. She doesn't seem keen on holding me by the hair."

Bluebeard barked a laugh as if this was a great joke and disappeared down the hall. When he returned, he had a lantern pole and a length of sky-blue ribbon. The lantern pole was the length of my leg with a decorative counterweight in the shape of a raven taking flight behind the handle, and a large lantern hanging from a chain on the other end. Bluebeard flung it onto the desk and began working to remove the lantern.

"I like this idea, wife. Perhaps Grosbeak can be of practical use to you. He knows this world enough to avoid the worst pitfalls. And if you fail her, you speaking pumpkin, you gourd of words, I'll feed you to the fire myself."

"Thank you," said the fire.

Bluebeard left the lantern on the desk and stalked over to Grosbeak, studying him as if deciding how to affix him to the end of the chain. It had a hook to hold the lantern. He gave a one-shoulder shrug and then began to dig the hook into Grosbeak's scalp.

Grosbeak grunted in pain.

I looked hurriedly away and tried to catch my breath. I was a practical girl. I was used to dealing with things as they were and not trying to imagine what they could be. Imagining, dreaming – that only made it harder to focus on what was in front of you. But all of this was pushing me to the very edge.

"Oh," Bluebeard said offhandedly. "There's a book in the top drawer of the desk. Would you fetch that?"

I was glad for a practical task. I opened the top drawer and found a book bound in blue leather. Everything was blue for these people. I was starting to long for red or yellow or any other color at all. By the time I'd turned back to my husband, he had Grosbeak fitted on the end of the pole and a ribbon tied to the tip where the chain hung down.

"There. That's delightful." He looked very satisfied with himself before he turned to me with a fierce glint in his eye. "The book is for you. You should keep it in the room the key opens."

At those words, a stab of fear shot through me. He could make me do a lot of things. He could dress me and bring me to homes carried on grouse wings. He could force my silence all night and be silent all the day long, but he could not make me go back to that place. I would not look his other wives in the eyes again or feel the horror of watching an hourglass measure my days.

I crossed my arms over my chest and gave him my most mulish look. There were limits. And this was where I'd set mine. Even if I felt a little sick to my stomach.

He was like the shadows when he slid across the floor to me, taking my shoulders in his hands and leaning in to whisper in my ear. I shuddered at the intimacy. This man was violence and desperation, intensity and focus. I did not like being the center of that focus.

"The book must go on the pedestal. Fail me in this and I will be sorely grieved."

He expected to slowly kill me and for me to spend that time … writing about it? Was that what this was?

He was insane. *That* was becoming obvious.

And his strange beauty as he hovered beside me glaring – all that coiled muscle waiting to spring, all those lean, hard lines – well, that did nothing to dull the danger and fury in his every look.

"Put the book in your private chambers, fire of my eyes. The chambers my key opens. And do it quickly for we are already late and there will be a penalty."

He drew back enough for me to see the threat in his eyes.

I swallowed, took out the key, and opened the door while he still held my shoulders in his grasp. The moment it was open, he released me, and I stumbled inside, trying not to cry with my frustration. These moods of his, harsh and fierce one moment and gentle the next, were impossible.

I set the book on the empty stand, the one nearest the door. My eyes clouded with unshed tears. I was furious. At him. At this situation. At everything. And fury made you do stupid things. I couldn't afford stupid things right now.

I took long breaths and dulled my fury, dashing the tears from my eyes. And that's when I saw a tiny roll of paper tucked into the ledge of the stand for my book. There, in the tiniest letters possible, someone had written, "open me."

I unrolled the tiny paper. Someone had written a note in tidy, round script:

All is not as it seems.

You'll be fine if you listen to him and stay out of the way.

It's not that bad.

M

I glanced at the stand next to mine where the brass plaque bore the name "Margaretta." She was dressed in soft gold with round, pink cheeks, long blonde hair to her waist, and a figure that would have looked good in any dress – but especially this one which made her round curves elegant and princess-like. She was almost shockingly like her niece, Princess Chasida. The family resemblance ran strong in their female line.

And she'd been kind enough to leave me a note. I felt a warmth at that. I wondered if it could possibly be true. Could this really not be so bad after all? Or was Margaretta just such a sweet girl that even being married to a monster hadn't shaken her?

I tucked her note into my book, my heart suddenly uncertain. It was easy enough to listen and stay out of the way. Perhaps I should follow her advice – at least until I knew more.

I looked around me furtively and snuck over to the first girl – the one on the other side of the horseshoe-shaped configuration. Her clothing was of a fashion I didn't recognize and the cloth was rough, the weaving not so fine as mine. I thought that perhaps this was Bluebeard's first wife.

Like the others, she was almost shockingly pretty, with delicate skin, a sea of freckles, and very long, straight hair the exact color of a fox. Foxes were embroidered all over her rough dress and a fox fur stole hung from her shoulders.

I opened her book and flipped quickly through the pages. There was nothing in it except for a small paragraph on the first page. Not even her name.

The paragraph was a riddle. It read:

I am sudden death to calm.

My roar breaks the hush.

My song the mind's somnolence.

What a strange thing to choose to write in your book. Nothing personal. No message to her family, just this strange little rhyme. Something about it tickled my memory. Hadn't I heard it before?

Shaking my head, I left the room and the strange women who had preceded me behind.

CHAPTER EIGHTEEN

I stepped out of the room and the door shut behind me. Before it had closed, Bluebeard crossed to me, lightning-fast and I didn't even have time to flinch before he flicked his wrist, and something cut my cheek just below my eye.

I gasped, barely biting back a cry, and my hand rose to touch the wound. He caught my hand in his, his chest heaving with emotion and his gaze latching on to mine so that I couldn't look away from those icy grey eyes if I wanted to.

"It's my mark," he said, turning his head ever so slightly and tilting his chin upward so I could see how the blood had dried into a very long tear-streak on his cheek. "Would you refuse it thus? You are my wife. You will wear it with pride."

I swallowed and nodded. After all, it didn't hurt too badly. A wife bore troubles for her husband and bore his name. Bearing his mark was no great thing.

He nodded sharply as if he approved of me and then spun toward the door of his home. He moved as he always did – with a kind of barely suppressed energy, as if he would have liked to run the width of Pensmoore and was only just holding himself back.

The sun was still not quite up when Bluebeard flung open the door to his home.

“In less than an hour,” he proclaimed to me, “the sun will rise and with it will dawn my silence. So, think on this, wife. I want you near me until we return to this home of mine. The world of the Wittenhame is a dangerous place and I dare not let you be stolen from my grasp.”

I gave him a wry look. After all, he only wanted me near to protect his investment. I was his well of power. It was like leaving the house with a bag of gold. You’d be a fool not to keep it near.

“Ah, here is my band,” he said, snatching my free hand to escort me down the steps of the house.

The house stayed relatively still as we made our descent. I tried to keep Grosbeak steady on the end of the lantern pole so that he didn’t swing into the railing.

“I think I might be ill,” Grosbeak groaned.

“You’ll get used to it,” I said firmly. “Keep your eyes on the horizon. It helps with motion sickness.”

“Where did you learn that?” he moaned.

“My father took me on a ship in the sea once. It was a mortifying experience.”

We reached the bottom of the steps, but Bluebeard did not let go of my hand as he inspected the double row of ten men on either side of the path. They stood in crisp blue uniforms that looked rather like Bluebeard’s but with arrows sewn up the arms in gold stitching and one across the breast with a whorl of scrollwork around it.

Vireo stood at their head, looking as if he’d hurried into his uniform, and Sparrow was on the other side of the rows, her head held high.

“Ibis?” Bluebeard inquired.

“Given to his family for rites.”

Bluebeard nodded sharply.

“All accounted for?” he asked, raising an eyebrow. There was a dangerous tone to his voice.

“For now,” Vireo replied, looking back and forth between me and Grosbeak. “What are you doing with the traitor?”

“My wife has made him her pet.”

Vireo’s eyebrows shot up and Grosbeak protested, “Here now!” but Bluebeard continued.

“We’ll make our formal entrance. We need to hurry.”

Vireo leaned in, concern etching his features. Across from him, Sparrow leaned in, too, an identical concern on her face.

“You bring her with you?” Vireo whispered. “Her who is mortal and key to our success?”

“I do,” Bluebeard said, his lip curling.

“You’ve not done so before, Arrow,” Sparrow said respectfully, but there was anxiety behind her eyes. “Far be it from us to question you on this, but would it not be better to bind her to her rooms as you did with the others? You could post us as guards. I would volunteer.”

“Speak to my riddle, Sparrow,” Bluebeard said with a dangerous smirk. “Who has a bed but does not sleep? Who has a heart that does not beat?”

“The dead,” she said, her eyebrows raising into a wry expression.

"And anyone who questions me on this," he said, pulling back and raising his voice. "We move with speed. Fall in."

And hurry we did.

I had expected Bluebeard to let go of my hand, but he kept a tight grip on it, and though I knew he would one day kill me and that he only kept me close because I was worth so much to him, I couldn't help but take a little comfort from the warmth of his grip as he led me through this strange world of his.

It was a puzzle that he had decided to keep me close. Sparrow's suggestion was very practical. If I was the magical equivalent to a well-stocked larder, didn't it make sense to keep me far from danger and guarded? And yet he'd reacted to that as if she had struck his face.

I shook my head and tried to take in the details around me. My brain kept trying to pretend that I was doing it so I could report on this world to my king. The rest of me knew that was a pleasant lie. My king could not cross into this world. He could not walk through the land of dreams or cross through the barrier of madness. I was too far gone to ever see another mortal again. I needed to adjust my thinking. I was weak and vulnerable as a hare in the snare. My only protection, a madman and murderer. But he did seem to want to protect me, and that was not without value.

And if I were to win his favor and extend my life, I would also have to pay attention.

The Grouse House, as I couldn't help but think of it, had taken us to the base of a strange cluster of blue and pink-tinged white fungus that rose so high in front of us that they dwarfed the palace of Pensmoore.

Icicles thicker than my waist hung in solid waterfalls from

one level to the next and pooled onto the ground, shining dangerously in the moonlight. The edges of these falls were clouded and frosty but the center portions were pure and transparent, and I found my eyes following the intricate pattern they formed as they rippled down the cluster of fungi.

To my horror, I realized that I really could see into the ice, and in its depths hands reached toward me and faces thrust forward with eyes and mouths gaping as if people had been frozen within the depths of the ice as they tried to claw their way free. And what people they were – for some had wings and some had claws, and some had the feet of hinds and goats.

I froze for a moment as the horror of their presence sank in. They were real people – I knew this somehow – not illusions. And they were trapped forever in the ice.

Bluebeard pulled me along after him, closer and closer to their last resting place. I did not want to go toward that ice.

But there was no way to avoid it. For it was to the fungi that we were hurrying as we made our way around the icy falls. Sounds of loud partying and celebration trickled down from the various levels and a wild dance spilled out around the base of the fungi as people whirled in the moonlight to the sound of fiddles and drums and tin whistles.

My feet were starting to grow lighter and my steps quicker as we drew near, as if my feet, too, wanted to join the dance despite my brain screaming at them that it was a terrible idea.

The moment the dancers caught sight of us, they froze, and then a cry went up.

"The Arrow! The arrow flies!" The tune changed, and a singer began to chant in a silken song, her words otherworldly and beautiful as they spread over the people. Each ear it touched seemed to warm to the tune and the people joined in with the song.

Fly with the Arrow,

Dance with the Sword,

Give Your Heart to the Barrow,

Die with your Lord

Bluebeard nodded to them as they sang and then some left the singers and the dancers and crowded around us so that his band escorting us had to make a path for Bluebeard and me to walk in. I could hardly hear the singing for all the cries of, "Arrow! Arrow!"

And if ever you be broken,

And gasp on the ground,

Hold up your fine token,

And join with the sound

Bluebeard turned to me with shining eyes, biting his lip as if he was planning something, and then he spun me around quickly as if we were dancing, too, and dipped me low. At the bottom of the dip, he seemed to pounce, like a cat on a songbird and he stole a kiss from my lips right there in front of the crowd.

My heart leapt in my throat. I couldn't breathe. I wasn't sure I wanted to. The pain in the tears on my back was agonizing but it mixed with the sweetness of his kiss in a way that made my head spin. He tasted like the sweet mint he'd eaten and his eyes were dancing when he pulled away and drew me back to my feet. I was still gasping when he made a throwing motion over the crowd on either side and people leapt to catch tiny blue sparks as they flew out.

To my shock, each person who caught one seemed to change.

Sing for your Sovereign,

Bow to your Dream,

Make Haste for the Fallen,

Rise in Esteem

One man with the feet of a faun leaned heavily on a cane, but when he caught the spark in his hand, he dropped the cane and leapt six feet into the air. Another woman, hacking and coughing to nearly double, caught a spark, and her brown-bark face cleared and her moss green eyes relaxed.

And if ever you be broken

And gasp on the ground,

The word may be spoken,

And salvation found!

We were almost to a door carved into ice and steps working their way through that doorway when Bluebeard held up his hands.

"No more today, my friends. I am spent."

And then he led me through the door and the sound of song and merriment began to fade as we climbed the steps. I paused on a stair and looked a question at him, and he scratched under his collar irritably.

"Five days," he said after a heartbeat. "Their healing cost five of your days."

I felt my face freeze as stone-cold as the ones pressing toward the surface of the ice behind him. They looked like they were trying to come through the wall to seize him and drag him into the ice with them. I felt the exact same way. But it was hard to begrudge others their health – even knowing that they were spending *my* days to get it.

I simply shook my head. It was only five days. But he'd spent them like candy, while he had wanted to save one to avoid healing me. Were these people so much more precious than I was?

A servant in a strange livery of leaves and brown swaths of fabric, with a crown of dried oak leaves around his tousled blond head, and strings of acorns across his chest, rushed up to us and made a hasty bow. His cat's eyes were wide, and his pupils narrow.

"My Lord and Prince, mighty Arrow," he said, his big eyes growing even larger as he spoke. His ears formed tight points at the end. His lips were very full for a man. "Please make haste."

He led us up the steps in the ice. After a moment, we reached a landing and an open door leading to a shelf of the fungus where the dancing continued, but here it was slow and sweet and couples swayed in each others' arms as tiny little multi-colored lights flitted around them.

Bluebeard guided me past the door. "We must make haste. We have but minutes until the dawn."

"Please," the servant begged from two steps above us. He swayed a little as if he wanted to sprint up the steps and was only holding himself back for our sakes. Tension filled his voice. "Please, the rest are seated."

They certainly started their days early if they were already partying before the sun came up, or maybe we were so very late that they'd been partying since yesterday and this was simply overflowing into today.

Along the stairway, portraits were hung. I paused slightly at the first one. A fair lady with hair like the servant's, and a crown of golden oak leaves. Her skin glowed like it held a candle inside, and her eyes – while blue – seemed almost to glow gold as well. She had a superior smile on her face that made me think of Princess Chasida. I did not like that smug look in her eyes. Those were eyes that would gut another woman and sell her meat at the market.

"That's Lady Tanglecott," Grosbeak informed me.

"She looks like she eats other women for a tea snack," I said precisely, and he snickered, to the horror of the servant two steps above us. The servant gasped and looked toward Bluebeard.

I chanced a glance at my husband, but his expression was carefully neutral.

The next landing showed me a feast so mouth-wateringly opulent that I couldn't prevent my belly from rumbling over the whole roasted pig and the scent of toasted nuts and berry pie.

"As I said, wife," Bluebeard growled as if I had spoken rather than my belly. "We have but minutes to spare."

I nodded and hurried on with him.

"There will be food up above," the servant said, a little breathless. He kept running a few steps up and then running back down to be sure we were following him, and then running up again. My father had a dog like that once.

We passed a series of other portraits like the first, all cruel-looking Wittenhame. Each one more other-worldly and inhuman-looking than the next.

I stumbled when we came to Bluebeard's portrait.

"Lord Riverbarrow," Grosbeak explained derisively. "Him who is called The Arrow. A prince among the Wittenhame."

I paused this time even though my husband's hand pulled at me. Because he looked so eerie in this portrait – so pale and so blue and so very inhuman that I felt choked at the reminder that I had married someone who was not of my world at all. On his cheek was a single red tear. Just like the one I bore.

"Hurry, wife," Bluebeard murmured, and to my eye, his pale skin looked blue among the ice and glowing fungi.

Something glinted in Grosbeak's eye and then he spoke.

"You call her 'wife,'" Grosbeak laughed, "but do you know what she calls you?" It felt to me like an act he was putting on. His voice sounded just a shade too high and his emotion just a tinge too desperate.

"What?" Bluebeard growled as he led me past two more landings.

The servant hopped from foot to foot as if he badly needed a quiet moment in the back house.

I was growing weary of all the stairs and every stitch in my back felt like it was pulling, but I didn't dare pause. Even if the servant hadn't looked about to cry, leaning against the wall was out of the question. It would mean leaning against the poor victims trapped within it.

Instead, I dug deep inside, battling both the pain of my stitches and the nausea and light-headedness that made it hard to concentrate.

Grosbeak remained silent, his expression turning smug. He was getting the reaction he wanted – though I didn't know why he wanted it.

We rounded another corner and Bluebeard spun me so my back was to the wall, but though his actions were full of frustration, he was careful not to press my wounded back against the ice . He let go of my hand and braced himself against the wall with a hand on either side of my head. He peeked a little look out at the worried servant on one side and his anxious men on the other, as if this was some grand joke that he was wasting time when he should be hurrying.

"You have a name for me, you stone-faced certainty?" His eyes were lit with some emotion I couldn't understand, and his lips parted slightly in anticipation. "It's not 'honey' or 'darling,' is it?"

I lifted a single eyebrow. I thought he said he was in a hurry. And even he should realize I was not a girl who would call him that.

"Please, for the love of the wind's name and the forest's caresses, please!" the servant begged, swaying side to side with urgency.

Bluebeard frowned as if he'd heard my thoughts and then tilted his head to one side, his cat's eyes still teasing. "It's not 'illegitimate son of a donkey' either, is it? What might that name be, wife of mine?"

I lifted the other eyebrow. Did he really want me to break my pact and speak aloud to him?

He waited a heartbeat before smiling savagely and winking at me.

"My prince?" Vireo said nervously. Now he sounded as

nervous as the servant. "The edge of darkness lifts."

"I shall hear the name at dawn, fire of my eyes," Bluebeard murmured for only my ears to hear.

I tilted my head as if asking, "But will you?"

Bluebeard growled in his throat, snatched my hand back, and led me up another spiral of the stairs to where they finally came out to a wide balcony. We stepped up into the bright moonlight there, where the thick lip of fungus made a fine, long hall looking out over the Wittenhame all around.

Though a fall from the edge of the fungus lip would be fatal, no railing was erected, nor a low wall. No provisions were made at all to guard guests.

A long table was laid out, made of woven bones and a tangle of interwoven weapons – bows, axes, swords, and anything else I could think of. Around it, were chairs that left my pulse racing. Who in all the world would choose chairs like these? I feared the stains on the dark wood were not made of age but of blood. Leather straps were dangling from them as if someone had once been strapped to them – or may still become imprisoned there.

The servant who had led us bowed until he was bent almost in half, and on either side of the door, a pair of other servants bowed in the same way.

They murmured something, but I was not listening to them. I was not even looking at the people surrounding the table as Bluebeard hustled me toward the one empty chair – the one at the end of the table.

I was looking at the figure seated at the head of the table.

He looked like a very large man – a head taller than Bluebeard and twice as thick. He was seated on a throne made of bones

I didn't recognize – large bones that were almost bird-like, or maybe lizard-like – and both he and the throne were half-encased by the ice of the wall. Frost covered what was still unencumbered by ice, coating his eyelids and his beard, decorating his grand crown with a lace of frostwork. His eyes were half-closed and his voice was speaking very quietly – and yet it seemed to fill the room.

"… wait no longer," it said slowly as Bluebeard drew me to the table. Someone had scattered fat white and blue hyacinths all over the table and everyone's drinks were interspersed with the sonsy blooms. "Only those who are seated …"

Bluebeard sat so quickly that it almost didn't look graceful – the first ungraceful movement I'd ever seen from him – and he pulled me down to sit on his knee like a child.

"…now, will be qualified to enter."

And when Bluebeard breathed out, I realized he'd been holding his breath.

Around the table, everyone else seemed to let out a breath, too, though their sighs sounded more like disappointment or resignation.

All the other eyes were on us. And they were the eyes from the portraits leading up the stairs.

"Did you feel the lack of my presence? Was it a howling wind echoing through your hearts?" Bluebeard asked lightly, throwing his leg up over the arm of his chair casually. He looked for all the world like a cat coming in late after a night of prowling.

Someone farther down the table growled.

A thrill of fear shot through me and with it the very strong desire to be ill for there was murder in every set of those eyes.

CHAPTER NINETEEN

"Let the game dawn," the sovereign's voice announced, and then his eyes closed as if he were going back to sleep.

"That's our sovereign," Grosbeak hissed to me. "He rules all of the Wittenhame. Any seated here could be his successor – if they earn the role."

I swallowed and very carefully did not touch the blood dripping down my cheek that everyone around the table was staring at.

Out on the horizon between the great trees, the first golden ray of dawn split the sky.

"You've married again," one of the men halfway down the table said, putting his feet up among the hyacinths as he spoke and crossing the ankles of his knee-high patent leather boots with delicate care.

I noted that he was absolutely not looking at Grosbeak's head and Grosbeak was looking very attentively at him, his mouth a straight line of fury. This, then, must be his master.

He wore a jacket like Bluebeard's, but it was crimson and trimmed in white. I counted three swords on his person. Two were crossed over his breast as if to show just how very addicted to swords he really was. He put his hands behind his head and leaned back in his chair as if he were going to fall asleep right here. Maybe they all were. After all, the man encased in ice seemed to be somnolent. Every now and then, his great face twitched under the frost as if he were dreaming.

Servants began to move quietly between those sitting, bringing steins, mugs, and glasses that steamed or seeped or bubbled depending on what manner of brew was within. One seemed to be hissing and another gave off a whine like a kettle at a boil. Those sitting around the table barely noticed the drinks or the servants, simply accepting them or waving them off as they chose. Bluebeard took a steaming, thick drink of a very pale green that smelled powerfully of mint. He must really like that flavor.

"And who exactly did you marry?" one of the women asked. She had dark hair and was missing two fingers and an ear. She'd placed a pair of small bearded axes before her, wedged into the table as if she thought she'd need them at a moment's notice.

Across from her, another woman laughed – one with pale blonde hair, but I barely looked at her hair. My breath froze in my throat when my gaze turned to a pet she was feeding from her hand. There was one on either side of her and they were silvery-bright, striped with black slashes, and bearing four small, feathered wings on their backs.

I froze, my eyes widening at the sight of them. Would I find my own flesh under their claws?

"I'm still finding out," Bluebeard said coldly, shifting me so that I had to meet his eye.

His gaze locked onto mine as a ray of gold washed over his face.

He wanted me to tell him what I called him to myself. His name. I could see the frustration building behind his visage just as it built in me when I couldn't speak to him in the night.

I bit my lip and thought about it. If I told it to him right now, it would tell him I was on his side, but it would also tell him that I could be cowed into doing whatever he said.

"I respond better to honey than to stings," I whispered. But I did not say his name, and though his lip twitched irritably right where that little scar nicked it, there was nothing he could say because dawn was bathing the sky.

"Do keep this one around longer than the last one," the man in the red coat said. He was missing the smallest finger on his left hand. "I like the taste of her spirit. Like black pepper and limes."

"You can still taste the spirits, Sword?" Bluebeard said with innocent eyes. "And here I thought you lost that ability in the last game."

There was laughter around the table and the Sword's expression went stiff. He was not amused.

Bluebeard caught my eye and there was something steely in his. He held my gaze and reached for the cords tying my cloak. I shied away but his free hand grabbed my knee and pinched it – hard – as if trying to tell me wordlessly to allow this.

I swallowed. It felt like a power game. And I was the one being made to look foolish. But showing my wounds to the table – which was what would happen if he removed my cloak and my backless dress showed everyone my stitched flesh – didn't make any sense to me. Why bother? What did it prove?

I was angled on his lap so that my back was to the table. I took a deep breath and judged the calculated look in Bluebeard's eye. He was planning something. If I wanted to know what it was – or know about any of this so I could report it to the King

– then I needed to play along. I gave an infinitesimal nod and let him loosen the string.

The cloak fell to the floor and behind me I heard a gasp.

"Someone has not been playing very nicely with his toys," the Sword drawled. "What a naughty boy. You should be conserving her. You'll need every bit of her you can barter."

Barter? Fear shot through me, and Bluebeard – his eyes still locked on mine – gave such a tiny shake of his head that I wasn't sure I'd seen it at all.

Someone cleared his throat – a man seated opposite to the Sword. He wore an opulent plum doublet with a jagged collar and golden powder surrounded his eyes. Unlike his fellows, he wasn't missing any fingers or ears.

His eyes held a calculating glance as he said, "As youngest and newest to the table, it is on my oath to offer the bones for the telling of the fates."

"Offer the bones then, boy," Bluebeard said in a bored tone. "Don't bore us all with talking about it."

Again, there were snickers, but the Sword spoke sourly. "We wouldn't have waited here until the exact last second if you hadn't delayed, Arrow. Your snide remarks notwithstanding. To be frank, I grow weary from a long night of indulgence. And you are its maker, not its victim."

The young man swallowed, looking back and forth between them as if waiting for someone to give him permission to move. Eventually, the woman from the first portrait I had seen on the stairs – Lady Tanglecott – raised an imperial hand. She was the one with the mist lion pets. Just glancing at them made my mouth taste sour. I did not like turning my back in their direction.

"Throw the bones, Coppertomb." She sipped on her pink drink and tiny pink sparks flew off of it when she blew on it, leaving black singes on the table and any clothing they hit.

The young man looked grateful. He lifted a horn up above his head and then stood, swirling it carefully in his hand before dashing the contents onto the table.

They looked something like dice but double the length and half the width. They were dark in color and etched with white, and they all landed face down except one.

Everyone around the table stared for a long minute at that one piece before Coppertomb gathered them up again with care.

The eyes of the Sword lit with what I thought might be pleasure or anticipation, but everyone else was properly stone-faced.

"What did that mean?" I whispered to Grosbeak.

"Shhh," he whispered back. "I'm concentrating."

"Leash your pet, Lord Riverbarrow," Lady Tanglecott said, and around me there were snickers. I realized, to my horror, that she was referring to me. My face felt hot.

"If I ever took a pet, Lady Tanglecott," Bluebeard said with care. "I would be sure to choose one that would claw your eyes out. And I don't mean those tame kitties you keep beside you. I think I would require something nearly as fearsome as I am."

"Enough." The word was cold, and it came from the other woman at the table – the one missing the eye and two of her fingers. She twirled one of the ones left in her dark hair. "We know the game. All that remains for today is to choose the playing piece. I grow weary and my pillow calls to me, so let's have this done and be off to our beds so that when darkness descends again, we are ready for the hazards."

"Why the hurry?" a man from the other end of the table whispered. He hadn't spoken until now, and he still didn't look up from a book he was reading. His head was crowned with antlers and his feet were up on the table just like the Sword's.

"I prefer my moves made in the game, not in boasting before it begins," the dark-haired lady said.

"I agree with Lady Wittentree," Lady Tanglecott said.

I committed the name to memory. If I was going to give a report on midsummer night, I would need all the information I could gather – surely, this was what he must have meant by spying. For we had no information about their rulers or courts or ways and that was something that I alone could discover for my people. And if I chose instead to throw in my lot with my husband, these details would make me a more canny ally.

"Bring the pieces," Coppertomb said nervously, and a pair of servants hurried through the ice door bearing a large copper cauldron between them on a pair of poles.

The servants wore padded gloves and long leather aprons, and they were both red-faced and sweating. After a heartbeat, I realized they were mortal just like me.

They struggled forward with the heavy cauldron and placed it alongside the table, next to Bluebeard. I could feel the heat of the cauldron from where I sat as the servants retreated, bowing and sweating, as they backed away from the swirling pot. It looked as though it were full of molten lead, and the top was streaked and crackled with impurities.

To my utter shock, Bluebeard thrust his left hand into his mug of minty drink and then into the molten lead beside us.

I screamed, clutching my throat. He was going to lose his hand. Cold sweat broke out across my brow and I leapt up from his lap, backing up to make space for him to crumple.

He did not crumple.

Along the table, vicious laughter rang out. Bluebeard brought his hand out and opened his fist to reveal a little figure in his palm. It looked exactly like the king of Pensmoore but it was the size of my index finger. Whoever had carved it had made his costume and features so perfect and so carefully detailed that he looked alive. That streak of grey in his hair was exactly as in life.

To my horror, the tiny figure blinked at me and then opened his mouth and screamed in silent, writhing agony.

"Pensmoore," Bluebeard announced casually, showing the others.

I clapped my hand over my mouth and he pocketed the piece, motioning to me with his hand to sit on his knee again.

His hand was untouched. Not even pink from the heat.

I felt like I might faint. Or perhaps be ill. Or perhaps throw myself off the edge of the fungi to end this madness. This could not be happening. Maybe I was still trapped in that wave of madness between the worlds. Maybe I'd never managed to get free of it.

Bluebeard's strong hand whipped out, snatched my wrist, and used it to guide me back to his knee.

The Sword was already getting up, swaggering over to the pot. He plunged his hand in the beer stein and then into the cauldron and came out with a glittering princess wrapped in silver swaths of fabric.

"Ayyadmoore," he said easily and sat again.

Behind him, a man in mason clothing began to tap chisel and hammer against the wall. Above him, I realized, were lists of countries and players. Tanglecott was listed beside Fraedrann. But the nation of Fraedrann had died in a terrible plague that swept the nation hundreds of years ago. My brow furrowed. What was this list?

The man's chisel began to tap and I could have sworn he was writing "Pensmoore" on the wall. My blood felt like ice.

"Ilkanmoore," Lady Tanglewood announced as she made her way back to her seat. The dark figure in her fist struggled, tiny arms and legs flailing.

"Rouranmoore," Lady Wittentree announced, leading a man made – it would seem – entirely of white roots that formed hair and beard and clothing. Two blue eyes peered from under the mass of roots while Lady Wittentree dipped his hand for him. When it emerged she announced, "And for Lord Marshyellow we have Moravidmoore."

Antlerdale never looked up, merely showing his piece to the others. Only the Sword's mutter of "Ptolemoore" tipped me off to who he had chosen.

"They play against each other," Grosbeak whispered to me. "The fates of mortals are their pieces and the whims of chance their dice. Although, that should be obvious to anyone possessing half a brain."

A thickly built man with jutting lower incisors and very thick black hair pulled his hood back and emerged from behind

Antlerdale. I didn't even notice him until he moved. He swayed as if he were under the influence of a substance.

"Gods have mercy," he muttered as he reached in and then cursed when he pulled out a woman with thick layers of skirts and a tall, conical hat on her head. "Qaramoore."

And that left only Coppertomb who hurried over, carefully soaking his hand in water until the sleeve was wet and the Sword was waggling his eyebrows at him, before reaching in and out as fast as a blink.

"Leaving me with Salamoore," he said, seeming relieved. But hadn't that been inevitable if it was the only piece left? The expressions on the other faces around the table suggested that maybe it was not.

The sovereign at the head of the table opened his eyes again, and the room fell silent. His voice – again – was authoritative, though barely louder than a whisper.

"Play resumes at Peak of Night."

Chapter Twenty

It was like a wildcat had been let loose in the room. The moment the Sovereign closed his eyes again, the Lords and Ladies of the Wittenbrand scattered.

Some leapt from the side of the fungi ledge. I gasped at that, but no one seemed concerned. Perhaps they could fly, or maybe they were athletic enough to twist and land on another ledge. Some rushed out the door. Some moved to watch the stonemason etching their names in the rocky wall, chatting loudly about the results of the nations drawn.

Bluebeard helped me up, leaving the cloak on the floor. Did he want my back on display? I opened my mouth, and he pressed a finger to his lips as if the two of us were sharing a delicious secret. I pressed my lips together tightly to show him how irritated I was. I was not cattle. I was not a prize dog. I was his wife, and if that meant to him that he could use me as he liked, to me it meant that I was his equal and deserved to be treated as such.

But I could wait until we were in private to tell him that. I could wait until it was just the two of us. And then I would show him how to treat his wife.

He'd wanted an answer on whether I would work with him. I wanted an answer on whether *he* would work with *me.*

I let my eyes glitter with suppressed anger but before I could do more than look at him, an icy hand touched my back and I flinched in pain. Something fumbled at my wrist. I spun in time to meet the gaze of the Sword. Something about the way he was looking at me made my mind go numb for just a moment.

Bluebeard's hand shot forward and caught the Sword's wrist, hauling his hand from my back. "Look all you want, but please don't touch," he said smoothly.

"Why ever not, Arrow?" the Sword asked, leaning smoothly against the woven table, his hip jutting out saucily as if he was completely at his ease. He picked a bloom up from the table, twirling it between finger and thumb before burying his nose in it. "It's not like you really touch them. You're more frigid than winter's bite."

"And more ruthless," Bluebeard countered. "I'll take more than your fingers if you touch her again. You'll be thinking fondly of the black of frozen flesh the frost steals when you compare it to what I demand in payment."

The Sword bit his lip at me and then the corner of his mouth turned up. "I think she's received the message."

He sauntered away, leaving Bluebeard standing there with his chest and fist thrust forward as if he were on the verge of giving chase. His lip curled up a little and he reached to take my hand.

Which was when I realized someone had tucked something into it. A scrap of paper, if I wasn't mistaken. I slid it between my fingers and offered my other hand to take his. Bluebeard whistled as he guided me down the steps and out of each doorway. His band joined him again, one by one, as if drawn by his low whistle.

They weren't the only ones. Little birds fluttered down,

landing on his head and shoulders and singing sweetly in harmony with him.

“A fine showing,” Grosbeak murmured. “The nations are all key ones and very close to one another. Close enough for the opening moves to be very interesting. They may already have agents in each others’ courts. It will be a fine Turning of Ages this time around. Very fine.”

“Are they truly playing on behalf of the nation whose leader they chose?” I asked Grosbeak, and was surprised when Bluebeard’s hand tightened on mine. It wasn’t painful, but more … tense … as if he feared the answer to this question.

“Haven’t you heard tell that the Wittenbrand play games with the fates of men?” Grosbeak asked me.

“I’ve heard the rumors.”

“Now you get to see it. A real game with real people and nations as the markers. If your nation is lost, you lose.”

“What do you mean by lost?” I asked weakly, conscious that Bluebeard was squeezing my hand even more tightly – and that in his other fist he held the king of my nation in miniature.

“Ever heard of the Eldenheim? The Corrindale? The Xan Tharan?”

“I have not,” I said, licking my dry lips.

“Well, there you go then. Lost means lost.”

Lost. My family. My home. My nation.

He held their fate in his palm.

Quite literally.

Which meant he must not fail. If he failed, he would lose everything I loved. Every*one* I cared for. And that meant that if I turned on him and gave him up to the King of Pensmoore – if that wasn't him shrunk to the size of a finger and stuffed into my husband's palm – then far, far worse would happen than simply me losing my life and all my days. And what if our king didn't know about this? Maybe he sould be told that much at least. It was hardly betraying anyone to tell him about his own fate – and possibly the best bit of information I could glean for him.

I felt dizzy.

At the last door, Vireo rejoined us.

"So," he asked my husband, "What is it to be then? I had a herd of pigs riding on famine."

"Famine?" I gasped. My eyes were so wide they were beginning to sting.

"War," Bluebeard said quietly. "It's to be war."

The band around us seemed grimmer somehow, their faces hardening, grips tightening on sword hilts. Did that mean they would fight?

"We're ready, Arrow," Sparrow said grimly.

"The flat tokens that Coppertomb threw determined the game," Grosbeak told me. "Famine, Pestilence, War, or Cataclysm. The games of the lives of men. Cataclysm is my favorite. Very dramatic. Most of it is determined by chance. War is the most strategic. It favors the thinkers and plotters. Like the Arrow here, or the Sword."

I risked a glance at my husband's face and shrank at what I saw there, for that was not concern or horror. In the lines of his face were anticipation and giddy eagerness. He couldn't wait to start. And if he lost, then everything would be lost to me.

Despite the frigid air, I felt hot all over.

"And could he have chosen not to play?"

Every eye was glaring at me now.

Grosbeak laughed. "Well, if he didn't play, he would no longer be a prince of the Wittenhame. He would forfeit his lands and people. Any claim he has laid on the mortal world and any magic he may derive from his claims there would be lost. He would lose his position and someone else would claim it. Vireo perhaps, or another Wittenbrand. Whoever made the claim would have to pass through a series of trials to take the role, but there would be many who would try to do that. If you don't play, then you are no prince of our land."

"Are we returning to your home, my lord Arrow?" Vireo asked crisply, refusing to look at Grosbeak or acknowledge the assumption that he was next in line for Bluebeard's position.

"Immediately. My wife needs feeding and sleep."

"And tomorrow?"

"You know none of us may act until the bets are placed," Bluebeard said briskly. Our escort shoved through the last of the stumbling dancers in the snow below the bottom steps. Around us, the day was bright and merry but the Wittenhame were stumbling to their homes nearby, putting their hands up to shield their eyes from the morning sun as if it was offensive to them and not the golden delight of the heavens.

"Others may choose to act sooner," Vireo replied, stone-faced.

Grosbeak chuckled. "You know the Sword will cheat. He'll already be sending messages. Nothing you can prove – just little things to pave the way."

"I am not the Sword," Bluebeard said menacingly. "I am so much worse than he could dare to be."

The Grouse House took that opportunity to make an appearance, fluttering down from one of the trees and landing in front of us so inelegantly that I was afraid it would crash.

Without a word, Bluebeard swept me off my feet and into his arms and marched up the stairs.

"Get sleep and food into you," he called over his shoulder. "And be back here before first dark. We have planning to do and strategies to make."

He yanked the door open and stepped inside with me still in his arms, pausing only when he saw there was barely room to stand inside.

"My people," he said, his voice ragged. "You have come to me."

My jaw dropped at the various people assembled in the room. Some sat or stood on or flapped over the desk. Some on the bookcases. Others on the hearth. The rest of the floor was packed with people of every size – one nearly the size of an oak tree, others so small they rivaled my fingernails. They had wings, or webbed feet, or horns that curled, or spiraled, or were straight. They had large, sharp teeth and broad, flat teeth. Some had papery skin like birch bark and others were ridged like a maple tree. Some hovered on dragonfly wings and some bore bird wings tucked modestly behind their backs. Some presented wide antlers and some hair like dandelion frills.

Bluebeard glanced at me, an odd expression on his face that looked almost like pride – but that could not be right. After a moment, he seemed to realize that he couldn't speak to me, so he spoke to them.

"This is my newest wife, Izolda of Pensmoore. I present her to you."

"Lady," the nearest one squeaked – a woman, perhaps? – who was shaped like a porcupine and completely covered in quills. "We thank you for your sacrifice."

And then they all swiveled away from me and toward Bluebeard and she spoke again. "We came together, but I was elected to speak. We suffer, Lord of Riverbarrow. All down the River the old ways die and the folk die with it. Our trees are cut, our swamps drained dry, our flowers plucked. We wane and die, we waste and grow hollow. We cry to you for salvation."

"Patience, my folk," Bluebeard said, but his face was pale and for the first time since I met him, he seemed afraid. "I work to buy it all back and make you free."

"We know you care, Lord of Riverbarrow," the porcupine lady said. "But we dwindle. Some of us are the last of our kind in your lands. And we fear that if you do not act quickly, there will be no folk for you to save."

He ran a hand over his face, and I could have sworn his lovely eyes were wet with tears. The blood streak on his cheek smeared and he bowed his head.

"I hear your words, my folk. And I listen. Please have faith in me for a little while longer."

They nodded gravely and then passed him one by one, leaving out the door. Each of them touching him as they left – as if just touching him would work some kind of magic.

Furtively, I stole a look at the tiny paper rolled up between my fingers.

I nearly dropped it in my shock. I could have sworn that the Sword had given it to me, and yet it was in my brother's hand. It read:

Izolda,

We will come for you. Have no fear.

Svetgin

My brother's words, in his hand. I looked up quickly. None had seen me reading the paper except Grosbeak, who raised a single eyebrow and smiled nastily. But even though I knew that my husband must win in this game with the lives of men, I couldn't help the glimmer of hope that seeing my brother's words drove into my heart. He knew where I was. He was coming for me.

Could that even be possible? He had sent a note – a feat I'd thought impossible. Perhaps the only limit here was my own imagination.

The last of the folk trooped out the door and Bluebeard shut it behind them, leaning his head against the doorframe. His shoulders slumped as if he was carrying a terrible load.

I ought to fight with him. I ought to tell him he was terrible and cruel and disrespectful and all the other things I'd observed since he put me on the back of his elk and ridden through the madness into this wild world. But how did you kick a man who was already so far down?

"I'll give you a hint," I said calmly, setting Grosbeak on the bookshelf.

Bluebeard spun and looked at me, his eyes blazing a question and irritated at my interruption all at once.

"The name I call you comes from a color," I said calmly.

His forehead wrinkled in puzzlement, but he no longer looked defeated.

I strode over to the edge of the fire and picked up one of the books on the hearth. Its name was on the spine. *Marvels of Modern Accountancy.*

Wait. Hadn't he thrown this book in the fire when he was reading it the night we were wed?

I shook my head. It was just a strange coincidence. I'd had a lot to think on that night. I couldn't trust my memory about the details.

Bluebeard moved to sit at his desk, poring over pages of what looked like poetry as if there were answers there. He opened his hand and put the little king down on the table so that he was standing, facing him. His feet were attached to a lead disc, so he could not move but he bellowed silently, shaking a fist. It made something cold seize in my chest.

No, I would not be the puppet of the little king. I needed to seal things with my husband. I had married him. He held my nation in his palm. It was with him that I must forge some kind of alliance.

"I would like to speak to you, husband," I said calmly.

He did not look up.

I swallowed.

This was going to be hard to manage when he couldn't speak to me but harder still if he wouldn't even look at me.

He gestured to a table in one corner of the jumbled room that was laden with food. I was not hungry. Okay, I was hungry, but I was not going to eat until I made my point.

"It's important that we talk." I made sure my voice was very clear.

He still didn't look up. He took out a pen, dipped it in an inkpot and began to write. I peeked over his shoulder. He was writing poetry. The fate of my world and the lives of those wild folk hung in the balance and he was writing poetry.

I shook my head and took a deep breath. Calm, Izolda. Losing your temper now will help nothing.

I waited and waited for what felt like an hour and still, he did not look up or even so much as glance toward me.

I needed to get his attention. I put my hands on my hips and then immediately let them drop again. The pain in my back was too intense. I was swaying on my feet from exhaustion and anxiety and hunger. I needed to eat and I needed my bed.

But if I left things like this, night would fall again and my voice would be lost to me before I could do anything to change what was.

The room was full of items – books and trinkets. Curiosities and precious things. The raven flapped over one bookshelf, tempting me, but it was important to choose things that were valuable enough that he'd notice but not so valuable that it would hurt him.

The raven walked across the desk and tilted his head at Bluebeard. My husband paused his writing and tilted his head in a mirror image of the bird, his cat's eyes flashing in the fire. So, he would not pause to hear me but he would pause to stare at a bird?

I shook my head. Well, that settled it.

With care, I strode to the hearth and picked up *Marvels of Modern Accountancy.* I cleared my throat and then threw it in the fire.

“Thank you,” the fire rumbled, puffing up to twice his height for a moment before calming back down.

Bluebeard’s head whipped up and he looked at the fire and then at me. I picked up the next book and this time I read the title aloud.

“*Crop Rotations: How to Account for Them Without Making Your Head Spin.* Clever.”

I threw it into the fire. Sparks puffed into the air and the fire belched loudly.

“Thank you.”

Bluebeard dropped his pen and rushed across the room as I picked up a third tome.

“*A Head Above the Rest: Ancestry of the Landholders of Pensmoore*. Well, don’t they think a lot of themselves.”

Bluebeard’s hand caught my wrist before I could throw it into the fire. His eyes blazed into mine.

“Don’t like the disrespect of having your books burned?” I asked Bluebeard acidly. “Well, I don’t like disrespect either. I’m your wife. I am not a broodmare to be auctioned off to the highest bidder. I am not cattle to be traded in and stalled. I am not a pretty necklace to be bought and placed within a jewelry box. I am a living woman with a mind and abilities and there are things I can offer you.”

"She speaks as though she possesses something I do not already own, my fire," Bluebeard said, shooting a glance at the fire.

"Yes, my master," the fire said.

"You drew my king from the molten lead," I said, catching his gaze again and looking into it with enough intensity to hold it. "You carry the fate of my nation in your hands."

He tilted his chin up arrogantly.

"And you carry the fates of those wild folk who came here to plead with you," I added, and he softened just a bit, his face relaxing slightly.

I felt my own brow furrowing. *That* was the path to his heart? This strange, violent man cared about that odd collection of creatures more than anything else? It was … surprisingly endearing.

"You think I am only of value to you for the days of mine that you can spend to get what you want."

He raised an eyebrow in response.

"You are wrong. You asked me if I would work with you. My answer is yes. But will *you* work with *me*? You will find it much easier to get what you want with me as your ally rather than your enemy."

He raised the other eyebrow as if he didn't believe I could be his enemy.

"I could speak during the night and take your magic away," I threatened. His grip on my wrist tightened, his eyes blazing with deadly warning. "Yes, you'd kill my family and nation, but you might already do that with foolishness in this game of war you are playing."

"She speaks as if I believe that she would doom us both, my fire." His voice was low and insinuating.

"Yes, my master," the fire said. "But have a care. There is a fire in this one. Like recognizes like."

"Have I mentioned you arc a rare fire beyond mortal worth?" Bluebeard said.

"You have not, my master."

I flicked my wrist and the book sailed into the fire's maw. He consumed it with a burst of orange flame and Bluebeard clenched his jaw so tightly that I heard his teeth click.

"Thank you," said the fire.

"That's what happens when you compliment things," Bluebeard said sourly. "It goes straight to their heads."

"Yes, my master."

I cleared my throat again.

"I can make your life miserable in a thousand small ways, husband. I can distract you from your purpose. I could even take my own life – and then what would you do? Would you have time to find a new bride?"

"Tell me she wouldn't do that," Bluebeard called to Grosbeak. "Tell me she has more sense than that."

Grosbeak opened his eyes and blinked slowly. "I doubt it. She took me on as a pet. That's hardly sensible."

"Ah, but had she not, you would have joined the heads of the other traitors in my crypt. An interesting prospect to be sure, but not quite as interesting as the fate she has granted you."

His crypt? He really did collect the heads of his enemies? I suppressed a shiver. There wasn't time for that when I was trying to make a point.

"I'm not asking for anything that doesn't benefit you to give," I insisted.

Bluebeard used his grip on my arm to lead me from the fire to the table full of food. He scooped up an apple.

"Care to eat, Grosbeak?"

"I do not, Lord Riverbarrow. I would like to sleep." Grosbeak promptly followed his words with closed eyes and a snore that could not possibly be real.

Bluebeard huffed and bit the apple, dropping my wrist.

I leaned in close. "Have any of your other wives helped you? Have they found ways to goad your enemies or sing the harmony to your melody?"

He shot a glance my way out of the corner of his eye. His eyes were rimmed in dark lashes, shockingly pretty for a man's.

"I am starting to think that they did nothing but sit in this house as you wiled away their days," I challenged.

He looked at me, chewing the apple and raising a single eyebrow.

"They did?" It was meant to be an exclamation, but it came out like a gasp. "But what did they do with themselves?"

He gave a one-shouldered shrug as if it was hardly his concern and tapped the key around my neck as if I could get all the answers I wanted if I just went and read their hideous books.

Which I supposed I would have to do … but I wasn't done with him yet.

I shook my head as he reached for a chicken leg but watching him eat was making my stomach rumble. I caught up a thin piece of bread that smelled of cardamom, lavished it with butter, and bit it. It was gone in moments and I followed it with dried plums and honeyed carrots, parsnips in mint sauce, a blue-veined cheese, something hot and bitter that poured from a kettle, and sweet spiced nuts that melted in my mouth. And when I'd eaten my fill, I met his eyes again and he was grinning at me as if my appetite amused him.

My cheeks grew hot, but I was not done. I leaned across the table, swallowing the terror inside me. I could do this and see some measure of freedom before my untimely death, or I could live shut up in this house for the rest of my days … with the warm fire and all the food and the books that seemed to never end. I pushed that thought aside before it became too tempting. I wasn't naturally bold or aggressive, but I needed him to hear me and to listen and if drama and bold words were the way he communicated, then they were probably the way he could hear me. I must use them or suffer for not using them.

"Only a fool leaves his sharpest sword behind when he goes into battle," I said, catching his eye. "Only a fool leaves one of his oxen behind when he goes to plow. Only a fool gets married in his second-best shirt. If you don't make use of me properly, then you've wasted what you have, and if you fail at whatever it is you are trying to achieve here, then you'll have no one to blame but yourself. Why bother asking me to work with you if you only plan to use me as your tool and not your equal?"

He chewed his food, watching me carefully, and then he took my hand. To my utter shock, he kissed the back of it and then winked at me. He stood and led me over to a settee beside the fire, sat, and motioned for me to come closer.

I watched him warily. It bothered me to no end that one of us must always be silent. It made me say more than I would usually say. And also less.

It was like a burr under my dress, like a splinter in the arch of my foot, like a buzzing mosquito in the small hours of the night.

He took my other hand and drew me so that I sat on his lap, straddling him, and then he smiled.

"I don't know what game this is," I said, still wary and worried. This intimacy was not what I was asking for. "But I would like an answer. Will you treat me like an ally? Will you show me the respect I deserve and see that I can work with you?"

He nodded very solemnly, his blue eyes locked on mine, and when I nodded, too, he smiled wickedly, and began to play with my hair.

I moved to get off his lap and he shook his head. He was tying little knots into my hair, oddly enough.

I might as well let him. I'd gotten what I asked for, after all. If all he wanted in return was to make a rat's nest of my hair, I'd still made the better bargain.

The fire felt good against my sore back and it was nice to sit without the wounds touching anything. The soft movement of his tying knots in the lengths of my hair began to lull me to sleep. I leaned forward enough that I could rest my forehead against the padded back of the settee. He made a sound in his throat that sounded almost contented.

And without meaning to, I drifted off to sleep.

CHAPTER TWENTY-ONE

I woke in the middle of the day. There was a knot in my stomach that made me feel like I was going to throw up. I pushed myself up from where I was slumped on the settee and pain flared through me like shards of glass under my skin. Sweat broke across my forehead.

I gasped, wavering on the edge of the settee. I'd fallen asleep half on top of Bluebeard and half on top of the settee. He was still sitting, head thrown back, breathing through his open mouth. It was shocking to see him so vulnerable, but I knew he was – that he'd left himself utterly at my mercy.

I could kill him right now if I wanted to and be free of him and his world of horrors.

I swallowed.

I could slit his throat before he woke. I could strike him on the head with the fire poker.

And then what? I would be a murderer just like him. My nation would be trampled in the game the Wittenbrand were playing. And it would be my fault.

I staggered to my feet. No. I'd told him I would back him. I'd made vows to him of marriage. I'd made my choice. Now came the part where I saw it through.

I was careful not to wake him as I stumbled out of the main room toward the dark corridor. I didn't know what was in the rest of the house, but I was hoping to draw a cool bath and ease the pain of these stitches.

I snuck past Grosbeak who was snoring on the shelf and carefully eased my way into the darkness. The corridor had no windows and I stubbed my toe on what turned out to be a staircase. I crept up it, step by step. The faintest sound of birdsong seemed to echo with each step, but there were no birds on the spiral stairs and eventually, they arrived at a wide, airy room.

It was as odd a room as I'd expected from this house.

A four-poster bed was strung with vines that formed a canopy and hung all around it in verdant tangles. From the vines bloomed such a display of coal-black flowers that the bed seemed to be made of them. They fluttered in a non-existent breeze, their petals dropping all around and fluttering through the air. To my surprise, they smelled faintly of vanilla.

Boots and gorgeous clothing were strewn everywhere, and among them were various swords, staves, bows, stacks of books, and more arrows than I could count. It was as if someone had been living a life in this room one layer on top of the other, on top of the other, without ever cleaning the layer below, or even checking to see if anything was growing inside of it.

My fingers twitched with the desire to tidy.

But this wasn't a room like one you'd find in a house. One wall was completely missing, showing a shoreline where waves rolled in one after another to smash against the rocks. The other walls were hung with thick tapestries and bookshelves jammed full of books and odd items, just like down below. Also like the room below, the ceiling was hung with a wide chandelier dripping with fat wax candles, and the ceiling above was so high that all I saw was darkness and mist.

To one side, the stone floor smoothed into slick rock and a pool was formed with water tumbling into it from a stream that started halfway up the stone wall. It steamed as though it was hot, and set beside it was a full-length mirror and a small table with a teapot and delicate cup.

To my surprise, the teapot was warm.

"Well, this is a curious place," I said.

"What do you find so curious?" asked the gargoyle at the top of the mirror.

I jumped. Little chills raced up my spine. But after a long breath, I answered him.

"There is hot tea but no servants."

"The house provides what is needed." I could have sworn that the gargoyle sniffed disdainfully.

"And if I drink the tea before he wakes?" I asked.

The gargoyle made a horrible face like children do when they are trying to terrify you. When I said nothing, he eventually replied.

"More will appear when he wants it, child of foolishness."

Well then. It only made sense to enjoy it if there would be more for him later.

I began to strip off my dress and then paused.

"I shall close my eyes," said the mirror, closing them but then opening just one a small sliver.

I shook my head. But I was being absurd. It was only a mirror.

I pulled off my dress, unwound the bandages carefully, and slipped into the stone pool. Every part of me hurt, from head to toe. The water made my wounds sting worse than ever, but at the same time it seemed to soothe them, so I stayed in the water, carefully nibbling on the toast and drinking the hot tea. If I couldn't sleep then I could at least take care of my body in other ways.

I needed to think.

Last night had gone well, all things considered. Bluebeard had agreed to respect me. I had settled in my mind that I would work with him. Note or no note. But if I was going to keep his respect, I would have to prove myself to him. What could I do that he couldn't? How could I make myself useful?

I pondered the question as I bathed and then I stepped out of the pool and found a somewhat clean pair of blue breeches and a loose white shirt with arrows stitched all over it. Dressed in these, I felt considerably better.

I felt my back with careful fingers. My stitches were no longer hot and puffy. They still stung, but they also itched. Bluebeard had been right. His silver stitching had quickened their healing.

Sitting down on the edge of the bed, I basked in the light coming from the beach on one side of the wall. I wasn't fool enough to walk through to it. For all I knew, it would leave me in another world. And I was on the second story of the house, so the sand that was drifting into the edge of the room and mixing with Bluebeard's discarded things made no sense at all.

I couldn't stay here, of course. This was his bed, in his room.

I would just sit for a moment to catch my breath. The warm sun began to relax me. Okay, I would just lie down for a moment and catch my breath.

I woke to the hooting of an owl and something that sounded like splashing. It was evening again.

"Ah, you're awake, fire of my eyes," Bluebeard said, his voice low and sultry. I blinked my eyes open and immediately shut them. Then, like the gargoyle, I cracked just one open a little bit.

The mirror snorted.

"Only you would enter *this* room, you devilish sensibility." He was sitting in a tufted chair beside the fire, one leg thrown over the arm of the chair with nothing on him but a pair of rumpled breeches. He had the teacup in one hand, his smallest finger on that hand pointed out delicately as he sipped. "You step where no one else dare pass."

I blinked, confused.

"The nightingale stairs decide where to bring the person who steps on them. Faithfully, they have carried fifteen brides to their own rooms and beds, but you, they have brought to *mine*."

I sat up. After all, he was the one who chose to sit half-naked while I was sleeping here. He could hardly feel modest now, could he? He was sipping his tea and reading a book called, *Avoiding Military Defeat and Assassination: Don't Lose Your Head.*

"I rather like you in my clothing," he said, watching me with a possessive gleam in his cat's eyes.

I felt my cheeks heat as I stole a little peek at him. He was made entirely of muscle and scars except for a dusting of dark hair over his chest and forearms that made my mouth unaccountably dry. It must have been whatever was in the tea I drank. I licked my upper lip and tried not to think of tea or of hair that clung to hard muscular planes. No, I definitely wasn't thinking of that.

Keep a clear head, Izolda. You may have agreed to work with him, but you know this marriage cannot exist in truth. You are simply working together. Besides, you have never let a pretty man turn your head before and you don't need to start making a fool of yourself now.

His hair was damp and little beads of water flecked his cheeks. I realized, with a feeling I wanted to hope was horror, but was something else entirely, that there were wet footsteps leading from the bath to his chair. I could have woken any time while he bathed.

Could you blush all over your body? I thought I might be.

"Your bag of things is over there, wife," he said, pointing to my saddlebag on the other side of the fire, "if you prefer something of your own. I don't know why you would. Your taste in clothing is sinfully plain."

My eyes widened. My things!

I hurried to them and to my delight, I found one of my woven dresses and tabards crumpled in the saddlebag, along with underthings and woolen socks. I was almost crying with the relief of something from home when I felt his eyes on me and turned to see him look suddenly away, his cheeks stained with sunset.

"Is it really too much to ask that you give your whole life to me?" he said, clearing his throat as if he were having trouble concentrating. "Is it really too much to ask that you risk the same way I do?"

"Mirror," I said, crossing to where the gargoyle looked down at me. Below him, I could see Bluebeard scowling in the reflection. "Tell my husband that sacrificing your wife's wellbeing isn't nearly the same risk as sacrificing your own."

"I'll tell him no such thing," the gargoyle said haughtily.

"What if there was a reward that came with the risk?" Bluebeard asked, tilting his chin.

"Mirror, tell my husband that if there is a reward, it would have to be vast to equal the risk to my life and future."

"I will not be your messenger," the gargoyle growled. "You are abusing me most sorely."

"Oh, the risk is great, I'll agree," Bluebeard said, his voice turned to coaxing. "So, let me offer you the greatest reward I can imagine to match it."

I quirked an eyebrow at him.

He grinned as if we were sharing a joke. "Me."

"Mirror, tell my husband that I already own him body and soul. That is what marriage means."

"That's torn it!" the gargoyle shouted and then he closed his eyes furiously and pursed his lips in concentration. The mirror went black and he was gone.

I heard a wet sound behind me and turned to find Bluebeard right there, leaning in close. I kept my eyes firmly on his and definitely nowhere else. But my cheeks felt hot enough to melt that lead from yesterday.

"There's owning and then there's possessing, you sober monstrosity," he whispered, leaning in so his lips brushed the shell of my ear. "You own me, as I own you, but I offer you more than that. Take this risk with me – offer your life up – and I will give myself to you beyond vows and bonds. I will give you heart and mind and my very soul."

I pulled back so I could look into his eyes, frowning. An offer like that was too extravagant. No wonder he lived in a little cottage instead of a palace. He had no sense of how to make a good bargain.

Maybe that was what he needed me for.

The predatory look in his eyes stole my breath away as he lifted my hand toward his lips. I expected him to kiss the back of it as a lord might. Instead, he caught my index finger in his teeth – not enough to hurt but enough to *suggest* he could hurt me. At the last second, his teeth released the tip of my finger, and his soft lips wrapped around it instead as his bite turned into a kiss. He let it slide between them and away and as my finger left his lips, he gave me a devilish smile.

"Now, I've put you on equal footing, my wife. You have offered your life in a gamble for the future. I offer you my soul. Do we have a bargain? If we do, then we have equal risk and equal reward."

It was what I wanted, wasn't it? Then why did my throat feel so dry?

I could not explain it, but I felt like I was at a disadvantage here.

He lifted his hand and offered it to me, as if to seal the bargain. Shaking, I took it. I hardly knew why. Why gamble for something I wasn't sure I wanted? Why gamble for something that technically I should already own? And yet my heart raced at the thought, and I could barely suppress the shiver that ran through my core.

“We have an accord,” he said with a fierce grin. “And we are late. The bids are supposed to begin at Peak of Night. I have held things up, but I cannot dally forever, or they will begin without me. So, dress and adorn yourself for a spectacle, for I have a task for you that will let you help me just as you offered to do.”

“Oh,” he said stalking across the room, reaching for something that hung over a dressing screen. “And wear this, my bride. We need all the spectacle we can muster.”

He handed me a filmy dress made of the finest silk and lace I’d ever seen and then pointed to a dressing screen in the corner. I looked longingly at my own dress in my other hand, but he snatched it away and threw it over the mirror.

“Quickly, unless you wish to lose one of our landholds before the game has even begun.”

That was all he needed to say. I hustled around to the back of the screen and began to dress in what he’d given me. It had a corset, but no back – to my relief. The boning of the corset merely kept the bodice in place, leaving my wounds free to air and heal.

Designed to look like a breastplate, the corset was trimmed in silver with sections that looked like overlapping plate armor. It fell to a frothy skirt and the lace at the top of the corset draped around the neckline in a way that hinted more than revealed. Dark and mysterious, the entire expanse of the full skirt was sewn in what looked like a battle scene, complete with charging horses, flying arrows, and dying corpses. I wasn’t sure if I should be impressed or horrified. I felt a little of both.

The people in the scene, I realized, were both human and Wittenbrand. And the Wittenbrand seemed to be leading them or cheering them on from behind the frontlines. I hoped it was not a picture of what was to come.

I strapped my sword belt back on over the dress. I was going to have to find someone to teach me how to use the sword.

I paused as I tucked the golden key into my neckline. Seeing it made me think of the riddle that the first of Bluebeard's wives had left behind. I was almost certain it was the words I'd heard when I first entered the room myself.

I am sudden death to calm.

My roar breaks the hush.

My song the mind's somnolence.

Was the answer a scream? That seemed appropriate for this strange land. But if that was the answer, then why had the first queen written it down? Was it some esoteric way to tell us she was screaming inside? She could have just come out and said that.

I shook my head and stepped out from behind the screen.

CHAPTER TWENTY-TWO

If I'd known then about the kinds of rituals the Wittenhame loves, I would have been a lot more nervous to see another of them. I might have even demanded a lesson in using the weapon at my side. But I was still flushed with pride at my triumph in securing my husband as an ally and I had not yet realized that even together we were not enough to rival this world.

Bluebeard had dressed in a midnight blue doublet slashed with crimson. He'd re-cut his cheek and with a quick flick of his little knife he recut mine so that the blood could drip and form that long red teardrop that apparently told everyone who we were. I gritted my teeth at the sting. For the sake of my nation, I could bear a tiny wound.

He looked grimly pleased and devastatingly handsome as his black hair shone with water and his short blue beard clung to the sharp angles of his face. There were tiny threads of silver at his temples and I wondered yet again exactly how old this husband of mine was.

His cat's eyes gleamed and narrowed. They made my stomach do little flip flops as if this were my lover escorting me to a feast rather than my co-conspirator leading me to battle.

I gave him a tiny nod.

"You look well, wife," he said, his eyes gleaming with something I couldn't quite place. "Did I mention that your sword has a name? I called it Angstbite when it was mine."

He led me down the stairs to the room below.

I lifted Grosbeak's pole and he yawned dramatically. "Ready to go?"

"For all the good you did me last time," I said sourly. "You were supposed to be a help to me, but you said nothing about what was going on and I had to figure it out on my own."

"Yeah, yeah, don't get too big for your britches."

"I'll remind you," I said primly, "that you do not wear britches and therefore require my good graces – which you will only have if you remain useful."

I was still frowning when Bluebeard draped a white fur stole over my shoulders. The ends of it had pockets for my hands and there was a deep hood attached.

"Keep your back visible," he said, looking at me like he was weighing me with his eyes. He raised the hood so it framed my face. "Yes, I think that's best. Let them all see your wounds."

Just the mention of them reminded me of their steady ache. I tried to push the thought aside. As long as I concentrated on other things, the pain of the cuts was easier to bear.

"We must make a grand entrance. When we arrive, I will make a bold move. If you want to be a help to me as you've said, then it would be good if you played along." He lifted an eyebrow. "Do you agree?"

I nodded. This was one way I could prove my worth to him. This, and maybe solving the riddle.

He offered me his hand and I followed him out the door and into the night.

"Why does everything happen at night?" I asked Grosbeak.

"In the Wittenhame, we live in the shadows and dusk and we sleep in the heat of the day."

I shook my head as I looked up at the crystal-clear stars. They splashed across the sky like a handful of snow flung into the air. Low on the horizon, the full moon clung to the edge of the earth as if afraid to show its face. Perhaps even the moon was wary of this mad place.

The Grouse House had moved while we were inside it, and now we were situated in a forest made entirely of tall, purplish mushrooms. They glowed just enough to make out their outlines in the darkness.

Bluebeard offered me a hand and leaned in close. "You're as wild-looking as this land and as lovely as the night and yet you feel as real as a stone in a world of shimmering shadow. You are cold iron to my Wittenbrand magic, hard bronze to my wafting vapor, heavy lead to my tumbling feathers. Anchor me, you obelisk. Keep me tethered to what is real."

It was an odd request, but it made sense that he would make it. Who wouldn't want to be firmly planted in reality? I nodded solemnly and then, with eyes that held a warmth I didn't recognize, he swept me into his arms.

"Ride with me to Hazard Hall. We have amusement to set to flight and revelry to take captive."

He leapt and we landed on something living. As he settled me on its back in front of him, I realized – to my surprise – that we were riding a black salamander with little flecks of blue in its shiny skin. It skittered along the ground so quickly that it almost felt like flying as we slid through the mushrooms all around. The salamander moved in a serpentine pattern so it looked as if we were hurrying straight for the stalk of a mushroom, only to suddenly avoid striking it as we veered in the other direction, and then the process repeated itself. I had to close my eyes to keep from being ill.

But closing my eyes was no help at all. It only made me more conscious of Bluebeard at my back, his warm body and all its hard and soft parts pressed against me. If we could be allies, couldn't we also be friends? If friends, why not a married couple in truth?

My cheeks flared hot at the thought.

There were the other wives to think of.

And the fact that when he had run me out of days, that I would be replaced by yet another girl who would look at my blank book with scorn and wonder if she should try to find happiness in the arms of this beautiful, wicked man while she could. The thought made me feel both cold and hot at the same time. And it also made me feel like a fool.

No man, no matter how pretty or fascinating, was worthy of having me for just a time. I wasn't a trinket to be enjoyed for an evening and discarded. I was more like a marriage sword, to be worn with honor for all your life.

I frowned at the thought. I wore Bluebeard's sword at my side, and he wore the one I'd given him. There had been a variety of weapons in his room, but no other fancy swords. No other marriage swords. And there had been none in the room with the wives. Had none of them exchanged swords with him?

"Keep your eyes open," he whispered in my ear. "When your

days are limited, you shouldn't waste even an hour of one of them. What if that hour is your very last?"

I wanted to ask him how a salamander was awake in such cold weather – didn't they sleep the cold months away? – but once again my question would go unanswered. If I could change one thing about my predicament, it would be that. To be able to speak and be spoken to was a gift I'd never fully realized before. I missed it sorely.

By the time we reached Hazard Hall, I was sick to my stomach and my head was spinning – but I'd enjoyed every minute of the ride. I'd let myself really look as the mushroom-covered landscape melted into a land with a mantle of snow and then went from flat to rocky and from rocky to the edge of an endless lake – calm and still as a summer pond and rimmed in giant cattails coated in frost. The edge of the lake was stiff with a ledge of ice, but a few steps out from the shore the water was still warm, and it lapped against the ice like a lover stealing kisses again and again.

We rounded a tuft of reeds and the sand of the beach opened to a cove where someone had painstakingly set blue stones into patterns that formed a mosaic in the sand. At the apex of the mosaic was a high stone that made a kind of platform or maybe an altar. It was set against the surrounding cliffs.

Beside it, a blue banner hung, with the names of those competing in the games and the nations they would represent emblazoned upon it. I saw Bluebeard's name immediately. Riverbarrow – Pensmoore.

On the other side of the rock, another banner hung that said "Hazards" at the top, but the rest of the banner was empty.

Behind the rock, set into the cliffside, the Sovereign slumbered. But this time he was not encased in ice, but rather mostly buried in sand, as if someone had begun to uncover him before growing bored and wandering away.

The other competitors were already arranged below the altar at a table heaped with so many kinds of food I couldn't have guessed at what some of them were.

The Sword was hacking flesh from a fish large enough to swallow me. His blade had carved through its silver, crackling skin to the soft orange flesh below. Beside him, Coppertomb bit into a golden apple and Marshyellow poured two separate jugs into one stein – one with a stream of silvery liquid and one with bronze.

And around them, tiered as they climbed the cliffsides, were the Wittenbrand gathered to watch. Their tables were also laden with food and each table was lit by a forest of white candles – some taller than I was. Some as thick as trees. Clusters of them wove between the tables and tiers of them in the spaces between groups of people. Thousands ringed the altar and the table where the players sat. Dancing and glinting, the lake reflected their light back to them in long smudges of brightness across its calm surface.

But in the shadows, I saw people whispering, and others kissing, and still others fighting with blades or fists. There was laughter everywhere and the occasional scream and something about the whole event that felt like the edge of a nightmare when a pleasant dream turns to something malevolent.

I shuddered and Bluebeard gripped my hand in his as he helped me down from the salamander.

"Do you think what you see is madness?" Bluebeard asked as I caught sight of a man grinning with teeth stained red. I could only hope that wasn't blood. "Then think about those folk you saw in my home. They wanted my help. Do you remember that? The people you're looking at right now are why they need help. These people took their whole lives from them."

"Lives worth no more than a beetle's," Grosbeak said from his place at the end of the pole. "Don't listen to your grandstanding husband, Izolda. The people you are watching now are those the gods truly love. The Tuathan. The true princes and princesses of all living things. And today they place their bets on the great game that will determine the fates of all the rest. If that isn't power, then what is? And having that power makes them almost immortal. It certainly sets them above all mortal ken."

"I think I preferred your pet when he didn't talk so much," Bluebeard said. "But do not fear. I have a use for him that will make listening to his ravings well worth the pain."

"You make it seem, Grosbeak," I said, "as if these people are not people at all but merely living versions of stories."

To my surprise, Bluebeard spoke, his eyes far away so that it looked like he was speaking to himself and not to me.

"We *are* stories. There's nothing more to us. This world we live in is no more real than any other. Life, death, these are ephemeral things no more solid than the steam that wafts from your cup of tea. We can none of us prove the world we see is the same as the world another sees. Our minds take in the sights but then they interpret those things into a story told just for us. We hear, we see, we touch, and our mind translates it to a tale. By rights, our hands should pass through each other, no more solid than the space between the stars. But one day, when we fly from this earth like the arrow loosed from the bow, we will enter whatever life comes after, and all we will have to bring with us will be the story – for that is what we are. We are the story of our choices, our grim failures, our crippled successes. We are the story of our molten passions, our loves and hates, our tears in the silence. We are the story of how others touched or shunned us, of loves returned, revenges enacted. When all flesh and glory melts away and there is nothing left of us, we will be only the story going on to what comes next."

I shivered at his words. No wonder he was willing to spend other people's days so blithely if he thought we were nothing more than stories. Did he think he was writing *my* story? If he did, he should think again. I would not let it be written by anyone else but me.

Bluebeard took something from a saddlebag hanging across the salamander's back. I hadn't even seen it was there until he slung a quiver over one shoulder and quickly strung a bow. The salamander dipped its head to my husband and slid away.

Bluebeard winked at me when he was finished.

"They call me Arrow and with good reason, wife. I fly just as fast and true."

I watched him as he arranged them the way he liked. He looked like an arrow himself – he was so slender and pointed and quick in his movements. His eyes flashed in the candle-light with intelligence and charm. If he hadn't been a murderer, I'd be proud to be a wife to a man like this. If he hadn't been so terribly unpredictable, I might have even liked it.

True to form, he reached for me, surprising me as he drew the wild curls of my hair forward with a gentle touch, making sure my back was exposed. Then he took my hand, lifting an eyebrow as if asking for permission, and when I nodded, he tucked it into his arm and began to stroll toward the party.

"So, what's your plan?" Grosbeak murmured. He was swaying in time with my steps, his expression flickering from worry to intensity and back to worry again. What would it be like to have your fate so much in the hands of another?

"You shall see and understand soon enough," Bluebeard murmured.

But I had other ideas. "Tell me what gossip you know about the players of this game, Grosbeak," I said. "Surely, you must know something."

"Ah! Finally, you are tapping into my potential. I can help you here. The Sword is – of course – a formidable player. Sharp and brutal, he will strike first and hardest. He is not known for finesse or spycraft."

Bluebeard snorted.

"Didn't he turn you on the Arrow?" I asked, watching Bluebeard stiffen a little out of the corner of my eye. "That seems like spycraft."

"Some people make it easy to betray them. The selfish. The arrogant."

"Keep talking," Bluebeard said in a low, calm voice that hinted at violence. "And we shall see whose arrogance makes them easy to betray."

He stalked beside me in a flowing stride that made me think of a black cat crossing a courtyard. His eyes were everywhere as if he were memorizing the position of each person and object in the riotous revel.

"Coppertomb is known for his callowness. This is his first time playing. They say he murdered his father to take his place. He used bitterbark poison – a woman's weapon."

I laughed and Bluebeard shot me a surprised glance. "Is the

insult in the death or the manner? You make it sound like it was worse that his death was womanish than that he was killed."

Grosbeak frowned. "Dying should be dignified. Look at how well I did it. The grandest of kings could not have surpassed me."

"At least we know your skills," I said glibly. "So, we should watch our cups around Coppertomb."

"Watch your cup around everyone," Bluebeard murmured. "You have no friends here but me. And possibly Vireo."

He nodded to the side and I saw Vireo with Bluebeard's band, playing a game of cards around a low table. There were already empty steins around them, and a half-eaten three-tiered cake to one side. Frosting dripped down like a waterfall across the cut side and my mouth watered. There was even a round orange fruit on top of it.

"In fact, it would be better if you didn't eat or drink anything until we return home. And now – no more gossip. We are nearly there."

We kept our eyes on the head table as we made our way forward, our path determined by the forest of white candles. They made the journey surprisingly warm in the frosty night and kept me from shivering despite my backless dress.

I heard murmurs as we passed tables and dancing couples. People were watching us.

At first, I thought it was because I was carrying a severed head, but after a while, I realized they were whispering about my back.

"Claws," someone said, curiosity thick in his voice. "Do you think he marked her on their first night?"

"Why not?" his companion asked but her voice sounded

intrigued. "He looks the type to mark what's his."

My face was hot when I realized what they were saying. They thought my husband had done this to my back – and rather than being repelled by that, they were intrigued.

When we reached the table, it was Lady Tanglecott who greeted us, her neutral expression unshakable.

"Will you bring your wife for every round, Riverbarrow? It seems somewhat gauche."

"Where I go, she will go, and what I despise, she shall despise also," he said lightly, but I noticed that everyone at the table was watching us. "Besides. I need her to set my target. Put your new pet over on that table, wife."

The large table was facing the crowd with all the players seated along one side of it. A place had been left for my husband at the end nearest us. Just one chair, I noted.

Off to the side past the far end of the table was a smaller table bearing a washbasin and towel and it was to that table that my husband gestured as he strode off in the opposite direction, fiddling with the string of his bow as he walked.

"Take one of those golden apples and put it on Grosbeak's head, sun of my world," Bluebeard continued lightly. I noticed he liked to give me extravagant pet names when he was being particularly overbearing.

I picked up two of the apples from the table and my eyes met the Sword's as I plucked them from the heap. I could eat the second one. There is no way they'd poison an apple on their own table.

"Just because you married him, doesn't mean you need to stay with him," the Sword drawled. "My claws may be bigger, but I don't feel the need to mark what is mine on the outside."

It was the words 'on the outside' that left me shivering. What sort of marks would he leave on the inside if I took him up on this offer? My eyes narrowed and I said nothing, simply gliding over to the table that my husband had indicated.

"Set the apple on his head when you have him in place, jewel of Wittenhame," Bluebeard said as he took an arrow from his quiver, looking down the shaft as if to judge how it might fly. "Grosbeak was a friend of yours, if I am not mistaken, Sword."

The Sword's mouth tightened. "No friend of mine."

"How odd," Bluebeard said, but his voice sounded more like a threat than a simple observation. "We Wittenhame cannot lie. And yet, I could have sworn he was a friend. Perhaps he was merely your plaything. As he is now the plaything of my wife."

"Don't let him do this to me," Grosbeak hissed. "He'll shoot me!"

"You're already dead," I said practically as I removed the wash basin from the table and set his head down on it.

"It will still hurt. And I will be humiliated." His hiss grew sharper. "You heard the Sword disavow me. They will all laugh at my torment."

I didn't feel the least bit bad for him. And yet I paused. My husband had asked me to play along to prove my loyalty. He was trying to make a spectacle here for all to see. Perhaps there was a way to show him how useful I could be. A way he hadn't even thought of himself.

"You sent me a message," Bluebeard continued as he chose a second shaft. "And in that message, you suggested I cannot win this game because I do not sacrifice enough. I am no risk taker, you said. You know every move I make before I make it, you said. Did you see this coming? Step back, wife."

I stepped back at the same time that the arrow flew, striking the apple on Grosbeak's head. He screamed, his face distorted with terror as juice sprayed across his face and the apple fell to the ground, pierced straight through with the arrow.

The crowd roared.

Bluebeard had their full attention. He made a little bow.

"Set up a second apple, wife. Once may be a coincidence. Twice will show my skill."

"I stand by your cowardice. What skill does it take to shoot at someone already dead?" the Sword said from his seat. He'd thrown his feet up onto the table, leaning back in his chair. "You won't take the risks I do. Which is why you won't win. And when I do, I will raze the ground of Pensmoore – I'm sick of how you treat it like your own fiefdom, snatching brides from there and letting your wild folk roam their bogs and woods."

He did? My brow furrowed.

He considered my land his?

"I can guess your every move," the Sword said.

"Did you guess this one?" I asked in a clear voice as I set the second apple not on Grosbeak's head but on my own.

There was a delighted gasp along the table, and when my eyes met my husband's, he had a look on his face as if he'd just found a particularly fine vintage of wine in his cellar he had not realized was there. He barely seemed to be able to tear his eye from me as he drew another arrow from the quiver.

He broke eye contact long enough to look down the shaft and then his gaze swung to mine again. He was drinking me in like I was life in a cup. He was watching me like I might evaporate with the dawn. Maybe he believed I would. After all, I was made of story to him. And I'd just given him an excellent story.

The party, I realized, had gone utterly still. I risked a glance to the side and saw they had all stopped their games of chance, their dances, their music, their trysts, and were arrayed to watch the spectacle before them.

My body was shaking all over, my head suddenly light.

He'd proven he could do it. Logic told me he could do it again. Logic was not working on my body, though. It was telling me that I needed to relieve myself. Promptly.

"Eyes on me," Bluebeard said as if he were seducing the entire crowd, but his words were for me, and as my gaze met his he gave me more instructions. "Hold your breath and watch me."

My fate was in his hands. But it had been there since I had greeted him. It only made sense to trust him with it again. The worst he could do was kill me. And he'd already promised to do that eventually.

I drew in a long, steadying breath. Despite my flawless logic, my knees were shaking, and my abdomen felt like water being sloshed around.

He drew his arrow. The point seemed aimed right at my head.

I couldn't help it. The tiniest moan of fear escaped my lips.

He raised an eyebrow.

I held my breath. I tried to keep my eyes on him, but I couldn't help the delicate scream that tore from my lips when the arrow loosed.

I heard it zip through the air. Heard the sound of it pierce the apple over my head. Felt apple juice spray across my scalp and the pulp of it fall into my hair.

I hadn't even shut my mouth when a second zip disturbed the air above me. An arrow took the apple a second time, splitting it right down the center. The halves fell to either side of me, bouncing off the fur of my stole.

Grosbeak cursed as loudly and vehemently as I wanted to, while around us the crowd cheered. Their voices washed across us over and again like waves smashing the shore. He had given them a spectacle. And they loved spectacles.

"I'm willing to place my hazard now," Bluebeard announced to the crowd. "And any sane man will be betting on me. My wife certainly did!"

That got him a laugh and another cheer. At the table, the Sword scowled grimly. He'd taken his feet off the table, but just like Bluebeard, his eyes never left me, as if he could steal me away by the power of his will and ruin all Bluebeard's plans in a single stroke.

There was a sudden chime, and everyone froze. The Sovereign spoke from his place half-covered in sand.

"Peak of Night is upon us. Make your hazards."

CHAPTER TWENTY-THREE

The Wittenhame, it would seem, took gambling very seriously indeed. The moment their Sovereign had finished announcing that they could make their hazards, a pair of creatures with large wings and hunched backs hurried to either side of the altar. They threw something at the ground that went up in a burst of bluish-white flame and continued to burn as they each pulled a silver cord and released a banner.

To the left of the altar, the official hazards of the players would be recorded. To the right, the official hazards of the spectators. I expected that list would be considerably longer.

The players rose, almost as one, to walk toward their banner. Bluebeard removed the string from his bow and approached me before he joined them.

To my utter shock, he kissed the top of my head almost reverently and murmured, "What courage. What blazing, maddening courage. You were right, wife of mine, you do make a better ally than an enemy. Wait here as I place my hazard."

And then he was gone. I gathered up Grosbeak and took him to the long table.

"I'm outraged that you did that to me," he sputtered. "Outraged."

There was still a little apple in his hair. I flicked it out and tried to ignore how tired I was and how much my back ached. There was no time for self-pity. If my husband's competitors had left anything incriminating at their table, now would be my chance to find it – and they had left so many things that I needed to move quickly to see if there was anything of value.

"I could have died, you know. He's not the best shot in all of history, just the best shot there is right now! And how did you know he wouldn't miss and kill us?"

"I guessed," I said.

I hadn't known. It was a calculated risk. I was the kind of person who took calculated risks because it was sometimes the only way to get ahead. You just had to be sensible about it.

"Guessed? You guessed? You gambled with our lives!"

"My life," I corrected. "You already lost yours by taking a stupid risk. I rather think that betting against Bluebeard – as you did – usually doesn't work out for people quite as well as betting on him winning does."

He was sputtering incoherently when I set him on the table and pretended to be grazing off the lavish food while I made my way slowly along it. I popped a grape in my mouth and looked over what Lady Tanglecott had left behind. A tiny fabric bag sewn with mouse skulls. A fan with a design of rats on it, their tales intertwined in a terrifying knot. A stole made of very delicate fur in a light brown color.

"Lady Tanglecott seems fond of rats," I murmured, but there was nothing here to lend me any guesses about her strategy. Her purse contained only a handkerchief and some mortal coins.

I moved on, plucking a tiny pickled egg from the dish and

popping it into my mouth as I looked at what Lord Antlerdale had left behind. It was a book.

Mist and Memories: The Memoirs of Lord Antlerdale, the cover read.

Wait. It was a book about him? I flipped open the cover.

"Don't think I don't see what you're doing," Grosbeak whispered. "And if you don't hurry, you're going to be caught. You won't find anything in there. The Arrow would have a copy of that book just like everyone else. Antlerdale gives them out like candy at a Nightwatch feast, and only the kindest of the Wittenhame agree to take a copy anymore. That's people who publish their own writing for you, forever hawking that tripe to everyone else."

I made a sound in the back of my throat, but I left the book and hurried onward, plucking a strawberry from the plate to hide my actions as I examined a hat left by Bluffroll. It was a simple, broadbrimmed black hat. Nothing of interest there except for the dried snakeskin tied around the crown of the hat.

I sighed and moved on to where Lord Marshyellow had left a walking staff as tall as he was. It was topped by the dried head of a cottonmouth snake, its mouth open and a small hat fitted to its head that matched the one Lord Bluffroll had been wearing exactly.

I shook my head. The Wittenbrand were an eclectic kind with the same taste in items you'd expect from a mad wizard, but there was nothing here that might help my husband.

Coppertomb had left nothing behind. Not even a hat or wrap. Wittentree had left a pipe carved to look like a small angry man.

The Sword had left his own copy of *Mist and Memories: The*

Memoirs of Lord Antlerdale. And that was all. In frustration, I sat down and began to chew on a roll.

"I told you," Grosbeak said, rolling his eyes. "Everyone has a copy. And you'd better get out of here before Lady Tanglecott places her bet and comes back here."

"Why do the players place bets anyway?" I asked. "I thought that was for spectators."

But I was hardly paying attention to the answer as a thought occurred to me. Grosbeak said only the kindest people still took copies of Lord Antlerdale's book. But the Sword was not a kind person. What was he doing with a copy?

I opened the book casually. It looked the same as every other. The title was on the first page. Lord Antlerdale had signed it.

"They have to have skin in the game. Literally. Those are the rules. They must bet with pain, or loss, or not at all. That's why some are missing eyes or ears or fingers from past games. Did you not notice?"

"Bluebeard is not missing anything," I said, opening the book and flipping through the pages. It was the right book. It hadn't been replaced with secret messages or hollowed out to hold something precious.

"He's missing wives," Grosbeak said a little nastily. "I'm sure you've noticed."

In the margins of the book, someone had written with pencil in a tiny, precise hand.

Raw timbers, ten carts full

Bridge builders tackle

Cart and horse

Wages

Cost: five hundred silver pieces, to be delivered when job is complete on the Alder River

Now, this was interesting.

"See," Grosbeak was saying, "Lady Tanglecott has bid her left hand. She must be very certain. I would have expected a finger or two, but the whole hand?"

I wasn't paying attention to their horrible game or the sudden burst of cheering around us. I was paying attention to those margins. The Sword had paid for a bridge to be built. And the nation he had received bordered Bluebeard's – mine – with only a river in between.

Six tons of quarry stone

Barges

Cable

Sail hands

Cost: three hundred gold sovereigns drawn from the coffers, half in advance

"You'd better hurry! She's on her way back. And look now! Antlerdale has bet his northern estate and one of his antlers."

There was a smattering of applause but nothing major.

"Why bid at all?" I asked. "Or why not bid something insignificant, to mitigate risk?"

But I was still distracted. These were the Sword's logistics notes. This one, I was sure, meant he was blockading a port somewhere. Logistics would tell us exactly what he was doing. I needed to read and remember as many as I could.

Cloth, uniforms, stitchery: five hundred gold sovereigns

How many uniforms could you get for that?

Stables and hands. Seven hundred and fifty silver pieces

I should have attended my father's lessons to my brothers about managing estates. I felt hot all over as I tried to remember how many horses you could house for a silver piece. How many uniforms could be made of a gold piece? This was all important.

My lips moved as I tried to memorize each entry.

"The highest bidders get the opening moves. And advantages. The key is to either convince your opponent to bid too high and thus, bleed him hard when you win, or to drive him to bid too low in his fear of how high you will go. There's no point making a huge bet if you are sure your opponent will outbid you. Usually, for instance, the Arrow is quite conservative. He bids the life of his wife."

"What?" I looked up then, my fingers still jammed in the book.

"Well, you had to know you were going to die soon," Grosbeak said unapologetically. "Maybe he'll keep *your* head on a ribbon, too." A hand clamped down on the back of my neck and I leapt in my seat.

"And what, pray tell, are you doing, mortal?" a silken voice asked me.

CHAPTER TWENTY-FOUR

The thing about allies is that they never end up being the people you expect. The same is true for enemies. Which makes them hard to distinguish.

I looked up into the cold eyes of Lord Coppertomb. His hand was soft and delicate, like he didn't perform even the lightest of tasks with it.

"Only competitors are allowed to be at this table," he said but there was a glint in his eye.

"I was only hungry," I said, popping an olive in my mouth. I chewed it deliberately, looking at him the whole time. Beside me, Grosbeak began to hum.

"What is your name, child of dust?" he asked, his plain face inscrutable. Almost everyone in the Wittenhame was either incredibly ugly or gloriously beautiful, but he was the one person here who was neither. He could have passed for human if he clipped the ends of his ears – and not even a very noticeable human if he wasn't dressed in cranberry uncut velvet and draped in strings of beads made to look just like human molars. My mind stuttered over that. I knew full well that they weren't made at all. They were taken. From people's mouths. I could only hope they were already dead.

"Izolda of Northpeak," I said calmly, keeping my face clear of any emotion. I had to remember that he was one of the players of this deadly game of lives, too. "What did you hazard for the game?"

"A finger," he said with a small smile. "And a month in a woven cage. I need no grand gestures for my debut game."

I suppressed a shudder. I knew how nature worked. If I seemed scared, the predators would gather.

"And you, Izolda, have already paid a price, haven't you? They say that those who fly with the arrow burn hot and bright and fast. And then they are gone. Like a shooting star in the sky."

"They say many things," I said coldly.

"Did he tell you that he has had sixteen brides before you?"

"Fifteen."

"She's not a fool, Coppertomb," Grosbeak said from beside me, breaking his hum for long enough to sneer.

A flash of irritation crept over Coppertomb's face, but Grosbeak only began his tune again.

Coppertomb turned his back to Grosbeak. "Then you know he will spend your days as water for his purposes."

I took another olive and ate it very slowly, trying to appear as though my heart wasn't racing so fast I could hardly breathe. But it was a lie. All calm in the face of this madness was a lie.

"He holds my nation in the palm of his hand," I said slowly.

Coppertomb looked surprised, but there was something off about it, as if he was very poor at performing and trying to make up for it.

"Oh. He's playing for your nation? It must seem noble to you – a woman who has never seen the game played before." I felt my face growing hot. I was not a fool and did not appreciate being spoken to like one. Coppertomb leaned in very close so that he could lower his voice almost to a whisper. "But what you don't know is this: he doesn't need to win to save your nation. In fact, he'll spend them like water just like he'll spend you. The faster he's out of the game, the sooner your people can go back to their normal lives. No plotting. No warring. No assassinations of minor nobles."

"What do you mean?" I asked, holding the next olive between my finger and thumb. My heart was beating so hard it felt like it would burst.

"We play this game to win, but we don't play it for the sake of the mortals. If one of us loses and the nation they were playing is still intact, then the country is left alone. We have no need to send our armies there. It's essentially out of play. If, for instance, your husband was delayed and missed his turn, that would be the end for him. And there would be no war in Pensmoore at all. No young soldiers dying on the field, wailing for their mothers. No children starving or women weeping. Just peace while the rest of the world battles it out."

I couldn't help myself. I saw the faces of my parents and brothers as he spoke. My heart galloped like a runaway horse.

"And wouldn't that be nice for you," I said acidly. "You could win."

"So, could you," he said slyly, as if letting me in on a joke. "I could send you home to be with them in such a way that he could never come after you again. It would be better for him. He could go attend to his folk. I've heard they have been much neglected as he's been amusing himself with wives. You could return to yours and comfort their hearts. Your nation would remain at peace. And all he would sacrifice is a little pride and one wife."

"Except that he's about to hazard me in this game and if he loses, my life is forfeit," I said.

"Let's watch and see," Coppertomb said, taking my shoulders gently in his hands and turning me so I could see the list of bets.

It read:

Tanglecott – left hand

Coppertomb – left pinkie, a month in a woven cage

Antlerdale – one antler and his northern estates

Bluffroll – a brace of stallions, his three consorts, a toe from the left foot

Marshyellow – a public flogging, a month of poisonings but not unto death

Towerrock – the child of his sister, his left eye

Riverbarrow –

I felt like I was holding my breath. I was going to burst. I was going to break apart.

And then the announcement.

"Lord Riverbarrow has bid –" There was a long pause as if the announcer had not expected what he saw here. "His immortality."

A gasp filled the air, and the shock was so intense that Grosbeak stopped his humming. Even I did not know what to say.

"See now?" Coppertomb whispered. "I can read a man's heart through his face, and I knew this year it would be different – that he would need your magic so much that he didn't dare bet you."

Was that the true reason? Because it felt as if he had taken a death sentence for me, and I did not know how to feel about that. My eyes sought his across the crowd. To my shock, his gaze met mine and something shot through me that felt exactly like lightning and fear all rolled into one.

"If I take your offer, he will lose his immortality," I said, and I was surprised to find my voice trembling.

Coppertomb's laugh sounded almost derisive. "What do you care if he loses something you never had? He will become like you. Is that such a terrible fate?"

It was not. I'd known many people who had lived and died natural lives. There was no shame in it.

"Think on it," Coppertomb said. "It is a solution to all of our problems, and if I use his magic to achieve it, it can be done with haste and perfect attention so that no one gets anything less than what they deserve."

"His magic?" I echoed. I felt stunned.

Coppertomb's hand drifted to my stricken back. I flinched from his touch. He must not have realized he was hurting me.

"Your days are represented somehow in his lair," Coppertomb whispered as Bluebeard began to stride toward us through the crowd. His brow was furrowed. "Bring me but one of them tomorrow at the Opening Spectacle and I will accomplish everything I have promised you."

I swallowed as he drifted away, and in my mind, I saw myself taking one of those garnets and giving it to Coppertomb.

"I don't trust him, and neither should you," Grosbeak opined.

But would it really be so terrible for all of us if I took this third way? The only one who would lose would be Bluebeard, and like Coppertomb said, he would only lose something I'd never had. It hardly even seemed like a loss when you put it like that.

"I can see you lying to yourself even though your back is turned," Grosbeak said. "It's fun, isn't it? Swallowing your own deceit? I always thought so, and then I ended up dead."

"I am not you," I said calmly.

"No, you're even more naïve."

CHAPTER TWENTY-FIVE

Husbands, it turned out, could be jealous even if their wife is nothing more than an ally in purpose.

We spent as little time at the event as we could. Bluebeard looked troubled, his eyes constantly flicking over to Coppertomb.

"Tell me what he said to her, Grosbeak," he whispered when the hazards were all made. "Tell me why she looks so pale."

"Or what?" Grosbeak asked. "Will you kill me?"

"There are worse things than being dead," my husband said through gritted teeth.

We were standing off to one side while he drank a small, foaming drink. He didn't offer one to me, and I didn't take one. My stomach had been rolling with nerves since Coppertomb spoke to me. To have a choice – a real, actual choice that could change everything – was both intoxicating and terrifying. Because whatever I chose tonight, it would seal the other path forever. Either way, I would be risking my family. Either way, I would be risking myself. And on top of that, I had given my word to Bluebeard that I would work with him. How could I betray him when he had not been faithless to me?

"Name one," Grosbeak countered.

"I shall name three. I could put you in a den of fire ants and let them leave you in stinging agony. With no hands to claw them away and no way to run, you would endure them long past your breaking point. I could make a death mask of your face with molten lead. Very slowly. One layer at a time. I could set you in a cupboard under my stairs, wrap your head in a towel so you could neither see nor hear and forget I put you there so that you may spend all of eternity with only your own thoughts for company."

Grosbeak did not answer, but he looked very green. I understood that feeling. I was swaying on my feet.

Eventually, Bluebeard sighed. "Enough. I will take you both home. Neither of you is much of a benefit to merrymaking."

He led us through the party, past screams, and chases, and bouts of swordplay. Past people laughing and drinking and feasting upon strange fruits. Past others passionately kissing in each other's embrace. Someone threw a crown of white flowers on his head and he left it there, slightly askew, as if he had already had too much of the wine.

And for the first time, I wasn't terrified. I felt as though I had a door I could open and step out at any time and that feeling gave me a coating of armor.

We had almost left the party behind us when we reached one last couple lurking in the shadows behind a rock. One of them looked up and as the candlelight caught her face, I realized it was Lady Wittentree.

"Leaving so soon, Riverbarrow?" she asked. Her teeth looked red and for a moment I worried she had not been kissing the man beside her, but harming him. But then he stepped out into the light and he was such a great ogre of a fellow, marked all over with green patterns, that I did not fear for him.

"The revelry grows tedious," Bluebeard said lightly.

"If you think to take an ally, consider me," she said, to my surprise. "Send that pretty one to deliver it. What is his name? Vireo?"

"I'll think on it," Bluebeard said, and then we were hurrying into the night and he was pulling me along as fast as our feet could carry us.

In the darkness, the laughter and screams seemed to echo everywhere.

"Sometimes I feel it, too," he whispered to me as we hurried into the velvet night. "The feeling that it's swallowing me up and I'll never be free of it."

I shivered. And then something landed in front of us. I sagged in relief when I realized it was the Grouse House.

Bluebeard swept me off my feet and mounted the steps two at a time, slamming the door behind us. I expected him to put me down then, but he murmured, "Leave Grosbeak to his napping here."

I set the head on the nearby bookshelf and Bluebeard carried me up the spiraling staircase, speaking barely above a whisper as the darkness caressed us.

"Your bravery touched me. My heart is not entirely ice. That someone – anyone – would choose to stand with me without bargain or coercion … You should know what it means to me. Though I do not have means to express it, I will have you know it all the same."

Guilt made my mouth dry. I didn't deserve his praise when I

was seriously tempted by the thought of betraying him.

We reached the top of the stairs again and found ourselves in his cluttered bedroom with the tall black-bloomed bed and the strange mirror, only now the open wall was showing a frozen lake with dancing bright lights across the crystal sky slung over it. The room was not cold despite the howling wind outside the open wall, because the other wall contained the hearth and the familiar fire. But this fire was twice as large as the last time we'd been in the room, and seemed to be dancing in tune to the howl of the wind.

"My fire," Bluebeard said tiredly.

"My master," the fire replied.

"Your greeting warms my heart as your flames warm my skin." Bluebeard turned to the bed and sighed. "There's still only one bed," he said tiredly. "I would have thought the house would realize there were two of us now. Ask the mirror and it will give you clothing for bed."

I went to the mirror and cleared my throat but before I could speak, it spat out a filmy white shift.

"Perhaps something with more fabric," I suggested shyly, my eyes glancing at that one bed. Bluebeard was beside it shrugging off his sword and more daggers than I realized he was carrying.

The mirror made a motion that looked like a shrug and spat out a long, trailing black nightgown made of a fabric so sheer it was nearly invisible. I sighed. It was so much worse than the shift.

Shaking my head, I went behind the screen, took off my dress and sword, and pulled the shift over my head. It was backless, too. Everything I wore these days was.

When I emerged, Bluebeard was sitting on the edge of the bed with a small clay pot in his hand. He motioned for me to join him.

I swallowed as I crossed his cluttered floor. Did he mean for us both to sleep in that bed? Had our strange way of sleeping the night before emboldened him? Would he want … I stumbled over the thought. To make matters worse, he was sitting there in only a thin pair of woolen trousers that hugged his legs like a second skin.

He saw me noticing and shrugged. "The mirror has odd tastes sometimes."

My face felt so hot that I wondered if I would need the fire.

"Lie down here," he said, patting the bed beside him.

I froze.

He looked at me, puzzled, and then his brow cleared in understanding and he sighed. "I want to tend your wounds. They do not look well to me."

I relaxed and nodded, making my way to the bed and lying down where he asked me to.

"With your back to me so I can rub in the ointment," he murmured, gently twisting me to where he liked. Then, he draped quilts over my legs and up to where I could hug them to my chest. "I can never understand why the house thinks a view is important when I sleep, but it never fails to provide one."

From where I lay on the bed, all I could see were the black blossoms hanging from the bed and the strange bright lights dancing over the pale snows beyond. I watched them weave and shudder, mesmerized by them.

After a moment, cold ointment touched my back and I

flinched.

"Easy. Easy there," he whispered to me as if calming a horse. "I must snip these stitches yet."

And yet, I did feel easier at his touch. It was light and while it certainly hurt my wounds, it was more sore than painful. They would heal. After a moment, his hands warmed and I leaned into the touch as he tended me, cutting the stitches and tugging them free and then soothing the skin with his salve. After long minutes, his hands left my wounds and began to gently knead the skin around them and up into the muscles of my shoulders and neck. I didn't know if this was part of his healing, but if it was, then it certainly was working. My whole body seemed to lose its tension, melting into his ministrations until I was certain I would let him do this forever if he wanted.

"I want to thank you, wife of mine, for coming to my aid. Speak to my riddle – what do you do with a sudden ally? An asset you didn't know you possessed?"

And I was imagining things, too. For a moment, I could have sworn I felt his hot breath on my neck and the faintest press of lips to my hair. But that was just dreams beginning before sleep had come. After a moment, I was pulled under into an exhausted rest where I dreamed of stolen kisses with a husband who had never had any other wives and had chosen me for love alone. And though he acted nothing at all like the man I married, he looked just like him and it made my heart hurt in a curious way I had not thought possible.

I woke in the pale light of pre-dawn to find him sleeping beside me, sprawled on his belly, the quilts wrapped around his waist. The fire drowsed in the hearth, snoring slightly with a burst of sparks whenever it did, and the rippling lights beyond had danced themselves away and left heavy snow drifting through the sky like fat feathers.

I blinked myself awake and found the chamber pot and a wash area in one of the doors leading out of the room. I cleaned myself up and leaned over the basin, thinking.

I didn't really want to think, if I was being honest. I didn't want to make a choice about what Coppertomb had offered. Partly because I was worried that Grosbeak was right, and I shouldn't trust Coppertomb. And partly because I was worried that even if he was right, I might still be tempted to snatch at the chance for everyone to be mostly happy.

It was the sensible solution. Falling in love with my captor was not.

I looked in the long mirror over the basin and took a deep breath. I was a mess. There were still knots in my long hair that Bluebeard had tied. My small shift was rumpled from sleep and the blood on my cheek had smeared in the night. I washed my face and took a long breath.

I didn't like to admit it to myself, but I was beginning to be almost attached to Bluebeard. It was likely only because he was fascinating. Everything he did was dramatic and vibrant – even among a people so dramatic that you could find death or glory around every turn. They made my head spin and my mouth feel dry – and he was worse than the rest. Taking that from him seemed like a crime.

But when I drew the golden key from its place between my breasts, I imagined all the other girls who had done the same thing. Murdering them had *also* been a crime. He would soon murder me, too. Would it just involve the stealing of all my days so that I collapsed on the floor lifeless because I had lost all my time, or would it have to turn … grisly? There had been no marks on the girls in the room. But what if he'd magically erased those? What if I was destined to die at his hand? Would it be ghastly and terrible? I swallowed down a knot of fear.

And if I chose to stick with his plan, then when he was done with me, he would take another bride and do the same to her.

Maybe I didn't have to choose yet, but maybe I could be prepared. What would it hurt to have one of the garnets … just in case?

But even making that decision felt like making *the* decision. I took a long breath and turned to go back to bed and then stopped. Why not just go into the room and take a look at it again? Maybe I would see something that would make sense of all this. It couldn't hurt. And avoiding the place didn't make all those other girls just go away.

I drew the key out, turned it in the air, and stepped lightly into the room that opened before me.

I was struck again by the incongruence of it – and the horror. It was a room outside of time and space and my husband used it to store the bodies of the women whose lives he'd stolen. How many of them had slept in his bed like I had last night? How many of them had he gently tended like he'd tended my wounds? My stomach twisted at the thought. It was bad enough when men were faithless, but worse when they killed the very women they were meant to be faithful to. Just looking at them nearly decided me.

I strode across the magical room to the eerie hourglass and worked my way around it. How would I steal a garnet from it? They were mine – my days and nights stored away within. And yet, they felt utterly inaccessible. I reached forward and set my hand against the glass bulb at the top. To my shock, my hand pressed right through the glass to the gems on the other side. My head spun and I felt ill – it was like seeing my own flesh cut up in front of me. Frantically, I snatched one of the garnets and drew it out, keeping it pressed tightly in my palm as I slumped to the ground and pressed my forehead to my knees. My breath wouldn't slow. I was getting lightheaded.

With a thrust of my will, I forced myself to concentrate. I mustn't let it get the better of me. It was my day to spend as I liked. If I gave it to Coppertomb … well, it was mine to give. And if I kept it for myself, wel,l it was still mine.

And yet, somehow, I didn't think that Bluebeard would feel the same way.

I stumbled back to my feet, my head still reeling. Apparently, stealing your own days was no easy task. I felt like I was intoxicated as I stumbled along the line of women. I kept glancing up at their clear, flawless faces, wondering if their spirits were watching and judging me. What would they have done in my place? None of them had betrayed Bluebeard, or they wouldn't be here. Was that because they didn't have the choice, or had they chosen to be faithful where I was thinking about faithlessness? Had they – possibly – loved him?

The thought put a stab of anger through my heart, and I froze at the feeling. Ridiculous, Izolda. To be jealous of women who had no more say in this than you did. To think you owned any part of him and could feel threatened by another's claim. Foolish. To want to own any part of him. Foolish and more foolish. I was falling down a fool's hole that I'd dug for myself, and the thought of that made me shake my head at myself.

Just to prove that I wasn't jealous, I opened the nearest book at random. It belonged to a woman who stood right beside Princess Margaretta. She had a very impressive figure clad in a silky dress that clung to every curve. I felt my cheeks growing hot just looking at her there, encased in his magic. It was like she might come to life and outshine me right here and now.

I opened her book at random and read a page from it.

I have always been considered a beauty. Desired by all.

Well, that part wasn't very surprising.

Princes from faraway lands had already come just to dance with me. Just to exchange heated looks and hidden kisses. So, when a lord of the Wittenbrand came to steal me away to be his wife, I was not surprised. An exquisite bride requires a rare groom.

I looked up at her again. She certainly thought a lot of herself.

Imagine my shock at discovering I was his fourteenth bride. To say it was an affront to my dignity would not be enough. I was horrified.

I felt a pang of sympathy. I had been horrified, too.

But I was not a fool. I never have been. I read the journals kept by those before me and I saw no hint of real attachment between them and their master.

Now that, actually, was quite interesting. And there had only been one more bride after her. Had he really not loved any of them? Not even a little?

So, I did what any thinking woman would do. I set out to seduce him.

Not what *any* thinking woman would do. I could think just fine, and I was seducing no one.

I started with fine foods and cut flowers. With well-thought compliments and careful turns of suggestive phrases. He proved impervious to suggestion and insensible to romance.

What? I was blushing just reading this.

Perhaps a more direct course of action was required. But my touches were rebuffed, and my kisses turned aside. In frustration, I revisited the journals of the others, looking to see if I had missed something. But if any of these others was somehow his one true love, it is not recorded on the pages of their journals. Nor is any hint of that in his home.

I snuck into his bedroom – you can coax the stairs to bring you there if you offer them pretty trinkets – dressed for love, but he took some time returning, so I searched it top to bottom and found no relic of the other wives there. No abandoned earring or lock of hair. No love missive or article of clothing. It was all his own property, all masculine.

She was certainly a bold one!

I grew bored and went back to the great room and when he found me there, he told me he was tired. When I offered to help him into bed, he told me he was perfectly capable of helping himself. When I offered to undress him, he looked as though he thought I was crazy. When I abased myself completely and told him I would do anything, anything at all for his pleasure, he told me he had left a cord of firewood outside the door and if I were to stack it in the shelf beside the fire, he'd certainly be grateful for my efforts. Then he took me by the elbows and gently shoved me away from him.

My eyes were huge. He'd done that? I doubted many men would. Particularly not when they were already married to the woman.

I was perplexed. Who would not be?

That night, emboldened by what might be the final option, I stripped down to my skin and waited in a bath of hot water and rose petals in his room. I had the mirror produce a bright, shining copper bath. You can get it to manifest any number of things.

She was relentless. I knew I should stop reading, but now I couldn't put it down. I wanted to know what was next. Where would these attempts end?

When he entered the room, his nose was in a book and he did not see me until I rose from the steaming water like a goddess from the depths.

I risked another glance at her and her very impressive figure. Yes, goddess seemed like an accurate descriptor.

He strode forward and lifted my wet body to his, and I thought I had finally won. I was just starting to smile in triumph when he threw me out his bedroom door. I skinned my knee on the floor and was just getting to my feet when he came out a second time … and threw the bathwater after me. I was left there sputtering, drenched, and rejected.

I covered my mouth to keep the laugh from escaping. I could see him doing that. I could see him striding back into his room and asking his fire to dry him.

I am not one to retreat from what I desire easily, but this man is too much for me. I have resorted to entertaining myself as I may, by flirting with his followers when they come here. If he feels any jealousy, he does not show it.

And now I felt bad for him. My face was burning with emotions I couldn't even put names to.

And I write this for those who come after me, so that they don't make the same mistake I did. It was humiliating for me to experience such depths of rejection, and I can assure you it will leave a bitter taste in your mouth to have the same happen to you. And it will, for none can outstrip me in beauty and desirability.

She was certainly right about that! If this happened to me, I would never live it down.

Was her whole journal like this? Curious, I flipped to the first page and found inscribed on it the same riddle that the first bride had in her book.

A sudden idea seized me, and I left her journal on the pedestal and hurried down the line, looking at the first page of each of the books.

And there it was.

The same riddle.

I am sudden death to calm.

My roar breaks the hush.

My song the mind's somnolence.

They each began the same way but in a different hand. Each of these women had heard those same words. And they'd faithfully written them down. And now that I was looking for them, I spotted them carved in a ring where the wall met the domed ceiling. The riddle was carved between roses and stars and strange symbols so that you had to either have them on your mind in order to see them. But it was plain as day.

Could one of the others have solved the riddle? But if they did, then wouldn't they have recorded the answer somewhere?

I shook my head in frustration. These were nothing but foolish guesses, and I had bigger problems to solve than riddles in books. I needed to decide whether to give Coppertomb my day.

But even though my mind should have been on that, it kept drifting back to the riddle as I left the room, crept back to the black-flowered bed, and crawled under the bright quilt.

The fire flared for a moment in a fiery yawn. I cuddled down into the warmth of the bed and let the rising sun's rays lull me to sleep as my mind turned the riddle around and around, looking for any kind of crack in its edges.

CHAPTER TWENTY-SIX

The next time I woke, it was to a surprisingly soft touch, and Bluebeard's cat's eyes regarding me carefully. He winked one of them and put a stack of clothing beside me.

"I have things I must say to you," I said blearily, and he sat down on the edge of the bed. I struggled to sit, wincing at the pain in my back.

I was surprised again when he helped me up, his hands strong and gentle and his dark lashes framing his cheeks as he looked down. His face was so close to mine that I could have kissed him if I pleased. Which was utter nonsense. Would I even be thinking that if I hadn't read about the fourteenth wife's attempt to seduce him? Would I ever consider it if he weren't so terminally beautiful that it hurt to look at him in the bright afternoon sun?

He bit his lip as he watched me, as if he was as nervous in this moment as I was.

"I don't know why you look nervous," I said irritably. "I am the one who has never been married before. You've had at least fifteen other women in your bed."

He raised an eyebrow condescendingly as if to dispute the matter. Maybe the journals hadn't been lying after all. I felt my cheeks growing warm – again.

"But that is not what I want to talk about." I paused and he sat back a little as I took the clothing from him so that I had something to do with my hands. Maybe I should take a page from his book. "Speak to my riddle, husband."

His answering grin was boyish. I would never get over how young he looked despite the blue beard.

"Who builds a bridge and does not use it to cross a river? Who gathers supplies to blockade a port with no intention of blockading it? Who orders uniforms for men who will never fight?"

He looked intrigued when I began and hungry when I ended my words, leaning forward as if his nearness could encourage me to speak more.

It did.

"While you were bidding, I took the liberty of investigating what your opponents left at the table," I said calmly. "People often forget that what they choose to keep or do not keep as possessions says a great deal about them. The Sword kept a book he shouldn't care about. And inside, he had notations. I can write them down for you. I remember them clearly."

He huffed a laugh through lips made soft with something that looked like a combination of pain and relief. His eyes met mine and a tiny thrill shot through me at the look in those liquid grey cat's eyes. In a human, that might almost be longing that he was letting me see behind the shutters of his eyes. Longing mixed with elation.

He held my gaze for a moment and then dove off the bed, moving too quick for a human and scrambling through the layers of his things. He came up like an otter with a fish in its mouth, holding an inkpot, a pen, and a half-filled page of crossed-out words and trailing verse. He flipped the parchment over, put it on a book and pushed everything toward me.

I took his quill, met his eyes with a proud look of my own, and began to faithfully copy everything I'd witnessed in my careful, clear hand.

"I am a good wife to have," I said coyly, and the smile he gave me in return looked sly. More than ever before, I wished he could speak at the same time as I could. This game where we each played mute was like chewing rocks for breakfast. I misliked it.

It ate at me constantly – termites to the wood of my mind.

"And by the way, I have a name to offer the sword I gave you. You called mine Angstbite. Yours can be Edgeworthy."

He barked a laugh.

When I was done, he kissed my forehead, gestured to the bath as if inviting me to take one, and left with the words I'd written.

I'd kept my left hand closed that whole time. The moment he was out of the room, I opened my palm and looked down at the rough-cut garnet concealed within it. It felt like a crime to be holding it. After that moment of his joy bursting from him so infectiously, it also felt like a betrayal.

But I kept it with me as I stripped out of the clinging shift and dropped into the hot pool. I kept it on the little tray beside the bath as I drank the steaming tea from the little teacup and tried to hold it like he did with my pinkie finger out. I kept glancing at it furtively as I washed my hair and then came out and dried my body with the cloth folded beside the stones of the pool. I donned the clothing Bluebeard had left for me – a tight pair of plum-colored velvet breeches, a tall pair of sturdy black boots, a creamy brocade doublet slashed in plum and sewn with gold, and a frothy white tunic sewn all over with downy grey feathers.

I was not in the habit of wearing breeches like a man. It made me feel bold. Just like my words that morning had.

I arranged my curls so that they framed my face in wild spirals – the best I could manage to make it do – and put the garnet carefully into a tiny hidden pocket of the doublet.

My marriage sword was nearby, and I strapped it on with hardly a thought. Perhaps I could convince Bluebeard to teach me to use it so it would not only be a decoration.

I made my way down the winding stairs, listening to the birdsong, and paused halfway down. I was growing used to this house and this world. If I was honest with myself, I would have to admit that I was even growing used to my feral husband. The thought should make me very careful. Instead, it brought a feeling of warmth rushing all through me.

And perhaps it was that moment, thinking those thoughts in complete betrayal of my original self, that doomed me the second time.

In the main room of the house, Bluebeard's band was clustered around his desk, poring over a map. Vireo studied Pensmoore, his index finger jammed right over Northpeak in a way that made my heart skip a beat. What was he planning with my home?

He spoke excitedly to the man next to him. "Five hundred. That must be the number of his new recruits and if he already has more uniforms being sewn for them then they'll be trained by the time we make our first move. We should expect that his will be the bridges. He'll need one to reach Southfallow. That has to be his first move."

"But why block the port off?" the other man said, shaking his head.

They were matching in their blue doublets and cat's eyes, and they both were eating from a spread of food all around the map as they spoke.

Sparrow looked up and caught my eye with a smirk as she took a delicate bite from a very tiny boiled egg.

"To keep his navy safe until he's ready to use them," Bluebeard said, considering the map. "He's planning to set against us the swollen weight of his empire like a river running after the melt of spring. Like so many, he exposes his vulnerability in his boldness. It will leave his rear unguarded. If we could just see our way clear to finding an ally to attack him there while he goes after us, then he'll be caught in a vice."

"Unless he's already persuaded the others to work with him," Vireo argued. "They'd love to see you unseated, Arrow. We all know the Bramble King favors you."

"The Bramble King favors no one," Grosbeak muttered bitterly from his place on a high shelf. Someone had elevated him so he could see the map over their heads.

"Is that the name of the Sovereign?" I asked from my place on the stairs.

Bluebeard froze, his eyes locked on me. Was he so surprised to see me? I lived here, too.

Vireo coughed, looking from Bluebeard to me and back. "As you say, lady, so it is."

"And you are tracking the Sword's plans on the map," I added.

"As you say," Vireo said, looking again to Bluebeard.

Bluebeard was still frozen in place, his eyes drinking me in as if he was watching for something. It made my cheeks hot. What would he be looking for in me? Betrayal? I had not yet planned to do that. And on top of it, I had proven to be a worthy spy.

"When do we make our first move?" I asked shyly.

"After the opening event – a grand showing of all the players and their retinues to kick off the games officially," Vireo said, his brow beginning to furrow now when he glanced at his master.

One of the others snickered and Bluebeard blinked suddenly and looked back at the map.

"A ball then?" I asked, face hot, trying to seem sophisticated and calm rather than off-balance. Why did my husband look at me so strangely? Was he that grateful for my spy work? It had only been common sense and a showing of good faith.

This made them all laugh. "A mortal might throw a ball, lady. But not the Wittenbrand. We prefer to show ourselves off in other ways."

"Like what?" I asked, crossing to the table and boldly helping myself to one of the spiced sweet buns. It was still steaming as I tore off a piece to bite.

His grin seemed eerie with the scars arching up from it. "Tonight, we will ride in the Spectacle. The competitors will choose two companions to ride with them on Wittensteeds which live a single night and then wither and die. We will ride them fast and hard and at each interval, a target will be high and far from the path. We must make a shot with an arrow. At the end of the night, the competitor whose arrows have pierced closest to the mark of each target will receive a boon. And all of Wittenhame will have seen us ride and shoot. It's an honor to be asked and I will ride with pride. As will Sparrow, I suppose, since Grosbeak has proven traitor."

"No," Bluebeard said firmly, and his eyes lock on mine again. There was something in them that I could not decipher. Something deep and swirling. "No insult to you, Sparrow, but you will be preparing for our first move against the Sword. We will not wait for him to strike us. We must strike first." His gaze returned to the map. "Here and here. Come, let Izolda advise us on her father's defenses and that of his neighbors. We will be relying on his ability to withstand attack from the sea."

I moved to his side and he leaned over the map to show me. As I leaned with him, his breath washed over my skin, making me shiver.

"If Sparrow does not ride with you, Arrow, then who will?" Vireo asked with a dangerous note to his voice.

"My wife will ride with me," he said, his eyes still on the map.

"Ridiculous!" Vireo snorted. "You jest."

"I do not jest today, but if you prefer that I did, then speak to my riddle. Who has two smiles and still makes me frown?" Bluebeard looked up and met Vireo's eyes, and I felt myself drawing back as their gazes locked. Vireo looked furious.

"Why begin down the path of a fool today, Arrow?" Vireo snarled. "You've never been one before. No fair ankles or delicate wrists have turned your head from battle. These mortals are to us as blades in the battle – we need them, but without us wielding them they are nothing."

Bluebeard made no reply, but I could see he was considering Vireo's words. I pulled back, taking a step from the table. I'd been a fool to think this could be a true partnership. Watching Bluebeard with his own made it so obvious that leading these people was what he was born for, and they were all faster and stronger and smarter than I was. Vireo made perfect sense. There was no reason to bring me when he had these others who were better.

My back hit the bookshelf and I hugged myself as I watched them all leaning in toward the growing conflict instead of away from it as men usually did. All but Sparrow, who rose unnoticed and made her way to stand beside me.

"You've never done this before," Vireo said, emboldened by Bluebeard's silence. "Why bring one of them into things now? Why dress her for a hunt instead of in silks to look pretty on your arm? Why involve her in your schemes?"

"Who do you think got us this information, Vireo," Bluebeard said mildly.

"You've stirred up a nest of wasps, mortal," Sparrow whispered beside me, looking casual, as if she'd chosen to stand beside me entirely at random.

"Then make her your spy. Dress her even prettier and foist her on your enemy. Don't bring her into our councils like this." Vireo gestured at the map and the silent men ringing it. They were watching him with intensity in their eyes, hanging on every word. "Don't offer her your secrets. You never have before. You know that they make you vulnerable. You can't afford to care if they live."

"I did not mean to cause such distress," I whispered back to Sparrow.

"Did you know," she said, "that he doesn't need to kiss you to take your days and use them as his own?"

I felt my face grow hot. Why else would he kiss me if not for that?

Vireo seemed like he couldn't stop now if he wanted to. "You can't afford to care if your wives are harmed. You can't afford not to use them up. And yet you have given this one true marriage vows. Don't deny it! I was there! You've given her a place at the table with you – not just at the events, but here where you discuss strategy. They whisper about it at every door of the Wittenhame! They roar with laughter when your back is turned. Your enemies have noticed, too. You have drawn their eyes to her. I saw how Coppertomb spoke to her last night. I saw how the Sword keeps one eye on her at all times. And worse yet – the fire suggested you tucked her into your bed last night!"

"Is that all?" Bluebeard asked in a low, dangerous voice. I felt my mouth go dry.

"We don't care who you bed," Vireo said in a low voice. "It's none of our business – so long as it isn't your wives."

I didn't mean to gasp, but I did. When Bluebeard turned to look at me when I did, there was something unreadable in his eyes – something that looked a little like fear.

He spun back to Vireo and in a voice so low I thought it might turn into a whisper, he began to speak, leaning over the table until his nose almost touched that of the other Wittenbrand. I could almost feel the violence crackling in the air, like lightning waiting to form.

"What has a head and no body?" my husband growled.

"Grosbeak," the Sparrow said with a laugh. She didn't seem at all worried by what was happening, and a quick look around the group told me that none of the rest of them looked particularly shaken either. They looked eager – like they were anticipating a particular treat.

"And what might soon have a body and no head?" my husband pushed.

"Vireo, if he doesn't remember why they call you 'Arrow,'" Sparrow drawled.

Vireo stormed out of the house, slamming the door loudly. The fire whooshed in response.

"Insulting!" it roared, flaring up.

Sparrow shook her head. "He's riled. That's all. Grosbeak was a friend."

"I could still be one," Grosbeak said from his perch.

Sparrow snorted, not even looking at the head. "No one else feels like that, Arrow. An exhibition is just a game. Take who you like." His eyes narrowed as he grinned. "Only let us win this game with you and we will be pleased."

There were murmurs of agreement from the others around the table, and my speeding heart began to slow. It would be fine. They would not all betray him just for me.

Bluebeard shot me a slightly guilty, slightly embarrassed look and then gestured toward the chair Vireo had been sitting in. I settled myself into it and Sparrow settled in with me.

"Now tell us, lady," Sparrow said with certainty in her voice. "Were there any other notations in the book?"

The rest of the afternoon was spent in strategy. The rest of the group seemed pleased enough as Bluebeard hammered out the details of how they would begin and what they would do to achieve it, what moves their competitors were sure to try, how they would counter. I offered what information I could about the land I'd come from and otherwise kept mostly quiet.

Bluebeard glanced at me often, an unreadable look in his eye. More than ever, I wished we could just speak honestly together. There was so much I would ask him. Every now and then, I felt the garnet in my hidden pocket, or remembered Vireo storming away, and I wondered if he had been right. Maybe I wasn't good for his master. Maybe I would ruin him.

And I also wondered if what Sparrow said was true. I'd thought he was kissing me because that was how he stole my days. Was it possible that he did it only because he liked it? Was it really true that he had married me in a different way, as his men had been complaining about since it happened? And if those things were true, was it possible that I could be his ruin like his enemies hoped and his followers feared?

CHAPTER TWENTY-SEVEN

I'm not given much to anxiety or supposing, but even if I had been, it would not have saved me from that night. There are some boxes that once opened, do not shut again. Some jewels that, once stolen, cannot be returned.

This time, as Bluebeard took my hand to lead me to the Spectacle, I wanted him to be able to speak to me so badly that I could almost taste it on the tip of my tongue. He looked me deep in the eyes and smiled a wicked smile full of promises he planned to break.

I left Grosbeak behind. He could not ride with us.

"She'll need both hands for her mount," Bluebeard told him. "She can't bring you."

But I was worried about leaving him on a shelf in the Grouse House.

"She could leave you in her secret room," Bluebeard suggested, and so that's what I did. I brought him into the little room and left his head on the pedestal meant for me.

"You can't just leave me here in a sepulchre," he raged. "It's filled with the bodies of the dead."

"Then you'll fit right in," I'd said shortly.

And so I stepped out into the evening beside my vicious husband and joined hundreds of people running like rain from the hills into a stream toward where the Spectacle would begin.

Rough wooden booths had been set up around the starting line and already – though the sun was only just sinking in the sky – they were lit from within. They roared to life as people served out strange drinks of every type – some that steamed and some that growled and some that turned the drinker's nose purple. There were booths with tight-wound breads and booths with evergreen wreaths to wear around the neck. One sold candies that were swirled white and red – so bright and glossy I could hardly believe they were real. Another booth had calling birds with tails almost as long as a man was tall. Those who bought them set them on a shoulder and the birds' tails trailed behind their owners like the train of a fancy bridal gown.

My eyes were wide as Bluebeard led me toward the event, but I stopped him just before the sun dipped below the horizon.

"Whatever happens next, you should know that you have my full confidence," I said.

If only I could be sure that was true of me, too. I was not at all confident in myself or in my own mind.

He gave me a puzzled look but waited a heartbeat as darkness took the place of golden sun, and when there was no more trace of gold in the sky, he looked at me with dangerous eyes and said, "Speak to my riddle, portentous one. Why do you wish me luck as if you think I will need it?"

But by the way his eyes glinted, I could tell he was joking. He had no notion of the garnet in my pocket. He had no idea that I was balanced on a knife's edge between loyalty and betrayal.

With a laugh, he threw a cloak around my shoulders – deep

blue and rippling like the night, trimmed in white fur around the hood and the edge, and then he drew me along with him toward the event.

The Bramble King – the Sovereign – was buried this time in snow and lit with bonfires at his feet. He watched sleepily over a scarlet line along the ground. Along the line, the other competitors already stood, their two chosen companions accompanying them. Vireo was already waiting for us.

He scowled when he saw our linked hands, but Bluebeard nodded to him and Vireo seemed to relax, as if he hadn't been sure whether he would still be welcome and was mollified to find that he was. It didn't seem very practical to keep a man so close who disagreed with you so vehemently, but Bluebeard greeted him, letting go of my hand to clasp his.

I was waiting to see the steeds we would ride. I had experience riding horses, and I even thought I could ride the elk that Bluebeard favored. But to my surprise, Bluebeard lifted up a handful of snow and blew on it, and from his breath, three pawing stallions sprang to life. They were made entirely of snow sparkle and frost, as if he had thrown the light snow into the air and it had simply decided to choose this form on the way down. They tossed their glittering rainbow manes and shook themselves, straining forward as if it were only his will holding them back.

"They respond to commands," Bluebeard told me. "'Halt' to stop. 'Forward' to go, and nudges of the knees to turn them."

All down the line, the other competitors were blowing on their handfuls of snow, but I privately thought that none of them had steeds quite so snorting and restless as Bluebeard's and certainly none of them were as shaggy and powerful looking. Perhaps there had been a storm in his breath but only calm summer breezes in theirs.

"I will guard your back to the end, brother," Vireo murmured as he mounted his steed. "Do not see my disagreement as disloyalty."

"I never did," Bluebeard said with a small smile.

He offered me a hand and I took it, meeting his gaze as he helped me into the saddle. He looked excited, barely containing his energy as he prowled from my mount to his, his eyes on everyone around him, looking for weaknesses. If I had to guess, I would say this spectacle would be fun for him.

The horses were far higher than I was used to, and though they were held back right now, I could feel in their magic bodies a desire to run that outstripped anything else I'd felt in a mount before. It was disconcerting to be able to see through them, catching only the movement and edges of their being in the glitter of shining snow, but I was determined to prove I was not afraid. If I chose loyalty to Bluebeard, he would need to know he could rely on me, and he could not rely on a coward.

The look he gave me from the back of his pawing stallion was one of both challenge and something that almost looked like respect. For one awful moment, I wondered if I could leave him even if I wanted to. I may never find a man who looked at me like that again. In Pensmoore, my best hope had been a man who would give me the dignity of marriage and children and – if I was very lucky – be faithful to me. Here, now, I could stay with this man who gave me devilish looks and bright magic horses and enchanted clothing and wondrous spectacles. And what if that meant my life was short and over before the winter? Was it really so bad to live thirty years in six months? Was it really a bad bargain?

Everything in me was screaming inside me that it was a very bad bargain, but when I looked into his glittering cats' eyes, I didn't believe any of it.

He whispered to his horse and it moved in close to me so that he could lean from the saddle and speak in a low whisper.

"Izolda, your beauty draws from me a confession I would not normally make, but I bare my throat to you. I am not certain that I can save your land as you hope. There, I have confessed it."

I felt my eyes going wide. He'd never seemed to lack confidence before.

"No," he said, shaking his head. "It is not that I think I shall lose, but rather that sometimes to win you must sacrifice everything. It is possible that I will need to destroy what you love, to let it burn and wail and die, if I am to win. I think it best that you know that before we start."

My mouth fell open, betrayal stark and bitter in my mouth.

A horn blared, haunting and dramatic, and Bluebeard's horse reared.

He shot me a last look, torn and haunted, and then he cried, "Forward!"

His sparkling mount it dashed across the line.

"Forward!" I called in a hollow voice, realizing the race had begun.

But the cold air streaming across my face could not compete with the ice solidifying my heart.

It was all I could do to cling to my horse's gossamer mane as he rushed forward, hot on the heels of Bluebeard's stallion. Beside me, Vireo cursed loudly, clinging to his own steed like a lamprey on the side of a fish. Even with my hesitation, we'd been first off the line.

We galloped up a narrow forest path between rounded boulders and groping pines, turning tightly to cling to the hill from the one direction, only to double back and cling in the other direction. The horses were wild, almost screaming as they ate the ground under their feet at a jolting, furious pace, nearly missing the turns as their hooves scrabbled over slick stone and tufts of grass.

I kept my gaze forward and clung tightly to the horse, letting him have his head. There was no way I could hope to steer him. I could only hope that he kept following Bluebeard's horse and was not lost in the tight turns and narrow trails.

My heart was in my throat, my cloak swirling behind me, my knuckles white where they gripped the icicle mane.

My husband was ahead of me. He rode with all the grace of a big cat – as if he had plucked this horse from the night sky and set it ablaze with his passion to bear him where he chose – which he had, I supposed. How many days had that cost me? Did I even care?

I should have been terrified. My heart should have been in my throat – and it was a bit – but there was also something else stealing over me. Something I hadn't expected. Elation.

I had never thought I would love the danger of a night ride like this one – and yet I did. Oh, how I did. All my inhibitions fled from me and it was just me and the horse and the ride, flying down the trail like an arrow loosed from a bow. There was no difficult decision. There was no betrayal. Just a magic horse and me and the ground below and the air above, forever.

I let out a delighted whoop and heard Vireo curse again from behind me.

I tried to catch a glance of him over my shoulder, but I saw nothing more than a blur of rider on horse and a vague impression of someone else very hot on his heels.

I had to turn again to catch my breath.

We neared the top of the high hill, where snow glazed the tops of rocks and trees like an iced bun. The moon was creeping high in the sky, and though it was small during this cycle, it seemed brighter than ever, flooding the landscape with its stark white gaze.

Bluebeard spoke to his horse and it reared, too excited to want to halt – even after racing up a hill so steep that I felt winded just thinking about it.

He drew the bow and arrows from the hanging quiver at the side of his magical saddle and fitted an arrow to the string.

I looked into the distance as Vireo pulled up beside me and there it was, the target. A ring of licking white fire surrounding what must be a solid target for the arrow to hit. It was far enough away that I wouldn't be able to see the arrow strike, but Vireo pulled out a long telescope and opened it, lifting it to his eye.

Bluebeard loosed the arrow and Vireo cried out in delight.

"Middle ring!"

But it wasn't Vireo that Bluebeard looked at with a wicked gleam in his eye, it was me. He grinned, and I found myself grinning back even as my heart was ice inside me. Our eyes met and for just a heartbeat I wondered what it would be like to be married to him in the normal way – the way where joys like this could be shared. My heart ached worse than the tears in my back at the thought of it.

"Now, how is that for shooting, mortal wife? Have you ever

seen the like?"

I wanted to tease him, wanted to remind him that I had let him shoot an apple from my head, but I dared not.

Vireo glanced at me. "I swear, Arrow, your wives leave tingles down my spine with their eerie silences and long looks. How you put up with it is beyond my ken."

Bluebeard frowned at Vireo, but he said nothing in my defense, simply calling to his horse, "Forward."

My face was burning with shame as the sounds of the next competitor warned me he was hot behind us. Vireo's horse leapt forward, and my horse was a heartbeat after as irritation simmered within me.

I could hardly be blamed for my silence when I'd been warned not to speak – ordered, even. Did he think that I didn't want to break the silence? Did he think I liked being mute when I had so many things to say?

But now some of the fun had been leeched out of the ride and while my horse still danced and leapt beneath me, its semi-translucent muscles bunching and lengthening with every stride, I did not revel in it as I had. I'd been given a bitter drink and told to swallow. Did he really mean that about sacrificing my family? Perhaps it had only been more drama. But could I be truly equal to the man while under this curse? While subject to his whim? I'd been fooling myself.

We rode down a steep hill and crossed an ankle-deep stream with ice crusting the edges, turning round a great tree's trunk and up through flowers encased in diamond frost that towered over my mortal head. And still, I was stewing.

I wanted to speak – of course I did! I wanted to congratulate him, to provoke him, to tease him. Did they think me less because I showed restraint for his sake?

I ground my teeth. If I could, I wouldn't just speak, I would demand, I would riposte, I would roar.

Roar.

We leapt over a low fence and I barely concentrated in time to stay astride the horse as he made the jump. The moment his diamond feet hit the hard ground again, my mind was back to spinning.

Roar.

That was in the riddle.

I am sudden death to calm.

My roar breaks the hush.

My song the mind's somnolence.

Could it be possible that the answer to the riddle was speech?

It was written in every journal – as if daring us to break his rule. If this was truly the answer to the riddle, then it was a gauntlet the magic had thrown down to each wife. One that had never been picked up. But why would it do that? Who had written those words in the room and why did it whisper those words to each of us? Had it been a ruse all along?

When he'd bid me silent, he'd said outright that we would lose the magic if I spoke out of turn. No wonder no one else had tried. And yet … this poem was written everywhere in the very heart of the magic he had possessed. What if he hadn't created the room, only brought his brides to it one by one? What if he was as much in the dark as we were about the provenance of the magic or the rules surrounding it? What if he'd been lied to?

I shook my head. I felt confused … but also curious.

Behind me, something snorted and I glanced over my shoulder to see the Sword right at my heels, his beast flaring with little bursts of fire.

"Forward," I whispered to my horse, leaning over its neck. "Forward."

The horse sped onward, but up ahead I'd lost sight of Bluebeard and Vireo. I'd been too occupied with the words of the riddle.

I heard a crack behind me, and my horse leapt forward, screaming.

I glanced back to see the Sword gaining ground. He was almost beside me now, a whip in his hand. He struck my horse with it and a tiny tear formed in the starlight-and-snow of my horse's hindquarters.

"Off on your own, mortal wife? What a delicious surprise!"

"Drawing their swords, they ran directly to Bluebeard. He knew them to be his wife's brothers ... but the two brothers pursued and overtook him."

- Charles Perrault, Bluebeard,

1697 as translated by Andrew Lang in The Blue Fairy Book 1889.

CHAPTER TWENTY-EIGHT

I wasn't sure what I was expecting him to do. Maybe whip me? Maybe speed by?

I didn't expect the shove when it came, hard and fast.

I fell from the back of the horse, smashing into a tuft of frozen flowers and hitting my shoulder hard against the ground.

I tumbled, momentum still at work, and then finally stilled, disoriented, head whirling and back screaming.

I forced myself to my feet, breathing hard. The pain of the impact only hit me as I tried to straighten. My entire left side – shoulder, ribs, arm – was in agony. Snow clung to me, melting and seeping through my clothes. And yet, as I saw the Sword plunging around the corner ahead, the pain seemed less important than what he was doing. He was tucking his whip into his belt and drawing his bow.

I knew, without knowing how, that he planned to use it on something other than the target.

Something nudged me from behind, and to my surprise, my horse was there, his velvet frost-nose pressing against my uninjured shoulder.

"Kneel, friend, and I will mount," I whispered.

He knelt and I scrambled onto his back as the Sword's two companions thundered by on horses that were mixtures of frost and flame. They were neck and neck as they took the corner ahead.

"Forward," I whispered, and my horse stood, reared, and pawed the air in a single motion.

I held on with gritted teeth as he plunged up the moonlit track, banking around the corner. As soon as we rounded the bend, everything before me stood out in the stark relief of the moonlight.

I gasped, my heart racing as I saw it all, my breath puffing out of me in ghastly clouds.

Vireo was down on the side of the trail, chasing after his horse. It looked like he'd been thrown on the corner. The Sword's two companions thundered off the trail toward him, their steeds kicking up clouds of snow as they galloped, whips at the ready and glinting in the moonlight. They were not playing fair.

That left Bluebeard alone and far ahead, his horse standing still as his back arched and he took aim with bow and arrow toward the second target.

Behind him, the Sword had stopped, too, his bow at the ready, arrow nocked. But he was not aiming at the target. He was aiming at my husband.

I couldn't get there in time to stop him. Or to do anything to warn my husband.

I could call his name and warn him. But only if I believed the riddle. Only if I thought I'd really solved it.

But something was sticking in my mind. Bluebeard had warned me personally not to speak or all would be lost.

And there was that last line speaking of "the mind's somnolence."

My heart was racing, my head seemed to spin, but there was no time to make a clever decision or be sensible about this. If I did not speak, it might be too late.

What good would any amount of magic do him if he were dead?

I opened my mouth, summoning all my courage.

And in that flash of a moment, my heart spoke to me.

The mind! The mind! It's in the mind.

I shut my mouth with a snap and thought with all my might.

Behind you! Bluebeard! Behind you!

Bluebeard's arrow flew from his bow and in the bright moonlight I saw it go wide from the target as he spun on his horse's back and ducked so quickly that it seemed to all be one motion. The Sword loosed at the same moment and his arrow flew over my husband.

He was fitting a second arrow to the string when a hand grabbed me from behind, spinning me.

"I've found you just in time, wife of the Arrow." Coppertomb's voice sounded triumphant.

"The Sword attacked him," I said stupidly, not sure how he came around the corner without me noticing. I felt like I was in shock, like Bluebeard really had heard my voice in his mind. How else would he have known to duck? The importance of it – the possibility of it – changed everything.

Coppertomb's horse was huffing in the cold, its frosty body

filled with dark swirls like eels living within it.

He leaned in close so that I could feel his warmth in the cold of the night, and his hands grabbed my jacket.

"Your day. Give me your day and let your brothers come and save you, or it will be too late. In a moment, the Sword will slay him, and your life will be forfeit with his. Only give me your day, and there is still hope for you."

"My brothers?"

I needed time to think. I needed time to consider what this new development might mean.

"You've done something. I can see it in your eyes, mortal. You are as open books to the Wittenbrand. You've broken your marriage somehow, haven't you?"

"What?" I peered toward Bluebeard but all I saw was his horse wheeling in the snow as the Sword took another run at him, sword held high. There was no sign that I'd done anything other than warn him.

"If your marriage was not broken, don't you think the Arrow would draw on your days to save himself now?" Coppertomb said impatiently. He grabbed my chin between a thumb and forefinger and turned my head back to the battle. "Look!"

In the distance, Bluebeard was battling the Sword – blade to blade. There were no bursts of light or strange occurrences, just the ring of blade on blade.

Could it be true? Had speaking within my mind been just as devastating as speaking with my mouth would have been?

"You've been a fool," Coppertomb said, confirming my thoughts. "Don't make it worse by continuing on that path."

"No," I began, but I was too distracted to notice when he grabbed me and started to pat at my pockets.

"Here!" he said, triumphant as he drew the garnet from my doublet. "Was that so hard? Mortals try to complicate everything."

He threw the garnet to the ground and when it hit, the earth shook and then tore open.

My horse screamed, rearing up.

It leapt over the tear in a cloud of starlight, wrenching me from Coppertomb's grasp.

His curses rang out behind me, but my horse's hooves pounded over the frozen ground as it tried to outrun the tear in the ground. Out of the fissure spilled dark figures that looked like armed men. They were dazed and stumbling, some of them calling out or raving like madmen.

"To me! To me!" Coppertomb cried, waving his arms to them.

I didn't know if he was rallying the men or trying to call me back, but my horse had a mind of its own and it was thundering straight toward Bluebeard.

Bluebeard raced toward the Sword. As I watched – shocked – he stood up on the back of his horse, crouching as the stallion galloped. The Sword had his weapon ready, aiming to sweep at Bluebeard's legs. But as he struck, my husband leapt to the Sword's horse, knocking his opponent off with him.

They rolled across the ground, sliding over the light skim of snow.

I put my hand over my mouth as my horse plunged toward them.

Bluebeard was going to break his neck. And then I was going to trample him.

He popped up from the ground and found his balance, wavering slightly. My breath hitched in my throat. A little sound like relief escaped my lips.

At his feet, the Sword reached for him – but too late. My horse galloped close at the same moment that Bluebeard lunged, leaping in a way that seemed almost effortless onto the back of my horse and then leaning almost over me as he clung to my horse's bright mane.

"Bluebeard?" he asked, horror in his voice. "This is what you name me?"

I squirmed on the horse's back so I could see him there, leaning over me like a black cat riding a charger.

You heard me. I … I solved the riddle.

His laugh was long and low. "Wondrous as it is, I do hear you, wife of mine, fire of my eyes, despair of my soul."

Coppertomb says I have broken our marriage.

"I think not. I feel your days. I can still reach for them. What riddle do you speak of?"

There was a riddle the room told me when I entered. It is written on the walls and in every book.

"A riddle," he said, his voice growing bright as if something had just finally made sense to him. "And it told you to speak to my mind?"

I thought so.

I looked up at his face – at the utter elation I saw there. He did not look angry at all.

He looked down at me for a half of a heartbeat and then back up again, but that tiny fraction of a second had shown me blazing pride and something that looked almost like fierce affection mixed in.

"Speak to my riddle, wife of mine. What manner of woman solves a puzzle that fifteen before her could not solve?"

The type who listens, I said dryly, but I didn't feel proud or smug. I felt nervous. I had not betrayed him by speaking aloud – but I had betrayed him far worse when I snuck into the room and stole one of my days. Even if I hadn't given it to Coppertomb with my own hand, he had it now, and he had used it to practice magic.

We plunged into a copse of trees and Bluebeard pushed the stallion onward as branches beat us from every direction.

"Something hunts us, solemn wife. Something not of this world."

Behind us, I heard a yell.

"They went in here!"

Our horse crashed into a small, roughly circular glen, bathed in moonlight. Light, swirling snow in flakes as tiny as dust motes whirled around us.

Bluebeard urged him to the center of the glen, and he drew his blade, one hand on the mane, one on the hilt of the sword.

"Do not fear, Izolda. You are under my protection wherever trees breathe and forests take root, wherever rain falls and water floods over the earth, wherever the angry wind blows or the rocks groan with age, there you are mine and always will be," he said in a low, dangerous way.

I met his eyes, but I did not see fear there. Instead, my pulse quickened for another reason entirely. He was looking at me with such open vulnerability in his eyes that it made me gasp.

"I have waited decade upon decade for a wife who is my equal – for a true partner in this adventure of mine." His lips quirked teasingly. "I had not expected her to mock me for my blue beard."

I wanted to answer him. I wanted to return his assurances with my own. But my words cleaved to the roof of my mouth. We had already been betrayed – and I was the traitor. I did not deserve his loyalty or his faith in me.

"They're here!" someone called, and just like that we were ringed by dark figures, coming out of the trees, their shadowy weapons raised and faces enshrouded in the dark hoods of their cloaks.

They charged before I had the chance to scream, weapons raised.

Our horse reared, pawing the ground, and I clung to his mane, Bluebeard at my back. My body pressed flat against his warmth and my breath hitched in my throat. I felt his breath coming hot and fast, his heart pounding through our clothing as it matched the speed of mine.

The horse crashed back to the earth and the fight began as Bluebeard clashed sword to sword, making our horse dance around to avoid contact as he fought.

I clenched my jaw, trying not to bite my tongue. Trying not to scream. I didn't dare distract him.

He was nimble and quick, his short sword lightning-fast as it swept a blade aside, twisting and flicking and sending it from the hand of an attacker. He was moving to the next one as I was still watching the first fall back – unarmed now.

Bluebeard urged the horse ahead at the exact right moment to get under a man's guard and then he plunged his blade through a chink between the man's breastplate and shoulder armor. We spun in a circle and his horse kicked back. There was a scream as the man charging us from behind fell to the ground, clutching his broken arm, his battle-axe skittering away across the frozen grass.

I didn't dare close my eyes. I didn't dare let myself scream. I was worried I might forget to breathe

Bluebeard moved like lightning, like time didn't touch him, like he was made of magic and wishes and songs of bards. He danced and wove and wheeled, one with the horse, one with the swirling snow, one with the night. And in his eyes, there was fierce violence and something that looked all too much like obsession. He lived for this, I realized. He loved it far too much.

Perhaps his men had not been joking when they said he collected heads.

And then someone cried "Hold!"

I gasped as Coppertomb rode out from the forest on his shadow-caging horse. The ring of soldiers encircling us drew back. All I could hear was panting breath and creaking leather and the squeak of boots on snow.

"There you are, Arrow. And with your lady wife, I see." Coppertomb looked far too smug. A shot of terror rippled down my spine. Bluebeard flicked the blood off the end of his sword, wheeling the horse to keep everyone in sight. "You should have stayed by my side, Izolda. It's harder to bring you to your brother with an angry husband crouched around you."

"Brother?" I gasped.

A dark figure stepped out from the ring, his shoulders back and head held high. He threw back his hood.

Svetgin.

It was both him and not him. My hand flew to my throat.

He looked to be thirty years old. Worn and filled out, his muscles bulky, his eyes narrowed in thought and a wicked scar decorating one cheek that looked old – a decade old. And yet it had not been there last week.

"Izolda," he said in wonder, looking at me as if he had seen a ghost. "You have not changed."

"What is this?" Bluebeard asked, his words thick with fury.

"Your lady wife gave me a single day – a day to save her family and her nation and free herself from your grasp."

"That's not –" I started.

"Shh," Bluebeard said gently, laying a finger over my lips. I bit his finger. He didn't even flinch. He merely turned to my brother. "You are here for your sister?"

Bluebeard tilted his head as he watched Svetgin and Svetgin stood a little straighter.

"We come for all the brides you've stolen."

There was a murmur from the rest of those in the ring, and with that murmur, I realized who they were. The Brotherhood of Stolen Sisters. And they had found a way into the Wittenhame because of me. Because of my betrayal. Because of the garnet I had stolen.

"My other wives have passed through this life," Bluebeard said calmly. "Izolda is the only one who still lives."

"Then we come for their revenge," Svetgin said harshly, his once boyish features twisted in a way so unfamiliar to me that they did not seem to be his at all.

Bluebeard turned my face gently toward him, his finger still on my lip. "Tell me only this, wife. Did he take your garnet, whether by your hand or by force?"

His grey cat's eyes held a depth of sadness that twisted in my belly. His finger left my lips.

He did, I said in my mind, feeling my eyes welling up.

Bluebeard's lips crashed into mine so unexpectedly that I didn't know what was happening at first and then he was kissing me with devouring passion so that I could hardly think, hardly breathe. Desire welled up in me, rising to match his. He moaned slightly into my mouth as if he was breaking apart even as he kissed me. I kissed him back, torn by the agony of my own betrayal. I was breaking, too, shattering apart even as I clung to him. A deep ache started in my heart and flooded through my body.

He broke away, leaving me gasping, his expression vulnerable and aching. His fingers caressed my cheek – longingly, almost lovingly. "You are beautiful, my betrayer, light of my eyes, breath of my lungs. For you, I would bend an oath and break the skies. Let that kiss be the memory you take of me as you leave me to my fate."

And then hand ripped me from the saddle and the sparkling snow horse under Bluebeard collapsed and dissipated in a puff of sparkling motes.

I couldn't see him – couldn't see anything as I was wrenched away, my hood pulled over my eyes, and dragged across the snow in strong, muscled arms.

I thought I might have screamed, but that, too, was muffled by my cloak.

Blade met blade in a sharp clang. A loud curse was abruptly cut off and then cries filled the air growing more and more frantic. I kicked and elbowed and lashed out wildly against whoever was holding me.

And then my brother's voice was in my ear, lower and rougher than I remembered. "Easy, now. Easy. We'll have you home soon. Trust us."

Someone smashed a cloth over my face, and everything went black.

***

Read more of Izolda and Bluebeard's story in Dance With the Sword.

BEHIND THE SCENES:

USA Today bestselling author, Sarah K. L. Wilson loves happy endings, stories that push things just a little further than you expect, heroes who actually act heroic, selfless acts of bravery and second chances. She writes young adult fantasy because fantasy is her home and apparently her internal monlogue is stuck in the late teens.

Sarah would like to thank **Melissa, and Eugenia**.Without their big hearts and passion for stories, this book would not be the same.

Sarah has the deepest regard for the talent of her phenomenal artist Kristen De Palma who created the gorgeous cover art that accompanies this book. She also wants to thank her editor, Melissa, who tried her best to make this book better. Any errors remaining are all Sarah's.

Thanks also to the Noble Order of Female Fantasy Authors who keep me sane – sort of. And for my beloved husband, Cale and sons Neville and Leif who are endlessly patient as I talk to them about bookish passions.

www.sarahklwilson.com